the WIDOWER'S *Wife*

A Novel

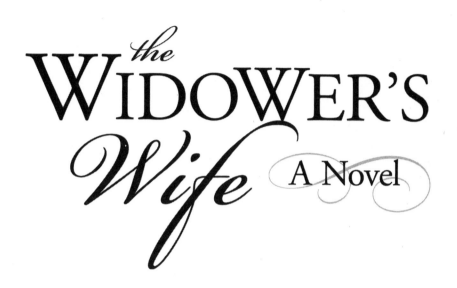

the WIDOWER'S Wife

A Novel

PRUDENCE BICE

BONNEVILLE BOOKS
SPRINGVILLE, UTAH

ISBN 13: 978-1-59955-411-2

Published by Bonneville Books, an imprint of Cedar Fort, Inc., 2373 W. 700 S., Springville, UT 84663
Distributed by Cedar Fort, Inc. www.cedarfort.com

LIBRARY OF CONGRESS CATALOGING-IN-PUBLICATION DATA

Bice, Prudence, 1967-
  The widower's wife / Prudence Bice.
    p. cm.
  ISBN 978-1-59955-411-2 (acid-free paper)
  1. Mail order brides--Fiction. 2. Widowers--Fiction. 3. Farm
life--Fiction. 4. Wisconsin--Fiction. I. Title.

  PS3602.I27W53 2010
  813'.6--dc22

  2010010337

Cover design by Tanya Quinlan
Cover design © 2010 by Lyle Mortimer
Edited and typeset by Megan E. Welton

Printed in the United States of America

10 9 8 7 6 5 4 3 2 1

Printed on acid-free paper

For Teila, Tasha, and Krista—my three hopeless romantics.

Acknowledgments

Thanks to my wonderful husband and family for their unending encouragement and patience, to my father-in-law, Virgil, for his horse-sense, and to Pam and Jocelyn—you are both irreplaceable.

One

As the train slowly pulled into Darlington Station, Jillian Grey anxiously searched the crowd, hoping to catch a glimpse of the man that she would begin her new life with. For a fleeting moment, she considered staying on the train and escaping the life she had chosen almost three months previously, but Jillian was a woman of integrity. She had given her word and was therefore honor bound to fulfill her commitment of marriage.

As she looked out the window, Jillian thought back to the night she had told her parents of her decision to become a mail-order bride.

Jillian's parents were shocked, disappointed, and angry. Her mother cried while her father threatened to both disown and disinherit her.

"How could you embarrass this family in such a way?" her father shouted. "What will people think? What will they say? I can already hear the gossipmongers whispering the tale of how my only daughter, heiress to a substantial fortune, has thrown everything away to go to some forsaken place and become the wife of a dirt poor farmer. Who, I might add, you've never even laid eyes on before! He could be a lunatic for all you know!"

Jillian knew her family was still recovering from the scandal that had rocked their quiet, comfortable existence in high society only months before. Visions of Nathan Shaw ran mercilessly through her mind. She shook her head to dispel the thoughts.

"Father," Jillian said anxiously, "you did not raise me to be a fool. I would not jump blindly into a marriage, even one of this nature. Mr. McCullough and I have been in correspondence for nearly two months now. He is a decent, hard-working man."

She chanced a glance over at Marcus, her brother, hoping to get any kind of clue as to what he was thinking. He sat in the corner lounge chair, not moving. His handsome face was strained and contorted in a mournful expression. Jillian wasn't even sure he was listening anymore. She knew he still blamed himself for what had happened to her months before. He felt that if he had not encouraged Nathan, had not helped set him up as a superior gentleman-like man, Jillian would have seen through him for the rake he was. Jillian wasn't so sure. They had grown up with Nathan. He had always been a little flirtatious and easily influenced, but she had chalked it up to the fickle tendencies of youth. She thought she'd sensed a deeper commitment beyond those temporary fractures in his character. Despite what she had said to her father, she had been a fool where Nathan Shaw had been concerned.

"Jillian." She winced under her father's glare. "This whole business is foolhardy, and I simply will not have my daughter traipsing off to some farm in Wisconsin to live with a complete stranger! Your mother and I have decided that you will go immediately to vacation with your Aunt Adelaide in Lexington for a time, just until you get your mind back where it ought to be. Then you will return to your studies at the university. We all need to get this whole sordid business behind us." Luckily, Jillian had predicted her father's reaction and prepared for it.

"It's too late, Father." Jillian gripped the couch to brace herself in the face of his anger. "I've already told the dean that I won't be returning this fall or ever, I've purchased my ticket, and I've sent a letter informing Mr. McCullough of my arrival date."

Even though she expected a harsh reaction from him, Jillian was still taken aback by her father's extreme anger. His frame shook with fury, and Jillian gripped the couch even harder.

"Jillian, how dare you go behind my back and do this! Does this family mean nothing to you?" His words stung, and moisture erupted from her eyes and began to stream down her cheeks. "I will speak to the dean," he continued, "and get things straightened out. You will get this foolish idea out of your head."

"No, Father." Jillian tried to call upon her inner courage. "I have given my word, and I will not break it. If I have to run away, I will. I'm turning eighteen in four months. I am not a child any longer!'

Jillian heard her mother sob more audibly and saw her frail hand reach up to grasp that of her husband. Suddenly, her father's shoulders slumped, and he groaned inwardly.

"Why, Jillian? We have worked so hard to give you all the things in life that could make you happy, not to mention an education—a privilege and rarity for most young women. Why choose this path and give up so much when you are free to accept any man that your heart desires?" New tears erupted from Jillian's eyes as Nathan came to mind, unbidden once more.

"Yes, Father, you have been very good to me"—she took a deep breath—"and I have tried doing things your way." Out of the corner of her eye, she saw Marcus wince noticeably. So he *was* still listening. "Father, I need to do this. I cannot bear it any other way."

"Jillian." This time his voice was soft and filled with tenderness. He held his arms out to her and she went eagerly into them. "I had not realized you were still hurting so. But you're still so young. You have plenty of time for your heart to heal. There are many honorable young men who would be proud and privileged to have a chance to win your affections as soon as you are ready to love again. So why do something so rash and dangerous? Go to your Aunt Adelaide's and mend your broken heart. You will see that I am right. One day you may even thank me for saving you from throwing your life away."

Reluctantly, Jillian pulled herself out of her father's arms and stood to her full height, lifting her chin slightly. "You may as well already consider me a married woman, Father. I am bound by my word. Mr. McCullough is expecting my arrival a week from Tuesday. We will be married that same day." She heard her mother's gasp. "I may not be in love, but I know I will find fulfillment and happiness in this man's home." She tried to soothe her father's anxious mind once more. "You would like him, Father. He is very much like you. I can feel his goodness in his words. Oh, he doesn't say too much about himself in his letters, but the way he talks about his children—his love for them, and his hopes for their future—"

Jillian stopped mid-sentence when she saw the look of pain seeping again into her father's eyes. How ironic it must seem to him. Here she was, leaving to care for a stranger's children, to give them hope, love,

and dreams while simultaneously shattering the dreams her father had for her.

Jillian's mother spoke for the first time since she had confessed her plans, causing Jillian to start.

"Life will not be easy out west, Jillian," her mother said. "I have heard many accounts of the horrors and hardships women are called on to bear in homes that are no more than broken-down shacks. You'll have no running water or indoor facilities. My love, you will be caring for what, three children besides?"—she paused as if to add emphasis to her next three words—"another woman's children?" She looked with sympathy at her daughter. Jillian attempted to say something in defense, but her mother placed a hand on her arm and squeezed lightly.

"Now, Jillian, I've no doubt you will be able to meet their physical needs. You have always been an industrious worker and willing to care for others. To your credit, you have had much experience helping the neighbors with their little ones." She gently lifted Jillian's chin to look into her eyes. "But have you truly thought this through? These children, at least the oldest one, will still be agonizing over the loss of their mother. You will most likely face a good deal of resentment from this child. Who will bear the brunt of your frustration when this child hurts you? Certainly not the child or her dear departed mother. This little girl will almost certainly see you as an enemy at first. How, my love, will you deal with the resentment she will feel toward you?"

Jillian's mother was wise, and her words cut deep into Jillian's heart. Jillian wished she had time to send Mr. McCullough another post and ask more questions, but there would be no time for a return letter.

Her only hope was that her newfound love for these children would be enough to overcome any obstacles they would face as a family.

"Mother, I know it won't be easy," Jillian said. "But I'm strong, and I'm willing to face this challenge," she said resolutely.

A tear silently traced its way down her mother's ivory cheek. What a beautiful woman her mother was. Her hair was an unusual shade of auburn, darker than Jillian's, but there was no question from whom Jillian and her brother had inherited their stunning green eyes. Though she was small and somewhat frail, Jillian's mother had always possessed an inner strength that Jillian had admired and tried to emulate. Jillian suddenly felt compelled to say more, as if it would ease the pain in her mother's eyes.

"I already love these children, Mother," she said. "I don't know how or why, but I do. Surely my love can endure any pain that may come my way." She was encouraged as she thought she saw a bit of hope leap into her mother's eyes at last. "You have taught me well. If I can but bring this family even a portion of the love and happiness you and Father have always given me, then I will have done a great work in my life."

Jillian sat next to her mother and laid her head against her shoulder. Instinctively, her mother began to caress her hair. She felt her mother's heart beating softly, and she closed her eyes reverently. She could feel the love in this home. The air was thick with it. She breathed in deeply, savoring the memories. She would treasure them and lock them up in her heart. Something told her inwardly that she would need to call upon them later for comfort and strength.

Jillian now scanned the crowd around her, noticing there were many more men at the station than women. Already she had seen many different men rudely stare at her, taking her in fully with their eyes. Although she had always considered herself plain, men seemed to find her attractive. Even as early as fifteen, she had been turning heads, and since that time, her figure had fully developed and she was too often forced to endure salacious stares from the male population, including some from well-bred men twice her age. It had always made her uncomfortable, and she couldn't abide how men could be so impolite.

Previously, Jillian had inquired how Mr. McCullough would recognize her at the station. His answer had simply been not to worry—apparently it wouldn't be a problem. She hadn't particularity liked his answer, for other than knowing the color of her hair and eyes and her height, he did not know much about her. She began to worry.

Unable to face the fear of being left standing alone in a new town among people with whom she had no acquaintance, Jillian's pragmatic nature overrode her confidence in this man's assumed ability to pick a total stranger out of a crowd. When she arrived in Chicago to change trains, she sent Mr. McCullough a telegram confirming her arrival time. At the last minute, she decided to add a quick note, which stated that when she exited the train, she would be carrying a yellow embroidered handkerchief.

Once the telegram was on its way, Jillian began to worry, particularly after checking two stores without any success in finding a handkerchief to match the one she had described to Mr. McCullough. As the time neared for her connecting train to depart, she ignored her hunger pains and dashed quickly into one last shop, praying she would find what she was looking for. She was greatly relieved to find a wide selection of colored handkerchiefs, including a yellow embroidered one. Thanking the shop owner emphatically, she made her purchase without delay and hurried back to the station, barely making it in time to catch her connecting train.

Jillian's worry increased as the platform and the station emptied out fast. Most people gathered their luggage and exited quickly, choosing more intimate places to continue their conversations. She wished she could move farther away from the tracks. It was slightly embarrassing to just stand there like she had been forgotten. She tried to drag her trunk a few feet, but when it fell back to the ground with a big "thunk," all she managed to do was bring attention to herself. Maybe if she tried to push it? She shook her head. *Oh,* she thought, exasperated. *Where is he?*

Sighing in frustration, Jillian slumped down in anguish on her trunk. A fear grew inside her that maybe Mr. McCullough had changed his mind. Surely he should have been here by now. It had been almost twenty minutes since she had stepped off the train. Would he be so cruel as to leave her standing in a strange train station with nobody she knew for hundreds of miles around? *No,* she thought, recalling his letters once more. *I'm convinced he wouldn't just leave me here.* Even if he had changed his mind, Jillian had learned some things about Dalton McCullough's character through the letters he had written. He was honorable and would do right by her. If she hadn't truly thought so, then she would have been foolish to even be here in the first place. Something must have happened to cause his delay.

Still, Jillian thought it wise to find out when the next train going back to Providence, Massachusetts, would be coming through. Standing up and clutching her valise, which held her small purse tucked inside, she was at once thankful for her mother's foresight.

As Jillian packed to leave, her mother slipped quietly into her room and handed her the small purse with an ample sum of money in it.

Jillian shook her head. "Mother, I will be fine. I can do this on my own." Her mother took both sides of her face in her warm hands.

"You are as stubborn and as strong willed as your father. I feared it would get you into trouble one day, and I am afraid that day has come." Her mother attempted a smile for Jillian's sake. "But I have a stubborn streak as well, and I refuse to send my only daughter off without at least a few dollars of her own. A woman needs to have a little something tucked away for good times as well as troubled ones. Trust me, you will not regret it."

"But Mother, this is more than a few dollars!" She tried to hand it back, but her mother would have none of it. Instead, she gathered Jillian up in a tender embrace before quickly fleeing the room in tears.

Jillian sighed. She knew that her impulsiveness would cost her family dearly, her mother most of all. They were close, and she cherished the heartfelt talks they had shared on their daily walks. She understood that she was also robbing her mother of the dream of seeing her only daughter wed. All the planning and the parties with flowers and frills would never be.

≈

Jillian turned and walked toward the ticket counter. It wasn't far, and she figured her trunk would be safe. A thief would have to be an idiot to think he could get away with it very quickly, as heavy as it was.

Before she reached the counter, a man came running into the station. He was breathtakingly handsome, and her eyes were immediately drawn to the perfect shape of his face. In fact, she couldn't help but take in the whole sight of him. He was quite tall, and though he wore a suit coat, she could see that he had large muscles beneath. His coat fit snugly around his arms and his chest. Even her brother Marcus, who prided himself on his build and strength, would be impressed.

Jillian quickly looked down as she felt her conscience send a blush of shame to her face. She would soon be a married woman. Could she be so disloyal already? She had no business staring and gawking at another man. Despite her shame, she felt her gaze being uncontrollably drawn back to this ruggedly attractive stranger.

He seemed to be looking for someone. A companion perhaps, coming in on the train? She had watched most of the passengers as they had exited the station. There were no other young women besides herself, and certainly no one she would consider to be an equal partner to this man. She couldn't help but wonder who he had come to see.

By the way he was dressed, she presumed it must be someone important to him. When he didn't appear to recognize anyone, she saw a worried look cross his face. As he started to turn back her way, Jillian quickly turned herself from him so he didn't notice her staring. She took the last few steps to the ticket counter.

"May I help you, miss?" the man behind the counter asked. He was quite a peculiar-looking young man with his hair parted in the middle and curled up on the sides. Thick, round glasses made him look older than he was, and an overgrown, unkempt mustache made it difficult to read his expression. When Jillian didn't answer right away, he cleared his throat loudly.

"Oh, yes," she quickly recovered. In her haste to reach the counter and avoid being caught staring, she had almost forgotten her reason for being there. However, the rude manner in which the clerk had cleared his throat had reminded her of her intentions. "I wanted to inquire about the cost of a ticket to Providence, Massachusetts, and when the next train would be through."

"Let me see," he replied, as he began looking though a list of train schedules while adding the numbers. "Your ticket will be twenty-seven dollars and thirty-five cents, and the next train will come through in three days. That would be Saturday, miss."

"Three days?" Jillian's heart began to beat faster. What would she do? Where would she stay? The clerk cleared his throat. Despite her good manners and upbringing, Jillian couldn't help but return a little of the clerk's bad behavior and flashed him a rude look of her own. He seemed to be taken aback, but when he again spoke, she noted his manner of voice seemed only slightly more polite.

"Excuse me, miss? Did you wish to purchase a ticket?" Jillian shook her head and worried he must think her strange.

"No, no, I was just inquiring." She turned to walk away, but her tutoring in good graces prompted her to add, "Thank you kindly for your time," though not before she caught the look of irritation return to the man's face.

As she headed back to her trunk, her annoyance at the ticket agent's lack of good manners faded quickly, though it was immediately replaced by frustration when her feelings of nervousness and worry returned. She dropped her head slightly, rubbing her hand across her forehead as she walked. Her mind was spinning, and she couldn't think straight. She needed to calm herself and make some decisions. Taking a deep breath, she closed her eyes for a moment to help her focus, though she continued walking. How long should she wait before leaving? Where would she go? What would she do with her trunk?

Just as she opened her eyes, she felt the wind being knocked out of her; she stumbled back, almost losing her balance. Mercifully, she was able to right herself again quickly before causing any damage to herself or anything else, saving herself from further embarrassment. She didn't remember any pillars on the way back to platform, but what she had hit had surely been as hard as one. She looked up quickly. To her great horror, she realized she had not run into a pillar, but a man—the same good-looking stranger in the suit coat she had been admiring moments before. She wanted to turn away and escape her embarrassment, but she was compelled to face her shame. There, at his feet, lay her valise, which she had dropped when she had collided with him.

The man didn't seem to be remotely jostled by their collision, but he turned just the same to see who his attacker had been. At first sight, he wore a look of irritation, but the look was quickly replaced by something akin to sympathy when he saw the look of sheer humiliation she felt on her face.

Before Jillian was able to apologize, another man came hurrying into the station lobby. Jillian and the stranger turned at the same time to observe the new arrival.

This new man appeared to be middle-aged, at least thirty-five or older. He was balding on the top of his head but had tried to hide it by growing the sides long and combing them over the space that was so obviously devoid of hair. His nose would have been a bit too large for his face had his face been normal sized, but too many sweets and not enough exercise had rounded his face out, thus helping to blend in his nose a bit. He wore a hideous plaid suit that wouldn't close across his ample stomach. Jillian eyed him curiously as he checked his pocket watch before scanning the small crowd that was still milling around the station.

The thought suddenly occurred to Jillian that this new arrival must be Dalton McCullough. He had somehow been delayed, just as she had thought. True, he wasn't much to look at, but she quickly hid the disappointed look that had crossed her face. Though he wasn't quite what she had expected, she had to admit she hadn't really known what to expect. The thought had once occurred to her that maybe she should suggest an exchange of photos. In the end, however, she had come to the conclusion that it wouldn't be fair to Mr. McCullough. She didn't want to judge him by how he looked but by what was in his heart, and she wanted no less for herself. He had been clear enough as to his expectations. He was not looking for someone to love, only someone to mother his children. In exchange, he would provide a good, comfortable home and a place of security. She couldn't imagine that it would matter too terribly if they did not find each other attractive.

The fact that he did not want a physical relationship was the reason his letter had interested her in the first place. Her sympathy for his plight in trying to raise three small children on his own had appealed to her heart. She had felt inexplicably drawn to his children and their need for a mother, but she was definitely not looking for a romantic relationship either.

For a moment, she observed this new man again and his lack of physical prowess. Mr. McCullough had told her of his living conditions and that he was a farmer. She had assumed farming required continuous hard physical work and discipline to be successful and had presumed he would be in better physical condition. This man didn't look like he did much of anything.

Jillian quickly chastised herself again. She would not judge him. He would have a fair chance to let his actions prove his character. She thought back on the letters he had written her. His capacity for love was entirely evident when he wrote of his children as well as when he briefly told of the passing of his wife. His reverence and adoration for her was so translucent, it had touched her deeply. No wonder he had no desire for an intimate relationship. She could sense how utterly complete his heartbreak was at losing his wife. Dalton McCullough was a man capable of great feeling. If this was the man who wrote those letters, then surely he was beautiful inside, and that was what was most important to her. Besides, she had had her fill of handsome men who flattered and spoke of love, but who on the inside were as black as coal.

The new arrival turned his head to scan the station again, obviously not seeing who he was looking for. Jillian stood a little taller, trying to catch his attention. Then she realized he must be looking for her yellow handkerchief! She must have dropped it during her collision with the tall stranger. She turned back to the man on the platform who stood before her. He was staring at her. A hot blush rushed to her cheeks again. Then she saw a small corner of her handkerchief just barely sticking out from under her valise, where it had fallen inches from his feet.

Jillian took a step toward the man, still not able to find her voice to utter an apology. As she bent down to retrieve her belongings, he bent down at the same time and their heads collided. Jillian quickly stood up again and placed her hand to her head. The man grabbed his head as well, but in his other hand he held her bag.

Finally, because she was sorely compelled to, she mumbled an apology. She feared the man in the lobby wearing the plaid suit would leave before she could get to her handkerchief. The man standing before her didn't move, though she was sure he had heard her. Jillian kept glancing back at the lobby, a worried look creasing her brow slightly as she did.

"Pardon me, sir," she tried again, "I don't know what's gotten into me today. I'm not usually so clumsy." She kept glancing at her bag as she spoke, hoping he would hand it over before she was left stranded in this horrible station. She chanced another quick look over her shoulder. The man in the lobby was starting to look irritated. She did not want their relationship to start out with him angry at her. She turned her head back again to eye her valise.

The man before her finally seemed to understand her urgency and stepped forward to giver her the bag he held. As he did, to Jillian's horror, his foot came to rest unknowingly on her handkerchief. Now, just a small corner of yellow embroidery poked out from under his right boot.

Two

Dalton McCullough looked into the face of the extraordinarily beautiful woman who stood before him. Her hair was the most beautiful color of strawberry blonde. It looked as soft as spun silk, although she wore it tightly held back in pins and not in a soft style with loose curls, a style he felt would do her more justice. And those eyes—he had never seen a color so green! Her lashes were thick and slightly darker than her hair, as were her perfectly shaped brows. She had obviously come from money by the style of her clothing.

He had noticed her when he had first run into the station, but he'd forced himself to look away. He hadn't driven such a long way to the train station only to admire women, even ones as lovely as she. He had come to greet the woman who was to be his new wife, and he was late. *Why didn't I get an earlier start?* he scolded himself again. He usually prided himself on being punctual, even with three small children to make ready. He had thought he had given himself plenty of time.

Dalton worked hard yesterday to complete some extra chores in order to save himself some time this morning. Things were going smoothly until his daughter Jenny slipped and cut her leg on a nail as they were all getting into the wagon.

Jenny, who usually remained calm in situations like this, went into hysterics. Dalton knew she was already extremely upset with him, and he had been walking on pins and needles all morning, hoping nothing would happen to make things worse. The flood of tears she had been holding back since the night before finally broke free of their dam, and she began to sob inconsolably. Lisa and Brenn, his two other children, weren't used to their older sister crying and wailed right along with her. He had to take all three children back into the house so both Lisa and Brenn could witness him doctoring Jenny's leg, making sure she would be okay.

It was times like these that Dalton sorely missed his wife, Laurellyn. In truth, he still thought of her nearly every waking moment of the day, and his dreams at night were filled with her as well. The dreams didn't hurt so much because he could fool his heart into believing that she was still lying there beside him. The days were different. There were constant reminders everywhere that she was gone, like her flower garden that lay ignored and overgrown.

Laurellyn had loved flowers. Her garden was her pride and joy. Every room in the house had contained a jar or vase filled with those beautiful reminders of her. She always smelled of flowers, especially lavender and roses. Dalton fought to hold back his own tears as the sweet memories of his wife threatened to be his undoing in front of his children, especially since he was the only member of the family not in tears at the moment. He managed to hold back the flood, but he could not hold back the memories.

Dalton forcibly pushed his thoughts back to the task at hand. He cleaned up Jenny's leg as best he could with lye soap and alcohol, like he'd seen their mother do many times before. It was actually quite a bad cut, and out on the frontier, it was impossible to be too careful when it came to injuries. A small, seemingly harmless wound could sometimes mean the loss of a limb, if not taken care of properly. He wrapped a clean strip of cotton cloth around her leg and tied it off. Then he gave her a quick kiss on the cheek and patted her on the back.

"Okay, Jenny Bugs, we need to get going. I really shouldn't be late." Jenny folded her arms across her chest and gave her father a stubborn glare. "Now, come on, Jenny, I've got to get you three over to Auntie Bet's right now. We talked about this last night. Miss Grey will be in a new town and won't know anyone but us. It wouldn't be polite or nice to leave her standing at the station alone."

"Maybe if you're late, she'll turn around and go back to where she

came from. And how come you got all fancied up just to go get her?" Jenny grumbled.

Dalton let out an exasperated breath of air. His daughter wasn't going to make this easy. He would surely be late now as it was.

"Jenny McCullough, you will get in that wagon right now or I will carry you out and put you in myself," he exploded out of frustration. And that's exactly what Dalton ended up doing, for Jenny was bound and determined to be difficult.

When they got to Aunt Betty's house, Jenny clung to him and cried. Of course, that started the other two children howling again. Luckily, Aunt Betty took charge immediately and had things under control in a relatively short time, all things considering.

"Come on, my little sprites, Auntie Bet has made some sugar cookies."

Dalton watched as Aunt Betty carried little Brenn and coaxed Lisa and Jenny into the house. She was actually Laurellyn's aunt, but she had always been there for them both, and he considered her his aunt as well. In fact, if it hadn't been for her, he was sure he couldn't have made it on his own this long since losing Laurellyn. He could still hear Jenny's sobs as she fought control over her emotions. *Laurellyn*, he thought as he hurried to the wagon, *I pray I've done the right thing*. He flung himself into the wagon and hurried through the gate.

Somewhere in the station a man laughed loudly, interrupting Dalton's thoughts and bringing him back to the present. The woman just stood there staring at him. It unnerved him somewhat because she kept fidgeting, nervously opening and shutting her mouth as if she wanted to say something. She also kept taking quick glances back over her shoulder at the odd-looking man standing in the lobby entrance. Dalton watched her as she spent an unusually long time making an observation of the man. Actually, he had been thoroughly captivated by the multitude of expressions that crossed her face, one after the other: shock, disappointment, resolve, relief, and finally admiration.

Surprised, Dalton turned to look at the man. Even though he tried not to be critical, he didn't know what she could have possibly seen that was worthy of her admiration. Maybe she knew him, knew his character. Nothing else made sense. But, somehow he couldn't see how this elegantly dressed, attractive woman could possibly run in the same social circles as this man. When he turned his attention back to the woman's face, the look of admiration had been replaced by a look of determination. Then she turned back to him and suddenly appeared overly nervous again, bordering on panic stricken. He was embarrassed to be caught staring, but he could not seem to pull his eyes away. He was too intrigued with this woman and admittedly a little amused too.

When she spoke to him, her voice was soft and low, and he could detect a slight tremor to it. He could barely make out what she said. He could only assume it was an embarrassed apology for bumping into him the way she had. A moment later, she spoke again—louder this time—and though she was polite, she was unable to keep the distress out of her voice. He knew he was being rude, but he couldn't seem to form the words in his mind to make a reply.

When she glanced down to his hand, it dawned on Dalton that he was still holding her bag. She finally looked relieved when he stepped forward and handed it to her. For a moment he was glad he had helped ease her worry and wiped the panicked look off her face. Then, to his dismay, the panic returned even worse than before.

Jillian had to do something quickly. She could hardly control her breathing. Her emotions were in such a state that she was starting to feel lightheaded and weak. All the worry and stress of the last hour were quickly becoming too much for her. She tried unsuccessfully to recall when she had last eaten. It had surely been too long since she had given her body proper nourishment. If she did not find a remedy to this distressing situation quickly, she would likely be in more trouble, and she wished to avoid any further humiliation.

"Pardon me again, sir." Her mouth was suddenly dry, and her body trembled slightly. "I believe—" she paused, swallowing hard, "I believe you're standing . . . on my handkerchief."

Between the fear of being stranded in a strange town and the panicked feeling that she needed to hurry, her emotions were unraveling quickly. She took another quick glance over her shoulder. The man in the lobby was gone. A look of horror crossed her face until gratefully, she spotted him talking to the clerk at the ticket counter. He would be inquiring about her, no doubt. A momentary feeling of relief washed

over her and she turned again, back to the man before her. He hadn't moved.

Dalton was beginning to worry about the woman standing before him. He feared she would faint, overcome by emotion. He needed to get someone to help this troubled woman so he could find out what had happened to his new wife-to-be.

He was again shaken by thoughts of Laurellyn. Would he ever be able to control the constant threat of tears, even at the slightest thought of his lost love? He would have to at least learn to hide his feelings in front of his new wife. Even though they would not share the same kind of relationship he had with Laurellyn, he did want her to feel comfortable and welcome in her new home.

Dalton glanced down at the ground to hide his face and to take a moment to recover himself. As he did, he saw something small and delicate sticking out from under his boot. What was he standing on? He tried to recall what the woman had said to him moments before, something about a handkerchief. He moved his foot aside and bent down to retrieve the dainty-looking thing. It had been soiled badly, no doubt by his boot, and he cringed guiltily. As he slowly stood back up, he looked at it more closely. He noticed the intricate yellow stitching that went around the border. A small, yellow rose completed its perfect design.

Suddenly, Dalton froze. His mind started to whirl, and he tried to think back to the exact words that had been printed on Miss Grey's last telegram. She had mentioned her arrival time—that was the main purpose for the telegram—but then there had been something else written, farther down. He had only briefly glanced over it. What had it said? He should have paid better attention. Dalton forced himself to return to the present. He was sure the telegram had mentioned something about a handkerchief, a yellow embroidered one. Yes, he remembered, she had written that she would be holding a yellow embroidered handkerchief so he would know who she was.

Suddenly, realization washed over him. The woman who stood before him was Miss Jillian Grey, soon to be Mrs. Jillian McCullough. But how could this be? She was definitely not what he had expected, though honestly, he wasn't sure what he had been expecting. He knew from their written correspondence that she was young—just seventeen.

He had been concerned about her age at first. Why would a girl so young sign up to be a mail-order bride? Did she have some strange affliction that made her chances of finding a husband the traditional way impossible? In her letters she had sounded so mature and sure of herself. Certainly her qualifications had been more than sufficient. She had even studied at a university for nearly a year, which would mean she could teach the children if needed. Jenny had fallen behind in her schooling in the last year. With the loss of their mother, it had been hard to adjust to running the house and the farm. She had missed too many days of school and had been unable to make up her work.

Dalton tried to remember the description Miss Grey had given him: she was about five foot seven, plain, with green eyes, and strawberry blonde hair. Had she really described herself as plain? Yes, he distinctly remembered her using that particular word. He looked her over more closely. He figured her height to be right, and her hair was most definitely the color she'd described—what he could see of it anyway. Her eyes . . . yes, they were the same stunning green he'd noticed when he'd first observed her. But plain? He questioned once again. No, this woman—this raving beauty that stood before him— was anything but plain!

And she certainly didn't look like any girl of seventeen he had ever seen. Of course, he didn't get to town much these days; he usually had too much work to get done. Besides, he was uncomfortable around all the single women in town who always seemed to find some excuse to talk and flirt with him. He usually just sent a list and some money with Aunt Betty. Sometimes she would take the children, so he didn't feel too guilty. No, he was definitely no expert on what young women of seventeen looked like these days, but he hadn't imagined them so . . . so womanly.

He had married Laurellyn when she was sixteen, and he didn't remember her figure being so well formed. Of course, he had only been seventeen at the time. Maybe he had seen things from a different perspective.

After eight years of marriage, he felt so much older. A seventeen-year-old girl had seemed young to him . . . and safe, he thought. Even though he knew girls out here married even younger than that, he had made it clear just what their relationship would be. Dalton shook his head slightly to get his thoughts straightened out. Not only had he not been expecting an attractive and grown-up looking woman, it was exactly what he hadn't wanted. He did not like the way she seemed to awaken feelings in him. Feelings and emotions that needed to stay locked away. He wasn't looking for romance and neither was she. She had been crystal clear to him about what she was expecting. He had been comforted by the fact that she had no expectations of him, other than providing a home and protection for her in return for caring for his children.

Besides, he had Laurellyn. Well, he had her memory anyway. His heart was full. There was no room for another woman. He'd stemmed the flow of love from his heart when Laurellyn had taken her last breath. His heart was dead to anyone else romantically.

As he looked at the young woman now standing before him, it was obvious that she didn't recognize him either. If nothing else, it was evident by the look of irritation she was giving him. They definitely needed to talk.

Jillian's frustration was getting worse. Just when she finally thought she had gotten through to this man, he seemed to freeze up again. Now he stood staring at her, just holding her handkerchief out in front of him, but making no move to hand it to her. He looked like he was trying to remember something for a moment, and then he seemed to shut down all together. She watched as a look of realization crossed over his face.

When he looked down at the handkerchief he was holding, his whole demeanor changed, as though he was seeing her for the first time. His eyes even moved over her whole figure, from head to toe, taking it in slowly. What was this man playing at? Jillian did not have any more time to waste on trying to be polite. Mr. McCullough appeared to be finishing his conversation with the ticket clerk. With one swift move, she reached out and snatched the handkerchief out of the hand of the man standing before her.

"Thank you!" Jillian said rather rudely and stomped her foot for emphasis. She was a little bit embarrassed to be acting with such impertinence, but the confusing man left her no choice. She was shocked when he grabbed her hand as she turned to walk away. Unprepared, Jillian felt a tingling sensation travel quickly up her arm, which only served to irritate her more.

"Let me go! What are you doing?" Jillian attempted to pull her hand out of his firm grip.

"Miss, I . . . uh, I think we need to talk," the man said, trying to get her to wait.

"We most certainly do not! Now let me go before I scream for help."

⌘

Dalton had no choice but to let go. The young woman darted across the station just as the stranger in the plaid suit moved away from the ticket counter.

All of a sudden, it dawned on him why she had been so anxious and irritated when he had not handed over her handkerchief more quickly. *No*, Dalton thought. *She couldn't possibly think . . . but she must!* It all made sense now, even all the panicked glances over her shoulder.

Dalton tried to keep a straight face. *Don't laugh*, he told himself. After all, it was apparent that the poor young woman was having an emotional time, which was probably his fault. He couldn't suppress a grin, however. He tried to stop her to explain who he was, but she wouldn't listen. So Dalton decided to wait and see how the scene before him played out.

Dalton really couldn't hold in a chortle as Miss Grey rushed to the balding man in the horrible plaid suit, practically waving her hand-kerchief in front of her. He still couldn't believe that she thought this man could be him. He couldn't hear what they were saying, but after a couple minutes had passed, he saw her wave her hankie again, a little more obviously this time, while still trying to be somewhat discreet.

Just then, Dalton felt someone tapping him on the shoulder. He turned to see an elderly man, roughly in his early sixties, standing behind him.

"Pardon me, sir, but my wife just got in on the afternoon train from a visit with her sister in Chicago. I'm always telling her when she travels, 'Now dear, you know you'll only be gone a few days, so pack only what you need.' " He grinned and shook his head. "They never listen. I wouldn't be surprised to find she's packed half of the house in that trunk."

Dalton looked across the station at the frail woman who was obviously the wife of this man. She was looking very chagrined. Surely she must suspect what her husband was saying. They appeared to be a sweet old couple, and he had always imagined that he and Laurellyn would look that way one day, growing old together. The little old man grinned again, boasting an almost toothless smile, and looked up at him hopefully. Dalton couldn't help thinking to himself that with any luck, he'd have a few more teeth when he reached that age.

He smiled at the couple. He understood what the old man was asking. Certainly it wouldn't do any harm to help him—it wouldn't take but a minute or two. Things seemed to be well in hand with Miss Grey and his substitute over at the platform lobby, although he would be sad to miss out on anything interesting. She would figure out her mistake eventually. As he grinned again, Dalton realized that he had smiled more since arriving at the train station today than he had in a very long time. Not wanting to miss anything, Dalton hurried over to the old woman's trunk, picked it up with almost no effort, and walked out the side door of the station to the old man's waiting wagon.

Jillian hurried across the lobby before the man in the awful plaid suit could reach the door. She held her handkerchief in front of her where it could not be missed.

"Excuse me, sir." Still a little out of breath from her mad dash across the platform to the lobby, she willed her voice to sound normal. "Were you looking for someone?"

The man looked startled at first, surprised that she had spoken to him, but then a satisfying smile slowing crossed his face. "Well now, I don't know. Were you looking for someone?"

Charles Richard Fitzgerald III, or Chuckles, as everyone down at the saloon usually called him, couldn't believe his luck. He had come to the station to fetch his brother. He had left a perfectly good game of cards to do it too, only to find that Jimmy had missed his connection in Chicago. The ticket clerk had had a telegram waiting for him at the booth.

That blasted brother of mine, Chuckles thought. He probably decided to pass the time in a nearby saloon and got drunk and passed out. Chuckles was willing to bet that was exactly what had happened, and Chuckles knew when a bet was good. He'd sure had a run of good luck lately. Even now, this fine-looking woman was talking to him. Maybe the long trip to the station had been worth it after all.

Jillian was puzzled by his reply at first. Maybe he was just being cautious. She thought maybe she ought to play it safe too. She gave the handkerchief another little wave in front of him to jog his memory. He looked at it, but didn't said anything. She thought maybe she ought to try a different approach.

"Were you expecting anyone in on the train from Chicago?" Jillian asked.

"Yep," he replied. He grinned a little wider as his eyes traveled slowly over her.

What is wrong with the men in this town? Getting a little angry and irritated, Jillian remembered how the handsome stranger had taken her in with his eyes in much the same way, just moments earlier. *Well no,* she admitted to herself, *that man definitely did not have the same look of hunger in his eyes as this man does.* She realized that the handsome stranger hadn't made her feel the least bit uncomfortable. Turning back to the balding man, she tried one more time for some sort of recognition. She was starting to feel uneasy.

"Well, who were you waiting for?" She was getting bold and she knew it, but frankly she was tired being ogled, tired of all these games, and especially tired of being in this train station!

"If I told you I had been waiting for you, could I take you home with me?" He reached out to grab a hold of her and missed, just as she realized her terrible mistake. She had no idea who he was, but one thing she knew for sure: This man was not the Dalton McCullough who had written those tender letters. What had she'd been thinking?

Now that the man in the plaid suit was standing closer to her, Jillian could smell the alcohol on his breath. He reached out to grab her again, got a good hold on her arm, and started moving her toward the door.

"Come on, little lady. I'll find you a nice warm bed to sleep in tonight."

"Let go of me, you horrible man!" Jillian felt hot tears start to burn her cheeks, and her knees weakened as fear coursed through her body, causing her to tremble.

"Oh, so now I'm horrible, am I? I seen you watching me since I came into the station. You think I didn't notice all them glances you were givin' me? I wasn't sure what you was all about, especially while you were standin' over there with that other feller. I reckon he wasn't so interested in your proposition. I figure that's why you come over a rushin' after me so quickly."

Jillian gasped. This new revelation only caused her to shake more uncontrollably than before. *He thinks I'm a*— She couldn't even finish the thought. What kind of awful place was this? Did she look to be that sort of woman?

Chuckles didn't like the look on the woman's face. Not only was she crying, but she was starting to shake something terrible, not to mention she had turned as pale as buttermilk.

He didn't want no trouble. He had misread her intentions was all. She obviously needed help from someone and it wasn't gonna be him. He was gettin' outta there fast and back to the saloon. Suddenly, Chuckles needed a drink, and he needed it badly.

Outside the station, the old man and woman thanked Dalton profusely. He smiled as he wondered how on earth they would ever get that trunk inside the house when they got home. He shook his head at the thought and hurried back to the platform.

Immediately, Dalton sensed something had gone terribly wrong in his absence. Jillian was crying and shaking uncontrollably. Her face had lost all color, and he could see she was in danger of fainting before too long, but apparently that wasn't the only danger she was facing. The balding man in the plaid suit had grabbed hold of her arm and appeared to be dragging her toward the station door. Dalton's anger took control, and he crossed the platform and was in the lobby in mere seconds. How dare he handle a woman in such a manner! And this was not just any woman; she was going to be his wife and mother to his children. The awful man would most certainly deserve the blow he would give him.

The room had just started to spin when Jillian thought she saw someone come up next to her and hit the horrible man in the face. Her knees finally buckled under her, and she felt herself falling. As she began to lose consciousness, she felt a pair of strong arms catch her. At the same time, she hit something hard and felt a maddening pain coursing through her head. A second later, everything went black.

As soon as Dalton had made contact with the man's face, he saw Jillian begin to fall. In one swift move, he caught her up in his arms, but not in time to prevent her head from hitting the wall directly behind her. Cringing at the sound, he quickly carried her over to one of the benches that lined the walls of the station and laid her down. He couldn't believe he had been laughing at her only minutes before. What had happened in the few moments he had stepped outside?

This was his fault. He shouldn't have let this happen. He should have insisted she talk to him and not have let her go to converse with that depraved man. What a way to start out their new life together. He hoped it was not a bad omen.

Three

Dalton felt a rush of relief run through him when he saw Miss Grey finally begin to stir. She had been out for almost twenty minutes, and he was beginning to seriously worry. One of the railway attendants had gone to fetch the sheriff, who arrived shortly after Dalton had knocked Chuckles out. Dalton wanted to take her to see the doctor, but the sheriff informed him that the doctor was out of town for the day. Dalton prayed her head injury wasn't serious. He felt the small bump on the back of her head and then looked down at the finger-sized bruises he could already see beginning to appear on the delicate ivory skin of her left arm.

Dalton felt anger rise in him once more. He knew she would recover from the physical injuries, but it was the emotional injuries that worried him most. Again he felt a great pang of guilt pass through him.

The sheriff had asked Dalton to come with him to the jailhouse to report what he had witnessed of the incident, but Dalton refused to leave Jillian's side. It was because of him that she lay there unconscious. He wouldn't leave her unattended again. Apparently though, according to the sheriff, there was some confusion as to who was truly at fault. He couldn't hide his disgust. How could anyone believe that this innocent woman could have possibly been the cause of any of the atrocities that had occurred here?

Both Chuckles and Jillian were unconscious and therefore unable to explain their sides of the story. Dalton had told the sheriff what he had witnessed. He thought the incident had been pretty clear, but as the sheriff had been making ready to leave, the ticket clerk, of all people, had called the sheriff over to his window and recounted an unbelievably different story. Something about how Miss Grey seemed mentally disturbed and how Chuckles was trying to help.

"Then that man there," the clerk said, pointing at Dalton, "barreled in the side door of the station, rushed into the lobby, and knocked Chuckles out cold. Next thing I know, that woman fainted and hit her head. Very convenient if you ask me."

Nobody asked you, Dalton thought, fighting to control his rising temper.

When the sheriff walked back over to Miss Grey to check on her one last time before he left, Dalton took a moment to speak to him. He explained who Miss Grey was, why she was here, and about how his tardiness had caused so much confusion. Just then, Chuckles started to come around, and the sheriff informed him that he would take Mr. Fitzgerald over to the jailhouse until they could sort everything out.

"As soon as the missus comes around and is able to get about," the sheriff said, "I'll be wantin' ya to come on over to my office to be makin' sure I got all yer stories straight. I'm sure I'll have gotten Chuckles's side by then." Dalton stood up and started to protest, but the sheriff shook his head. "Now don't go gettin' them feathers all ruffled up again, boy. I believe what you been tellin' me. Chuckles ain't been no stranger down at the jailhouse over the years." This did not surprise Dalton. "I ain't daft in the head. I can see this woman is a genuine lady, as plain as day. Now it's just a formality, ya see, because of that other witness. I won't even be makin' ya bring her inside with ya. She can wait out in yer wagon. Don't want the sight of old Chuckles causin' her to faint again in my jailhouse. You just come on in, look over what I wrote down 'bout what you've been tellin' me happened here today, and sign it fer the both of ya. If the story you've been tellin' me is true, you'll shortly be man and wife anyhow, so I don't mind ya signing fer the lady."

The sheriff paused for a moment and scratched at the side of his head. "Though I can't figure it, I ain't never seen no mail-order bride lookin' as good as that one there. Shoot, if I weren't already married, I might be signin' up fer one of them gals real quick-like m'self!" He grinned and gave Dalton a wink. "Though I suspect you're just one heck of a lucky guy. Bet they only come that good lookin' one in a million." He chuckled a bit to himself and then added, "Bet you're relieved,

though. I never figured how any man could go sending off fer some woman, promisin' to marry her afore he ever even got a good look at her. I'd be offering up some extra prayers of thanks tonight if I was you, boy."

He gave Dalton a friendly jab, took one more look at Jillian before giving a low whistle, and turned back to go assist his deputy. Chuckles was being uncooperative, and it took both the sheriff and the deputy to maneuver the big man out through the train station door.

Dalton took a few steps toward the ticket counter, and the clerk gave him a scowl. He had obviously been eavesdropping. Dalton couldn't help but clench his fist. He suspected there had been more than one man in this train station today in need of a good lesson about the proper way to treat a lady. He gave the clerk a warning look that made the younger man visibly nervous. *Good*, Dalton thought. *Let him think on that awhile.*

Walking back over to where Jillian lay, Dalton gazed down at her tenderly. It disturbed him how his heart had begun to beat so fast in his chest when he caught her from falling and held her soft, warm body in his arms. Panicked at the sudden rush of emotion, he had quickly laid her down. He'd removed and folded his suit coat and placed it beneath her head, gently inspecting her injury as he did. It had swelled slightly, but was not bleeding.

She looked so peaceful and beautiful lying there now. All evidence of the fear and panic that had disturbed her perfect features earlier was gone. Some of the coloring had even returned to her face. That was a good sign.

In her struggle with Mr. Fitzgerald, a number of her hairpins had fallen out, and now a cascade of strawberry curls fell around her face. Surprisingly, he felt himself fighting the impulse to reach out and feel the softness of those curls between his fingers. A sense of guilt washed over him. Dalton forced himself to turn his back to her. As he did, his hand unconsciously went into his pants pocket and desperately clasped the small, delicate cameo that lay hidden there. He did not want this temptation. He purposely called on a memory of his late wife.

Laurellyn was baking bread early one Saturday when Dalton came in from doing his morning chores. Little Jenny, just two and a half, was playing on the kitchen floor by Laurellyn's feet with the wooden blocks Dalton had made last Christmas.

Baking had always been a struggle for Laurellyn, and it pained her deeply that she was not more efficient at it. Aunt Betty had always been a marvelous cook, and she often wished she had inherited more of her aunt's talent. The biggest problem, he suspected, wasn't that she couldn't improve her cooking skills with practice. She did try to from time to time, but her heart just wasn't in it. The truth of it was that she would rather be digging her hands into a garden full of rich, dark soil than in a bowl full of flour.

Laurellyn knew just enough to get by, but Dalton had not suffered. Aunt Betty was forever sneaking some sweets or a small treat, wrapped in a napkin, into his hands or his pocket when he'd leave her house after one of his frequent visits. Besides, if he had to eat burnt hotcakes every morning for breakfast, he would do it willingly and with a smile on his face, as long as his sweetheart was there at his side.

Laurellyn spent most of her free time in either her gardens or with the animals, her other love. Old Decker, Dalton's horse, was her particular favorite. That morning, however, she felt guilty for not baking homemade treats more often for Dalton. She had it in her mind to make him a batch of cinnamon rolls and had even ridden over to Aunt Betty's the afternoon before to get a copy of her recipe and instructions. When he came into the house, she was trying to knead the dough, but obviously something had gone terribly wrong with it. It was much too sticky. Her fingers were covered with the stuff, and she was desperately trying to free her fingers from the caked-on mess.

Laurellyn looked up at Dalton when she heard the door close. A look of frustration pained her face, what he could see of it anyway. He feared she had more flour on her face and in her hair than she had started with in the bowl. No wonder the dough was so sticky! He couldn't help but laugh. Her look of frustration turned to a glare, and then, just as quickly, a grin began to turn up the corners of her mouth. He could read in her eyes what she was thinking.

"Oh, no you don't, Mrs. Laurellyn McCullough. I will turn you over my knee and tan your hide but good if you do what I think you're wanting to do," he threatened.

It was too late. He saw the look of mischief in her eyes. Before he could open his mouth again, he felt something moist and sticky hit the

side of his head and begin to slowly creep down his face. He feigned a look of anger before turning briefly to hang his hat on the hook by the door. Before he even had a chance to turn around again, he felt something else hit him squarely on his back. On the floor, little Jenny squealed with delight and clapped her hands.

"Ooh, Daddy sticky," she laughed.

"Yes, Jenny Bugs, Daddy's sticky, and Mommy will be too, in a second." Jenny squealed again as Dalton took two large steps forward and grabbed the bowl of dough from off the table.

"Oh, no you don't, Dalton." She started to back away and maneuvered herself so that the table stood between them. "You deserved it, you know, for laughing at me." She pretended to pout. "Here I've been, slaving away in this hot kitchen for half of the morning, trying to make something nice for you, and you . . . you laugh!" He could tell she wanted to put her hands on her hips to make her indignation abundantly clear, but she didn't want to get more of the botched dough on her dress. Instead, she lifted her chin and turned her head to the side and said, "Humph!"

Dalton smiled to himself. "You're right. I shouldn't have laughed." He forced a serious and penitent look to his face and set the bowl back on the table. "Here . . . truce . . . see?" He raised his hands a few inches higher. Laurellyn tried to look upset, but Dalton could tell by the merriment in her eyes that she was not really angry with him.

"Now look at what a mess I've made of things!" she exclaimed. "I suppose I'll clean this up while you go wash up for lunch."

Dalton raised one eyebrow. "Maybe I should clean this mess up while you go wash up for lunch." He chuckled softly.

"Maybe you're right, Dalton McCullough. I must look awfully horrible." Unfortunately, he missed the look of mischief that had returned to her eyes. "Come, let's kiss and make up before I go and try to make myself a bit more presentable." Laurellyn walked back around the table and stood in front of him.

Dalton leaned toward Laurellyn. He tried to make sure that the least amount of him might touch her as possible for fear she would transfer her floury mess onto him. Just as their lips met, though, two sticky hands grabbed both sides of his face.

"Ha!" she shouted in triumph.

Dalton released his hold on the cameo in his pocket and turned back to Miss Grey, strengthened again in his resolve not to think of this woman beyond friendship. She stirred again and moaned softly. He decided to get a cool cloth for her head and a drink of water. She would surely have a headache and be thirsty when she woke.

❧

Jillian felt something cool and wet being pressed gently to the back of her head and then to her forehead. The feel of it both shocked her tender skin and refreshed her aching head at the same time. Her limbs were heavy and weak, and she didn't dare try to move them yet. She was vaguely aware that she was lying on something hard and uncomfortable and that there was a tender spot on the back of her head. She was grateful for the folded cloth underneath it. It had an unfamiliar but pleasant scent of leather and soap that tickled her nose. She willed her eyes to open.

The light that assaulted her eyes immediately triggered a throbbing in her temples. She grimaced, closed her eyes again, and, despite the pain, tried to sit up.

"Whoa, Miss Grey, hold up there. You shouldn't try to sit up just yet. Take it easy awhile longer. I have a glass of water for you."

At once, Jillian felt a pair of strong but gentle hands push tenderly against her shoulders, forcing her to lie back down. She kept her eyes closed; the darkness was soothing. She tried to collect her thoughts. Who had spoken to her? His voice was vaguely familiar, but how had he known her name? There could be only one man at this station who would know who she was. Again she willed her eyes to open, this time forcing them to stay that way. Slowly her vision adjusted to the light, and she was able to focus on her surroundings.

For a moment, Jillian couldn't remember everything that had happened, just that things hadn't gone as she had expected them to. She remembered being worried about being late and that there had been no one waiting for her upon her arrival. All of a sudden, a flood of images came rushing back at once. Her first impulse was to flee as a feeling of fear gripped at her heart. However, when she attempted to push herself up to a vertical position for a second time, she felt the room spin, and a sudden feeling of nausea turn her stomach.

Relaxing back down to the bench, Jillian took a deep breath, closed

her eyes, and concentrated on settling her stomach and slowing her racing heart. She felt a glass being pressed lightly to her lips and a cool liquid travel slowly down her throat. It felt soothing and revitalizing, and she summoned her strength. She was suddenly all too aware of the strong need rising within her to see the man who had spoken to her a moment ago.

Jillian struggled to force herself up again and felt those same gentle hands on her once more. This time though, they helped her to a sitting position. As she swung her legs around her so that her feet were planted on the floor, she was compelled to place her head in her hands to stop the sudden rush of blood that made the throbbing sensation and the pain worsen.

"Miss Grey, please . . . take it easy. You've had a terrible ordeal. You were quite shaken and you've hit your head. You have been out for about twenty minutes now."

There was that voice again, soft and pleading, and somehow familiar. Mr. McCullough had finally come for her—she knew it. Jillian lifted her head to look up into the face of her husband-to-be.

"Miss Grey," Dalton hurried and spoke first. He could see that she immediately looked flustered. "I am Dalton McCullough." He paused when she looked back down, away from him. "You are Miss Jillian Grey, aren't you?" He noticed a slight nod of her head. A rush of relief flooded over him. "I'm afraid I owe you an apology. If it hadn't been for me—" his voice broke slightly—"I mean, if I hadn't been so late getting to the station—" again, he paused before continuing—"I fear none of this would have happened."

Jillian lifted her head back up and stared at him for a moment before she could respond. She was having a hard time taking in the fact that this man was who he said he was. She knew she was staring, and it occurred to her that he'd probably think her rude, but then a thought much worse than that seized her mind.

What must he think of her? Jillian tried to recall everything that had happened since she'd first seen him running into the station. What of all the things she had said and done? She felt the heat in her cheeks as she recalled one embarrassing encounter after another.

She had run into him. She could still feel the bruised skin on her shoulder under her dress. There was a pain on her forehead too, though not as bad as the one on the back of her head. Yes, she remembered they had bumped heads while both trying to retrieve her valise at the same time. *Maybe this would be easier if I just felt around for bruises and tried to remember how I got them*, Jillian thought ruefully.

As though her body had been listening to her, she was suddenly and painfully aware of the ache in her left forearm. The face of the plaid-suited man and all the horror that came with it flashed before her eyes. Her face burned unbearably hot. What must Mr. McCullough think of her, rudely brushing him off and practically chasing after that other man? He must have known who she was by then. *Oh*, she thought, *the handkerchief!* The more she remembered, the worse she felt. Had she actually snatched it out of his hand before running off? To his credit, she remembered that he had tried to stop her and again she had been rude to him. She pressed her hands to her forehead and looked down. She had to stop the flow of memories. Her humiliation was already complete.

After a moment, she finally found her voice and looked timidly into his face again. She couldn't help but be touched by the worry and compassion evident in the deep blue hue of his eyes.

"Mr. McCullough, I am sure much of the blame rests with me. You've no need to trouble yourself about it any longer," she said quietly. She then leaned forward to gather her belongings that lay on the floor beside her feet. As she did, strands of her hair fell forward and hung in front of her face. It wasn't until that moment she had even considered how deplorable she must look. Reaching up, she felt the back of her head to check her bun and examine the damage that had been done, noting the tender bump. She had lost too many of her hair pins and knew that any hope of salvaging the bun was hopeless. Reluctantly, she reached back and pulled the remainder of the pins out and stowed them in her pocket. Her hair fell instantly past her shoulders, stopping just short of her waist. To her shame, all her unruly curls were clearly on display. She was painfully aware of her audience and fixed her eyes in front of her while she began to work.

With nimble fingers and years of practice, she quickly gathered her hair in her hands and braided it. She wrapped a small ribbon around

the end to secure it, which she had retrieved from her pocket. She often kept ribbon in a pocket or handbag in case of just such a necessity.

Her hair was forever giving her trouble and falling out of its trappings at the most inopportune times. As a child, she had cried many nights, wishing she had inherited the tame, soft waves of her mother's auburn hair instead of the unruly curls of her father's. She was grateful, though it was indeed unruly and seemingly had a mind of its own most days, that she had at least inherited some of the softness of her mother's hair. In truth, she hated to do her hair up at all. Maybe it was because she was forever fighting it, but she had grown accustomed to wearing it down as a child. It had always been a fight to tame the curls, and her mother had often given in and allowed it to be worn loose. When she had turned fourteen, however, her mother had insisted she start wearing it up, as was the proper fashion for her age. But the first chance she got every night, out would come the pins.

When Jillian finished her braid, she dared to look up at Dalton. He was watching her closely. It unnerved her slightly. He was so handsome. She had never seen anyone quite like him. His dark hair was thick and wavy. He wore it shorter than some men she had seen, but not so short that it couldn't fall in perfect waves around his face. He was glad to see that he was clean shaven. She didn't care much for men who wore their beards thick and heavy, and she definitely preferred none at all. For some reason, she had pictured that he would have a beard. Farmers were busy men; to shave every morning would only serve to take up precious time that could be spent in more productive ways. At least that's what she had always thought. At any rate, she had prepared herself to be married to a man who wore a beard.

Dalton's eyes were so blue. They made her recall the sky over the ocean the morning after a storm, when the sun burned bright and full of hope. As for the rest of him, well, not even the most eligible and sought-after bachelors back in Providence could hold a candle to the Adonis-like features of Dalton McCullough. He wore a white shirt with no coat. He had rolled up the sleeves, and she could see the muscles in his tanned forearms twitch every so often, as though they were not used to holding still for very long. A couple of the buttons on his shirt had come undone, and the upper part of his chest was exposed. She tried to pull her eyes away, but found it surprisingly difficult to do so.

A sudden thought puzzled her for a moment. He had been wearing a dark blue suit coat when he had come into the station. She glanced around, looking for where it might have gone. She spotted it next to her, folded into a neat pile. She hadn't noticed it there before. As Jillian gathered her things, she reached over to retrieve the coat as well and slowly stood.

"I believe this is yours." She handed the coat across to him. As she did, she briefly caught the pleasant scent that had tickled her nose earlier. She then realized why his coat had been placed there, and again she was touched, this time by his concern for her comfort. "Thank you, Mr. McCullough, for your kind consideration on my behalf."

Dalton watched Jillian closely as she reached back and felt the hair that had come loose from its intended place at the back of her head. Ever since he had admired her strawberry curls tenderly laying about her face as she had lain there unconscious, he was curious to see how her hair would look hanging free in all its glory. For a moment he was disappointed, thinking she would attempt to pull the loose strands back into the bun. All of a sudden, she reluctantly pulled out the rest of the pins, and her hair came tumbling down around her. He wasn't prepared for his reaction and was glad she was looking forward and didn't notice his quick, but sharp intake of breath.

Almost as quickly as those stubborn curls had escaped from their imprisonment, they were whisked back with her slight fingers and quickly worked into a soft braid that hung down the length of her back. He liked it better that way. He could never understand why some women would grow such beautifully long hair and then wear it all day tightly wound and hidden at the back of their necks. Laurellyn had worn her hair down loose often enough. She knew he liked it that way, and though he knew that she didn't, she would wear it down to please him.

Looking back at Miss Grey, he realized she was handing him his coat. He reached across and took the coat from her hand, but made no move to put in on. He looked thoughtfully at Miss Grey and soon realized he was being rude not to respond to her polite thanks.

"It was the least I could do, Miss Grey, seeing as I was the cause of all your troubles."

Jillian considered arguing with him about whose blame this awkward situation truly was, but she was extremely tired and hungry, not to mention that her head was still throbbing incessantly. She was ready to leave the station.

"Listen." Dalton's face suddenly became serious. "I know this has all been terribly difficult for you. I didn't mean for things to go so wrong." He paused. "I would understand if you . . . well, if you've changed your mind about our whole arrangement. I could buy you a ticket home and rent a room over at the hotel for you until the train comes back through."

Jillian felt as if the breath had been knocked out of her. He wanted her to leave. She must have embarrassed him beyond forgiveness. Maybe he thought she would be more attractive, though she had specifically described herself as plain. She hadn't wanted him to have any preconceived notions of what to expect. When he hadn't stopped writing, she had assumed he wasn't concerned with her appearance.

Sighing, she considered herself for a moment. Even though she wasn't the most beautiful woman, she knew she wasn't horrible to look at. Besides, their relationship would be purely platonic. No, it mustn't be her looks that concerned him. Something else was bothering him.

The thought suddenly occurred that maybe he was worried about the children. The way she had acted! He must have decided that she would not be a good choice for a mother. She should try to explain why she had acted so out of character. But would he think she was begging him to keep her? The thought made her cringe. She thought of the children again and felt a tug at the corner of her heart. She couldn't leave. She didn't understand why, but she already loved this man's children and felt a need to protect them. Surely they were expecting her. She couldn't disappoint them.

"I see no reason to sever our agreement, unless—" Jillian paused to gather her courage, "—unless you feel the need to do so." Instinctively, she closed her eyes to try to shield herself from his reply.

Dalton was torn. A part of him wished she had agreed to go back home. Already he was fighting to keep thoughts of this woman from his mind, thoughts that were crowding Laurellyn's space in his heart. Still, there was another part of him that feared if he allowed her to go, it would be one of the biggest mistakes he ever made. The children needed her, were waiting for her. He couldn't explain it, but he felt that somehow, despite his frustrations about his attraction to her, this woman was meant to come into their family.

He had felt it as he had read her letters, when she wrote of her home, her loving family, and the mother she greatly admired. It was as though Laurellyn had whispered her blessing to his heart. How could he deny that? How could he stand here and hope Jillian might leave and go back for his own selfish reasons? Dalton knew he could sustain himself with thoughts of Laurellyn, but what about little Lisa and Brenn? They didn't remember their mother. They needed a woman to love them, nurture them, and help them grow. Jenny, whether she knew it or not, did too.

All doubt was suddenly washed from his mind and from his heart. Dalton knew. Yes, he knew, without a doubt, that even though Jenny would fight against her, Miss Jillian Grey would be the one that would heal his oldest daughter's heart. Dalton smiled and reached over to unburden Jillian of her bag.

"No, Miss Grey, I have no objections." He looked around. "Well," he paused. "Maybe I do have one objection." Dalton saw Jillian stiffen slightly. "I object to spending one minute longer than I have to in this blasted train station!" She visibly relaxed then, and he smiled again, a little wider this time. "Now, if you will kindly point me in the right direction in order to collect your trunk, we can be on our way."

Dalton walked to the middle of the platform. The station was at this point entirely vacant with the exception of the ticket clerk, who was still scowling at them from behind his glass window. The only other exception was the one single, solitary, and very lonely looking trunk sitting unattended in the middle of the platform. Despite all that had happened, Jillian couldn't help but smile as well.

Four

Jillian sat alone in the wagon out in front of the jailhouse, hungry and still weakened from her ordeal. She shuddered to think of the man in plaid who was locked up inside. Dalton had promised he would only be a moment. Jillian immediately felt a surge of fear when Dalton first mentioned the delay. The sheriff had made it plain that they were to stop in at the jailhouse before they could go to the courthouse. Dalton quickly explained that the sheriff had agreed she could wait in the wagon while he took care of everything. He had told Jillian that he felt the need to explain their circumstances to the sheriff in order to shed some light on everything that had happened at the station. Aside from the fiasco with Mr. Fitzgerald, she wondered what the sheriff must think of her. Mail-order brides were not uncommon, but still, she had to wonder what others thought about her for choosing to become one.

Jillian breathed in deeply. She couldn't believe she was finally out in the fresh air again. It had been almost two hours since her train had arrived. Jillian's stomach growled, reminding her of how long it had been since she had eaten. She wished she had thought to pack something to nibble on just in case. The apple she ate on the train was long gone, yet she didn't feel comfortable mentioning her plight to Dalton. She was sure he was anxious to get home. They had already lost a lot of time, and she was sure that no matter what time they finally did get home, there would be chores waiting for him. She prayed her stomach would not give her away.

The moment Dalton entered the jailhouse, his good mood instantly faded away, and he felt himself getting angry again. The man nick-named "Chuckles" sat glaring at him from his jail cell. Dalton resolved to make this meeting as quick as possible. That man made his skin crawl, and he wanted to be done with him and this whole business. The sheriff greeted him from behind his desk.

"Howdy, Mr. McCullough, I've been hopin' you'd be arrivin' soon. I'm needin' to get home early today, and I'm wantin' to be finished with this here whole train station business. Me and the missus are expectin' company come mornin', and she has a list as long as my arm here that she's a-wantin' me to get done tonight. So iffin' you don't mind comin' right on over and takin' a look at this here report, we'll get on with it. Then, if everythin' looks to be about how you remember it all happenin', just put your 'John Hancock' right here and yer soon-to-be wife's right there." He pointed to where he wanted Dalton to sign.

Dalton picked up the book and read the account. It all seemed accurate, so he first signed his name and then wrote 'Miss Jillian Grey' on the other line. He laid the book back down on the sheriff's desk. The sheriff closed it and stood up, extending his hand to Dalton. Dalton took his hand.

"Well, that'll do," the sheriff said and placed his free hand on Dalton's shoulder and gave it a squeeze. "Thank you for coming by. Oh and . . . " he gave Dalton a sly look and then a wink, "congratulations on the upcomin' nuptials!"

"Thank you, Sheriff," Dalton said as the sheriff shook his hand heartily before releasing it. He turned to go, pausing briefly to look back once more at Chuckles. By the look of sheer hatred in the man's eyes, Dalton knew he had made a true enemy. Even though the man was less than formidable, Chuckles had no scruples, and such a man was capable of anything. As Dalton stepped out through the door, an ominous feeling came over him despite the warmth of the day. He felt a shiver run down his spine.

A sense of nervousness assaulted Jillian as soon as Dalton pulled the wagon to a stop in front of the courthouse. The ride from the jailhouse had been short, and they hadn't talked much. Jillian felt that something was bothering Dalton. She didn't know what had gone on inside the

jailhouse, but when she saw him approach the wagon, she thought she saw his body tremble slightly.

He didn't jump down from the wagon right away. Instead, he sat for a moment, absentmindedly twisting the reins in his hands. Jillian thought again of the offer he had made in the train station. Maybe he was having doubts again. She felt like he wanted to say something, but he remained silent. Just as she was gathering the courage to address him first, her stomach beat her to the punch and growled loudly.

The noise startled Dalton out of his deep contemplation, and he looked up. "You're hungry." It was a statement, not a question. Dalton tried to think when she would have last been able to eat. The train ride from Chicago was a long one. There would have been a few stops in between, but only one long enough to get anything to eat. That would have been about four hours before her arrival time. With the ordeal at the station and the stop at the jailhouse, he knew he had to add at least another two. Six hours was a long time to go without something to eat, and that was if she had indeed eaten since Chicago. Once again today, he was guilty of being thoughtless. "There's a café across the street. The courthouse is open for a little while yet. Why don't we have something to eat first?"

Jillian was embarrassed at her stomach and its obnoxious protest, but she knew it would be foolish not take him up on his offer.

"That would be nice, thank you. I must admit it has been a while since I have eaten," she said gratefully.

Dalton helped her down from the wagon. Jillian struggled to keep the surprised look off her face when he took her hand. She was having trouble dealing with the thrill that went through her every time he even brushed against her. She wasn't accustomed to riding in a wagon and was jostled around a bit before she figured out that if she held onto the seat with one hand on either side of her, she could manage to keep her balance somewhat. Even then, she felt tingles pass through her each time she was haphazardly thrown into him.

The café was larger than she had expected for a town this size because the building doubled as a hotel. The smell of food that assaulted her nose when they stepped through the doors started her mouth watering instantly. She felt the pains in her stomach increase in ferocity as her body demanded immediate attention. The restaurant didn't have many patrons. Anyone coming from the station to dine would have already eaten and gone home. This proved fortunate, because they were served a pleasant home-style meal in an adequate amount of time.

&

When they both finished eating, neither of them made any immediate motion to leave. Dalton was nervous. Ever since they'd left the jailhouse and the vile man within, Dalton had tried to shake the uncomfortable feeling that had come over him.

He looked over at Jillian. Full color had now come back into her face, and, other than looking a bit uncomfortable, her health looked completely restored. He knew, though, that the bruises and blow to her head would pain her for some time.

She had been hungry, he could tell, and he couldn't avoid the new feelings of guilt. No wonder she had fainted earlier in the station! The situation had been emotional enough, but then to add to that the lack of sustenance . . . Dalton knew it wasn't a good combination, especially for a woman. He was intensely relieved that she appeared to be recovering.

When he noticed Jillian fidgeting in her seat slightly, he realized that he wasn't doing much to help repair her already negative view of him. She was most likely starting to wonder whether he could hold an intelligent conversation by now.

"Thank you for the meal. I do feel much better," Jillian said suddenly, offering him a slight smile. She paused a moment, giving him a chance to respond. When he said nothing, she continued, though her voice was a little less confident this time. "I suppose we ought to get over to the courthouse." She looked down at her hands and Dalton stood up quickly.

"Yes, of course. You must be tired from your journey, and I am sure Aunt Betty will be starting to worry by now," he agreed.

"I am anxious to meet the children." She smiled beautifully when she mentioned them, and his heart skipped a beat.

"Yes, the children will be anxious, as well. The drive home will take us about two hours."

Dalton swallowed hard, his nervousness suddenly increasing. They still had an important task to do before they left town. He came around the table, helped Jillian with her chair, paid for their meal, and thanked the hostess for the fine service before they headed out the door and back across the street.

Jillian worked to steady her breathing as they walked slowly toward the courthouse. She knew the ceremony would be simple—just Dalton, herself, a justice of the peace, and whoever was called in to witness the ceremony.

She suppressed a slight, unexpected feeling of disappointment. *It's better this way,* she told herself. *Something more would almost seem a farce.* She knew Dalton would honor and care for her and provide for her needs, but his obligations ended there. Both of their hearts were closed, and love would not be the reason for their union here today.

Dalton could tell Jillian was trying to keep herself calm, simply because he was trying to do the same. He was also trying to hold back the thoughts of Laurellyn that were fighting for their rightful place. He would not dishonor Jillian by thinking of his first wife while they were being married. He might never be in love with her, but he would owe her a great deal one day, especially where his children were concerned. He could start right now by paying her the proper respect she deserved.

With newfound resolve, Dalton walked up to the courthouse and held the door for Miss Jillian Grey—for the last time. The next time they walked through these doors, she would be Mrs. Dalton McCullough.

Five

Dalton tried to find the smoothest parts of the road. He knew wagon rides could be hard on a woman, especially when it was her first time riding in one. Jillian hadn't written too much about her family's financial situation, but the way she had struggled at first to keep her balance told him that she must have been used to riding in a carriage, not a wagon.

The first part of the road home had been unusually rough. He hadn't paid much attention to it on his way to the train station that morning—he had been in too much of a hurry to notice. Eventually the road got better, and when he glanced over at Jillian, he could tell she was relieved. It wasn't long after that she began to nod off.

Dalton looked down at her head now resting on his shoulder. Her head felt heavy there, if only for the weight of the emotions he was again fighting. He noticed that her face looked troubled as she slept, not peaceful as it had in the train station when she lay unconscious. He wondered what was going through her mind.

The wedding ceremony hadn't been much. He felt sorry for her. Surely, it wasn't the wedding she might have dreamed of as a young girl. Jillian suddenly sighed in her sleep as though agreeing with his unspoken thoughts. A twinge of guilt shot through him as he remembered what a special and glorious day it had been when he had married Laurellyn. As he pondered for a moment on that beautiful spring morning, it felt just like it had been yesterday.

❧

Neither Dalton nor Laurellyn wanted a big wedding. They invited mostly family and a few close friends. Walking into the church, the first thing Dalton noticed was all the flowers. "Of course," he thought. There were so many different kinds, most of which were wildflowers. No wonder she had made him wait until May to marry her. He imagined there was not a wildflower left in any meadow or garden for miles.

He walked to where Reverend Jenkins was waiting for him at the front of the altar. The reverend's wife, Mrs. Jenkins, began to play the piano. A few short moments later, the doors to the church opened again. The next moments were trance-like for Dalton. He no longer noticed anything else in the room. The piano had even become silent to his ears. All he could see was the vision of his love standing before him. Laurellyn and her Aunt Betty had worked on her dress together for months. He was sure it was beautiful, but all Dalton could see was her face smiling at him as she slowly walked down the aisle on her Uncle Ned's arm.

His sweetheart was so beautiful. A wreath of woven flowers adorned her hair, and her cheeks were flushed pink with the excitement of the moment. Dalton stared into Laurellyn's smiling eyes and mouthed the word "forever" before they both turned and faced the reverend.

They were coming to the outskirts of Uncle Ned and Aunt Betty's farm. Dalton pushed the memory back to its treasured place in his mind. He wondered if he should wake Jillian up before they arrived to give her a minute to compose herself. He was glad she had been able to nap, even though he had felt uncomfortable with her being so close.

The sun was low in the sky. He thought of Jenny and the battle he was likely to face. Most folks around these parts would be winding down for the night because they rose so early in the morning. He himself had been up since five o'clock that morning and was finding it difficult to suppress the desire to yawn. Knowing Jenny, he worried that their evening was only just beginning.

Dalton was still trying to decide whether to wake Jillian when the wagon wheel hit an unusually large rut in the road and lurched to the side. Jillian flew away from him toward the right. Dalton reached over and caught her by the arm, quickly settling her to rights once again.

Jillian looked around, disoriented for a moment. She realized she must have fallen asleep and was sorely embarrassed. *How long have I been out?* she wondered. She was all too aware of Dalton's hand that still held her upper arm, trying to keep her steady. She must have nearly fallen out of the wagon when it suddenly pitched to one side. She looked up at him, embarrassed, and smiled her thanks. He hesitantly let go of her when she appeared to have her balance once more. Looking around again, slowly this time, Jillian was pleased with the beauty that surrounded her and sighed deeply. They were passing a meadow of wildflowers on the left and a massive field of green cornstalks on the right. They must be coming up onto a farm. I wonder how much farther, she thought.

It seemed that Dalton could read her mind; he smiled at her obvious pleasure. He looked down at her and spoke. "That's Aunt Betty and Uncle Ned's house just up ahead."

Jillian was relieved to finally be nearing the end of her journey. "I'm afraid I must look a fright by now," she remarked. Her hands went immediately back to her hair. Her braid had indeed come loose again. She wasn't surprised. Swiftly pulling it out, she was able to braid it again in no time. She was just retying the ribbon when they turned past the gate and headed up to the house.

Before the wagon could come to a full stop, the door burst open and a slight but energetic little girl came tumbling out. She quickly regained her footing and hurried down the stairs.

Dalton set the brake and hopped off the wagon. He swept the little one up into his arms, giving her a twirl and a kiss on the cheek before setting her back down.

"Pa, you was gone forever!" she complained, but the smile never left her face or her eyes. "Jenny was so ornery all day. She's still mad about her leg," she paused—*This must be Lisa*, Jillian thought—and glanced over at Jillian, then continued quietly, " . . . and our new ma." She gave Jillian a shy smile. "I'm not mad though, Pa. She's pretty." Jillian smiled, and the child continued talking. "Are ya glad with her, Pa? Is she as pretty as our real ma was?" She paused to look up into her father's eyes, as his face paled a little. "Jenny says no one will ever be as pretty as our real ma, but I think she's real pretty. What does Jenny mean by 'real,' anyhow?" She didn't even stop to take a breath. "Jenny can be so mean sometimes. Auntie Bet says that Jenny's still got a big hurt inside here," Lisa put her hand over her heart, "and that she really doesn't want to be so mean to me. I do hear her cryin' in her room at night sometimes when she thinks I'm already sleepin'. I told her one day that if she was so sad about somethin', she should talk to you or Auntie Bet 'bout it. She got all mad and told me that I didn't know nothin'. Then she says . . ."

Lisa stopped talking when Jillian walked over and knelt down on one knee beside her so they were eye level. Her eyes got big when Jillian reached out and took one of her hands and placed her other hand lovingly on her cheek. She smiled shyly, and Jillian smiled in return.

"You must be Lisa." *What a delightful child this is*, Jillian thought to herself, *and such a talker!* "I am very pleased to meet you at last. Your father wrote me many wonderful things about you, and I can see why you are so deserving of his praise." She looked over at Dalton. He still looked a bit taken aback at Lisa's string of questions, but at least the color had come back into his face. He wouldn't have had time to answer them anyway, because Lisa started up again.

"Jenny says you probably wouldn't come 'cause Pa was late," she said. "He was late 'cause Jenny cut her leg. He tried real hard to be on time, so you wouldn't be scared bein' alone and not knowin' anyone . . . but Jenny says it don't matter if you do come 'cause you probably won't stay long anyhow. " For the first time since Lisa had tumbled through the door, her smile disappeared and was replaced by a sad pout as she quietly asked, "You will stay . . . won't you?" She looked deep into Jillian's eyes questioningly. "Even if Jenny's got a hurt that makes her so mean?" The questioning look turned to pleading. "I've been waitin' a real long time for a new ma, been prayin' too . . . real hard."

Before Jillian could answer her, the door to the house burst open again. Jenny walked out and down the steps with her arms folded across her chest. She was shocked by the contrast in the looks of the two girls.

Lisa's long hair was a golden, honey-colored blonde, and her eyes were bright blue. They seemed to dance and sparkle when they caught your attention. Jenny's hair was dark and cut just a bit shorter. Her eyes were also blue, but with flecks of grey around the edges. There seemed to be a storm brewing just under their surface.

From the corner of her eye, Jillian saw Dalton smile and take a tentative step toward her. Jenny gave him a glare that stopped him dead in his tracks, and she noticed his shoulders slump slightly in defeat.

Lisa turned and saw that Jenny had come out of the house, her worry forgotten momentarily as she smiled at Jenny genuinely. Jillian could tell she loved and admired her sister, despite all her frustrations.

"Jenny!" she exclaimed. "Look, our new ma is here! I told you she would come! See how pretty she is?" She pointed toward Jillian as if to prove her point. "Told you so," she added a bit more smugly, looking triumphantly back over at Jenny.

Jillian braced herself for Jenny's angry glare and was not disappointed. Jenny looked back at her father, and this time the defiant look she gave him was mixed with a questioning pain. Without warning, Jenny took off running, favoring one leg just a little as she ran between the house and the barn. She headed quickly into the meadow that lay just beyond. Dalton sighed.

Jillian wished she could comfort him but knew that was not her place. She saw that Lisa started crying. Jillian took her protectively into her arms and held her close and smoothed her hair.

"Jenny's going to ruin everything." Lisa's voice trembled. "She's going to make you want to leave." Jillian took her shoulders and held her back so she could look into her eyes.

"Nothing is going to be ruined, little one, you just wait and see." But as Jillian saw the look of sadness on Dalton's face as he stared after his willful and broken daughter, she wasn't so sure herself.

Dalton was torn. He wondered if he should go right after Jenny or let her brood awhile. He knew where she would be headed. Maybe she would find comfort there. He realized that his delay in speaking with her was not only making this more difficult for him, but was hurting Jillian's feelings as well. Little Lisa was also being affected by his thoughtlessness. All he could do now was pray that they could work this out as quickly as possible.

His smallest daughter's questions had been almost unbearable. How could he answer them? He was relieved when Jillian seemed to sense that he was being overwhelmed and had come to his rescue. When she knelt down beside his tiny daughter, with no thought of soiling her lovely dress and took one of her small hands into her own, placing the other softly on little Lisa's cheek, his heart confirmed to him again that this woman would be a source of healing and comfort in their home.

The door to the house opened again for the third time. Aunt Betty stepped out, carrying a little blond-headed boy. He was the spitting image of his father, with the exception of his hair color. He was still rubbing the sleep from his eyes when he spotted Dalton. He stretched his arms out toward him and squealed with delight. Aunt Betty walked forward, and, after giving Dalton a knowing look, she nodded her head out toward the meadow questioningly. As Aunt Betty deposited little Brenn into his father's arms, Jillian saw Dalton slightly nod his head affirmatively. A troubled look crossed Aunt Betty's face, disappearing as she turned and came toward Jillian, arms outstretched.

"Ah, here you are at last!" she exclaimed as she gathered Jillian up into her ample arms. "We've been expecting you for quite some time now, you know. I was beginning to wonder if you had missed your train." She pulled Jillian back enough to see her face and to give her a teasing look before gathering her back into her arms for another hug.

Jillian was glad her face was hidden for a moment so Aunt Betty didn't see the blush that had come to her cheeks. She wondered what Aunt Betty thought of Dalton's method of obtaining a wife and mother for his children. Sensing they were close, she assumed that they were in each other's confidence and was sure that the subject had been discussed at length, probably more than once. Aunt Betty released her and smiled. Despite her teasing, this woman had already made her feel loved by her warm welcome. Jillian knew this woman would be easy to love in return. She felt she would have a friend—perhaps even an ally—in Aunt Betty. Her heart and her mind told her both would come in handy in the very near future.

"Well, my boy." Aunt Betty turned back to Dalton. "I suppose you'd best hand that boy back over and go find that stubborn child of yours." She took Brenn from his arms. Brenn made a sound of protest, but she paid him no mind. "It is gettin' late. I made up some supper to send home with you." She glanced back at Jillian and smiled. "Figured you'd be plum tuckered out by the time ya got here, dear, and I reckon you still have your evening chores to do, Dalton." She motioned Jillian to follow her. "Come on into the house with me, Jillian, and grab the children's things while I gather up your supper."

Jillian obediently followed her into the house, adoring the woman already. Lisa was close at her heels, while Dalton headed in the direction Jenny had disappeared. Their things, along with dinner, were packed in the wagon long before Dalton and Jenny returned. Aunt Betty excused herself to go back inside the house to get their own dinner finished up. Her husband, Ned, had made an afternoon trip into town and would be returning home shortly.

Rather than wait in the wagon, Jillian sat down on the porch. Little Brenn was sleepy again and rested his head against her right shoulder as she patted his back. Lisa had taken the opportunity to snuggle up under her left arm. She began humming a soft melody she remembered hearing somewhere. Her arms felt full and warmed by the tender souls tucked safely there. She smiled peacefully to herself.

Dalton came around the corner of the house, dragging a reluctant Jenny behind him. All at once, he came to an abrupt halt.

Jillian sat on the front porch steps with his two youngest children. Brenn was sleeping soundly on one shoulder, while Lisa was nodding off, snuggled under her other arm. The feeling of *déjà vu* came over him. How much more could his heart take? In a flood of emotions, he was taken back in time once again.

"Dalton!" Laurellyn came running out through the door as he headed through the gate.

"Whoa!" he called to the horses and brought the wagon to a halt. He wondered what he had forgotten, and then he saw the pail in her hand.

"Dalton!" she called again. She was out of breath by the time she reached the wagon. "You forgot your lunch." As she reached up to hand it to him, Dalton bent down and with hardly any effort at all, lifted her up and set her on his lap. By her smile, he knew she'd caught the look of mischief in his eyes.

"So you decided to come with me after all, did you?"

Laurellyn playfully punched him on the arm. "Now, Dalton McCullough, you put me down this minute. You know I can't go with you. I promised Aunt Betty I'd help her put up beans today." She sighed.

A whole day in the kitchen would be sheer torture for her. She loved to raise vegetables and fruit, but cooking and canning them, well, those were all very different things to her.

"Well, seeing as you came running out this way, why don't I make it worth your while?" He winked and wrapped his arms around her a little tighter. She giggled and snuggled in a little closer. Just then Jenny came barreling down the walk. Reluctantly, he loosened his hold. "Well, my lady, you were saved from your devouring . . . I mean, *devoted* husband by a four-year-old chaperone with a keen sense of the wrong time to interrupt." She laughed and kissed his cheek, and he let her back down to the ground.

"I'll be back about an hour or so before sunset." Smiling, he added, "Have fun with Aunt Betty today!" Dalton watched as she visibly cringed before he chuckled and drove the wagon away.

He was driving into Darlington to buy supplies and some new equipment for the farm. Most of his trips went by without incident, but this trip wouldn't prove to be one of those times. It was fraught with problems from the beginning. A little over halfway there, Old Decker was spooked by a rattler that had ventured onto the road, and the horse bolted, dragging the other horse along. Dalton quickly got both horses under control, but not before the wagon had veered off hard to the left. The rim was knocked loose from the back left wheel when it hit a rock in the ditch.

"Confounded horse," he grumbled. "You're always spooking too easily for your own good." Years ago, his father had bought Old Decker as a favor to an old gambler who was passing through town and was down on his luck. The horse had been old then, but hadn't minded hard work—an important requirement for farm life. When he was finished with the harvest come summer, Dalton had already decided that he would have to start looking for another horse. It was time to put Old Decker out to pasture. He was getting too lazy and stubborn in his old age. It had taken Dalton an hour to patch the wheel well enough to get him the rest of the way into town.

When Dalton had finally made it to Darlington, it hadn't been easy to find a blacksmith that was both reasonable and available to fix the wheel in a relatively short amount of time. As he waited for the repair, he purchased the items he had come for; walking them one at a time back to the blacksmith's to load them into his wagon. The sun was already setting when he left town and headed for home.

With the trouble-filled day finally almost over, he was both frustrated and exhausted when he turned the wagon into the gate and started up to the house. His family hadn't noticed his arrival yet, so he brought the wagon to a stop as he contemplated the scene before him.

Laurellyn was perched on the porch and strands of her long blonde hair were lifting in turns as the light breeze caught beneath them. It almost had an ethereal look to it. One-year-old Lisa was snuggled up under her chin, and Jenny was leaning on her lap, listening intently. He could hear the faint but beautiful musical strains of a melody carry over to him on the breeze.

Suddenly, she looked over at him and their gazes locked. The love that passed between them at that moment was so pure, so strong; he could feel the bands that tied their hearts together pulling him even closer to her. A feeling of knowing and belonging washed over him. A feeling of "coming home." Something whispered then and confirmed what he already knew: this was his heaven on earth.

As Dalton stood looking at Jillian and he heard the soft melody she was humming, the same feeling had overcome him. At once, he put up his defenses to fight against it. In a futile attempt to hold back the new emotions, he reached into his pocket and desperately closed his fingers around Laurellyn's cameo for the second time that day. *Laurellyn is my home*, he reassured himself. His heart was hers and hers alone.

"Jenny!"

Startled, Jillian stopped humming and looked up when she heard Dalton's voice. He was looking directly at her, seemingly frozen in place, and Jenny was standing a few feet behind him. His voice was tinged with frustration, but the look on his face was painful.

"Go get in the wagon!" he called over his shoulder at his daughter. Jenny made no move toward the wagon, and this time Dalton turned to look at her when he spoke.

"Jennifer Laura McCullough." He hadn't raised his voice, but Jillian could tell he meant business. "You go get in the wagon this minute." The little girl was stubborn, for sure. Jillian could see she was trembling,

but she wore a look of sheer willpower and determination.

For a moment, Jillian thought Jenny would remain standing where she was, but then her stubborn look broke and she walked toward the wagon. Jenny climbed in, but not before sending Jillian a venomous glare. Then she sat down hard, with her back to her family.

Just as Jillian stood up to walk over to the wagon herself, Aunt Betty came back out of the house. Jillian could tell Aunt Betty was assessing the situation with a quick sweep of her eyes. She turned to Jillian and gave her an encouraging smile and then turned and spoke to Dalton.

"Well, you seem to have found Jenny all right. You best be gettin' on home now." To Jillian, she added, "I'll drop on by in a few days to check on how you're doin' and see if I can help you out with anything."

Jillian nodded and smiled her thanks before taking Lisa's hand and heading over to the wagon, still carrying the sleeping Brenn in her arms. As she walked, her eyes were drawn back to Dalton's pain-stricken face. Seeing that look of pain again made her suddenly apprehensive, and she quickly turned her own gaze back toward the wagon, but not before noticing the stern look and nod Aunt Betty gave Dalton in her direction. He was at her side in an instant, lifting little Lisa in the wagon beside Jenny and taking Brenn from her as he helped her up on to the wagon seat. She noticed, however, that he tried to keep their contact as brief as possible and avoided looking into her eyes.

After handing the sleeping babe back up to her, Dalton did something she hadn't expected. He walked back to the porch where Aunt Betty still stood watching and gathered the older woman up into a loving embrace. He held her for a long moment before he began speaking softly. His back was to her, and Jillian could not make out what he was saying, but as he whispered into Aunt Betty's ear, she could see a pool of emotions ripple across the older woman's face. The first was love. Jillian already had a deep sense of how much Aunt Betty loved Dalton and his children, so she was not surprised. The next were worry, understanding, and then sorrow. Jillian's apprehension returned. She wished she could hear what Dalton was saying. The last emotion to float across Aunt Betty's face was one of peace, and its afterglow was not wasted on Jillian.

Dalton didn't know why he had such a strong impulse to go back and hug Aunt Betty, but suddenly he felt an overwhelming need for the comfort and reassurance he knew he would find in her warm embrace. She understood his pain and his loss. She and Uncle Ned had raised Laurellyn since she was a small child. When Laurellyn's father had died during the war, she and her mother had come to live with her mother's sister, Betty. Her mother, who had never been able to get over the loss of her husband, had succumbed to a lingering illness the following winter. Uncle Ned and Aunt Betty had loved Laurellyn as their own, and he knew they now loved him like a son too. He needed any strength he could glean from his aunt right then. He had almost lost control of his emotions a moment ago. Why was this woman he hardly knew challenging his resolve to never love again?

He had made the right decision, hadn't he? Though he was torn and frustrated, he knew he shouldn't question his choice. It would be the same as questioning his faith in God. He had received an answer to his prayers, a confirmation that marrying this woman and bringing her here was the right thing to do. He could feel in his heart that she was a loving woman who would nurture and care unconditionally for his three young children. They needed her love and compassion—especially Jenny. This was what he had prayed so earnestly for. It was all that he wanted. He wasn't looking for love himself. He had long ago become resolved to the fact that though he had only been given such a short time with Laurellyn, it had been enough to sustain him until they were together again in the next life. Why then was he being assaulted today with one emotion after another—challenging his commitment to his departed wife?

Before he released Aunt Betty, a new sense of resolve came over him. He would be stronger. It wouldn't be hard. He had many memories to call upon. If he kept Laurellyn alive in his mind and in his heart, this arrangement would work. Now he needed to comfort Aunt Betty. She worried about the children and him too much. She and Uncle Ned were getting older, and maybe now, with Jillian here, she wouldn't have to worry so much.

He leaned back a little and whispered in her ear. "I know you worry about me and the children, but you need to know I am sure I have done the right thing . . . for them anyway. I have felt that much in my heart, and my prayers have been confirmed. Laurellyn will be pleased

I have fulfilled my promise to her. The only part I intend to fulfill, anyway." He paused, sighing deeply, and then continued, "I know you don't agree with our arrangement, but you know how it was with Laurellyn and me. She will always own my heart. I have nothing else to offer another woman. If it weren't for the children—" he paused again. He was about to say that if it weren't for the children, Jillian wouldn't be here, but he couldn't bring himself to say it. Why? He was tempted to look back at her, but he forced himself to remain as he was. "Aunt Betty, you'll see. It'll work out as I have planned. . . . All will be well." A feeling he didn't understand washed over him, and he felt compelled to say the words again, this time a little more reverently. "All will be well." He then turned, walked back to the wagon, and climbed in.

They were just exiting the gate and heading for home when Dalton saw Uncle Ned approaching in his own wagon. Dalton felt compelled to stop momentarily, out of respect, to offer a polite greeting. He reined in the horses.

"Good evening, Uncle Ned. It's good to see you." Ned had been good to him and his parents over the years.

"Well, hello there, Dalton! I expected you would have fetched those young'uns and been long gone by now!" Uncle Ned exclaimed.

Dalton answered, "Had a bit of trouble at the station, I'm afraid. I was late getting there, and it caused us quite the mishap."

Uncle Ned raised his eyebrow but didn't inquire further. Instead, he looked over at Jillian and gave her a warm grin. "You must be the new missus, I presume." He winked. "I didn't think our Dalton would ever get around to marryin' again. I'd be pleased if you'd be helpin' to put some of the fun back into him. He's as sour as an old pickle most of the time." He chuckled softly to himself. "Well, seein' as you're so late gettin' back, I suppose I ought to let you be on your way. It was nice makin' your acquaintance, dear. I'm sure we'll be seein' a lot of you."

As Dalton was pulling the wagon the rest of the way through the gate, he heard Uncle Ned insist, "Now, Jenny Bugs, don't you be givin' your new ma a hard time now. You make your Uncle Ned proud, ya hear?"

Dalton thought to himself, *It's a little late for that.*

Uncle Ned parked the wagon and joined his wife on the porch.

He stood next to her, and they both watched Dalton's wagon turn the corner up the road until it was eventually out of sight.

"That there new wife of his sure is a looker," Uncle Ned commented.

"Poor Dalton," Aunt Betty answered her husband absentmindedly. She was still thinking about what Dalton had said to her before he left. "He's been havin' a real hard time of it today. I imagine he got the worst of it at the train station . . . wasn't expectin' such a pretty thing to come steppin' off the train, that's for sure—the stubborn boy." She suddenly smiled knowingly. "He thinks he can keep his heart sealed up and closed off by gettin' married this way. Has it all planned out, I imagine—sleepin' in separate rooms and everything. He doesn't realize that it's hard to keep from lovin' a woman who loves your children so. She'd never even met those babes until today, and she's already endeared them in her heart. I have a real good feelin' about this right now, a real good feelin'." She put her arm through her husband's and gave it a squeeze. She reverently added, "I wouldn't be surprised if our Laurellyn had a hand in this." With that, she wiped a tear away with the corner of her apron and went into the house to serve her husband his dinner.

Little Brenn had snuggled into Jillian's chest as they rode away and fallen asleep immediately. What a special feeling it was to mother a child. Jillian had tended other people's children many times, but at the end of the day, she knew she would go her way and leave them with their mothers. Even though she had loved them, it wasn't the same. There was always that separation and lack of belonging. She was the mother of these children now, and their faces were branded onto her heart already. She couldn't explain the joy that filled her bosom. She smiled down again at the little boy in her arms. She thought of little Lisa and her whimsical ways. Last, she turned to look at Jenny. She could tell the child was straining to hold back a flow of tears. *Oh, Jenny,* she thought. *Please don't lock me out. Just let me love you. I won't try to replace your mother but . . . please, please . . . just let me love you.* Jillian then sent a fervent plea heavenward and turned back to face the road. She missed the single tear that escaped its confines and traveled slowly down Jenny's face.

W e're home! We're home!" Lisa exclaimed. "Pa, hurry, help me out!" Just then, a scrawny little brown and white pup came bounding from around the corner, barking out his welcome.

Dalton set the brake on the wagon and climbed down. Lisa, in her anticipation, began jumping enthusiastically, consequently shaking the wagon and waking her little brother.

"Now hold you britches, Lisa." Dalton lifted her out and set her on the ground. She sat down at once and gathered the puppy into her arms, letting him lick her face.

"Digger! I missed you so much. Did you miss me? I wish Pa would have let me take you to Auntie Bet's. Jenny was no fun at all." She held the pup up and turned him to face the wagon. "Look, Digger, that's our new ma. She's come all the way from Masse . . . Masse . . . from far away."

Jillian sat watching in amusement. What a character Lisa was, but she wasn't finished. Lisa held her lips to the dog's ears and whispered as he wiggled and squirmed about.

"I can't let you sleep on my bed tonight 'til I know if our new ma will let ya. So wait outside my window and if I'm not allowed, I'll let you in when everybody else is asleep, okay?"

The pup licked her face again, and Lisa giggled in delight.

Jillian noticed that Jenny had climbed down from the wagon and stood watching Lisa too. It was apparent that she wanted to say something to her sister but was struggling to bite her tongue.

Jillian was the last one left in the wagon. Dalton had just claimed Brenn from her and set him down. He toddled over to where Lisa was and began to maul the pup with as much enthusiasm as his big sister.

Dalton returned and held his hand out to her. She couldn't help purposely avoiding looking into eyes when he helped her down. She worried about what she'd see there and didn't want to spoil the fun she was having watching his two youngest children. She remembered the tortured look he had given her back at Aunt Betty's when he had returned with Jenny.

Dalton then finished unhitching the horses and started to lead them to the barn. Abruptly, he stopped and turned. "Jenny, help your ma carry dinner in and show her where things are." His voice was firm. He looked at Jillian. "As soon as I'm done tending to the horses, I'll be in to eat. Please, you don't need to wait for me." Dalton turned and led the horses to the barn. Jillian stared after him until the barn doors closed behind him.

Turning back to the children, Jillian gathered her courage and spoke. "Well, I suppose it would be best to do as your father asks." Abruptly, Jenny ran past her into the house and disappeared through the door. A moment later, she felt a small hand find its way into hers. She looked down into to the face of her other new little daughter.

"I'll show you," Lisa said.

Jillian picked up Brenn, and while still holding Lisa's hand, walked toward the house. As she neared the steps, she noticed for the first time the beautiful flower garden that framed the house. It started on each side of the porch steps and extended partially around the house on both sides. There was even a small white picket fence that acted as a border. The garden was sorely neglected and badly in need of some work, but it was filled with a large variety of flowers of different shapes and colors. Jillian knew the names of many of them, though some were unfamiliar. She felt another surge of hope rise within her, and her step felt a little lighter as she walked through the door of her new home.

Dalton was having trouble sleeping. His glance finally wandered over to Laurellyn's cameo, which was placed on his bedside table. He examined it a moment and recalled the day he had first seen it displayed in the shop window.

Dalton had convinced Laurellyn to ride into Darlington with him that day. It was time to purchase supplies, and he dreaded making the trip alone. Auntie Betty was always offering to tend Jenny so the two of them could have some time alone. They hadn't had a good long time to spend together in awhile. So, after much coaxing, Laurellyn finally agreed to come.

With Laurellyn by his side, the day seemed to fly by. They had just finished lunch at the café and were walking down the boardwalk, when Laurellyn stopped to look in the window of the small five-and-dime store. There was a wide selection of trinkets of all types and sizes on display, from small delicate pins and combs, to loud and obnoxious looking broaches and hats. Laurellyn admired a small, delicate cameo because it reminded her of the one her mother used to wear. Later that afternoon, before they started for home, Dalton slipped away from Laurellyn for a moment and purchased it for her birthday gift that year. She had worn the cameo every day from then on.

When Laurellyn died, Dalton considered burying the cameo with her, but in the end, he couldn't part with it. Now, he carried it with him daily in his pocket and at night he would place it on the stand next to his bed.

"Well, Laurellyn," he whispered, "your children have a new mother . . . .just like I promised." He suppressed the twinge of guilt he felt about the other half of the promise he had made and rolled over on his side, closing his eyes. He couldn't think about that right now. Morning would be here before he knew it. His last thought before closing his eyes was of Laurellyn, as always.

Jillian took another look about her room. It was smaller than her bedroom back home, but it was warm and comfortable. She smiled. Little Lisa had been so excited to show her every little detail, running from this thing to that. Apparently, Aunt Betty had come over a few days before and thoroughly cleaned it, putting a new quilt on the bed and adding other homey touches. At the time the girls hadn't known why.

When Dalton had brought her trunk and other things in, Lisa had begged to help her unpack. Jillian had told Lisa that she was much too tired to do it tonight and promised her she could help when she got around to it in the next day or two.

Jenny hadn't come out of her room since she had raced into the house earlier that evening. When Dalton had come in from tending the horses, Jillian had sent him in to her with a small plate. He had returned with it untouched. She could tell by the look on his face that they had not smoothed things over. Jillian was a little worried about Jenny not eating at first, but then she saw Lisa sneak a roll and wrap it up in her napkin. The child tucked it under the table and into her apron before she asked to be excused from the table. Lisa had a soft heart.

Jillian sighed and sank a little deeper into her pillow. It had been a long day. Her emotions had swung back and forth, over and over again, from one side of the pendulum to the other. But when she had laid little sleeping Brenn into his cradle for the night, she'd felt a feeling of peace settling within her again. She'd then stooped to pick up Lisa's fallen blanket, tucking it in under her chin and bending down to kiss the little angel on her forehead. The child had stirred lightly and spoken.

" 'Night, Ma."

Hearing those simple words had caused Jillian's heart to swell. After turning to take one more look at the sleeping children before closing the door, she knew how right it had been to come here. With these children to love and to nurture, and with poor Jenny who needed a mother so badly, her heart would not become cold and bitter, as it had tried to do over the last few months.

Jillian blew out the lantern beside her bed. Rolling over onto her side, she gazed out the window for a moment at the stars that brightened the night sky. She felt soothed and calmed as she watched the limbs of the old oak gently sway back and forth in the slight breeze. She knew she would sleep well. Nothing would disturb her slumber—not even the tortured face of one Mr. Dalton McCullough that flashed across her mind as she drifted off.

Seven

"Good morning." Jillian smiled tentatively at Dalton as he walked through the door after his morning chores were through. After two weeks, they had settled into a relatively comfortable routine. Jenny still avoided Jillian as much as possible, but the other children were a constant delight, filling her days with laughter and surprises.

Jillian set the platter of hotcakes on the table. After she had made them for breakfast the morning after her arrival, Lisa had begged for them every day since. She was going to have to find out from Aunt Betty what other things the children liked to eat so they could have a little variety. She pondered on Aunt Betty for a moment. The woman had been true to her word. She had come over for a visit a couple of days after Jillian arrived, bringing a blueberry pie and a loaf of freshly baked bread with her. Aunt Betty was a wonderful cook, Jillian had soon discovered. She enjoyed cooking herself and was fairly skillful at it, but she looked forward to learning some new things and perhaps sharing some recipes with Dalton's aunt. They had talked about how the children were adjusting to the change. Jillian knew Aunt Betty was referring mostly to Jenny, and it pained her that she didn't have much improvement to report, other than that it appeared the cut on her leg had healed nicely. But all in all, they had a good visit.

Jillian didn't see too much of Dalton. He seemed to be working hard in the fields. In three months, he'd told her, it would be time for the harvest. Then, everyone would have more work than they knew how to manage.

Jillian was anxious to get started in the flower garden. It had been neglected so long that the weeds had taken over, and it was going to take quite a bit of work to get them under control. She had brought a few seeds with her from home, and she knew they would make a beautiful addition to the garden. Hopefully, she would be able to find some time to plant them soon or she would have to wait until next spring.

She was disappointed that it was too late to plant a vegetable garden this year. One afternoon, she had taken the younger children over on a walk to Aunt Betty's and had found the dear woman working vigorously in her own vegetable garden. Jillian had been quite impressed. She had only ever planted flowers before and was looking forward to trying something new. Since growing their own vegetables was the only way to ensure that they had a healthy variety for the family's needs, she was thankful when Aunt Betty had assured her that she had planted an extra large garden this year and would have more than enough to share with them.

Just then, Jenny came trudging into the kitchen and sat down at the far end of the table, interrupting Jillian's thoughts. Dalton's oldest daughter had been attending school for two weeks now. Jillian hoped the girl would be more excited to go back, but she seemed to dread going more and more with each passing school day.

It troubled Jillian to see Jenny so disheartened. Jillian had always loved school. Each day had brought the opportunity to learn something new and exciting she hadn't known the day before. She wondered just how far behind Jenny was in her studies. Jillian was anxious to begin tutoring her, but as yet, their relationship was still too tense. On her next trip to town she would have to make a point of stopping by and speaking with the schoolmaster. For now, she would just have to pray that Jenny's heart would quickly soften so she would accept Jillian's help. Jillian sent a familiar prayer heavenward, along with a new one for patience. Thankfully, thoughts of her mother and her tender ways helped give her guidance as to how she should approach her challenges with Jenny.

Lisa wouldn't be attending school for another year. The child was pure energy, and though Jillian enjoyed her immensely, she was difficult to keep up with sometimes.

After Jenny left for school, Jillian cleaned up the kitchen and continued through the house, getting things in order. Even after two weeks, there was plenty to do in order to thoroughly clean and straighten things up. Dalton had been doing what he could, but many of the household chores had fallen to Jenny, and a girl of eight could only accomplish so much. Lisa followed her around all morning, happily mimicking her work. Brenn toddled after Lisa, sometimes undoing what Jillian had just completed.

As soon as lunch was over, Jillian coaxed Brenn into taking a nap and then took Lisa by the hand and went to her room to begin the task of going through her trunk. She'd unpacked the essentials when she had arrived but hadn't yet unpacked any of her precious reminders of home.

The moment she opened her trunk, Lisa eyes lit up with delight. Everything was fascinating to the child. She "oohed" and "ahhed" over each item Jillian removed from the trunk, especially the party dresses she'd brought, with all their frills and lace. Then Jillian showed Lisa the fabric that her mother had given her.

"Look," Jillian told her. "Maybe this winter we'll make you a new Sunday dress." The mere idea caused Lisa to go into fits of anticipation.

"Will it be pretty like this one?" Lisa ran her hand over one of Jillian's dresses. Jillian held a piece of blue floral cloth with small pink roses up in front of the enchanted girl. The color was perfect, matching her eyes exactly.

"I think it will be the most beautiful dress in the world, especially on you," she predicted.

Lisa giggled with delight, stood up, and did a couple of twirls as she imagined wearing her new dress. Then she sat back down by the trunk next to Jillian, waiting for the next surprise.

Jillian slowly took out the books that she'd brought, showing them to Lisa one by one. She looked forward to working with her this winter to get her ready for school. She sincerely hoped that Jenny would be caught up by then.

Lisa gently handed the books back one at time. Jillian put them back into the trunk to be stored, except for a few children's storybooks and fairy tales that she intended on reading to the children during the long winter months. Lisa was so enthralled as she turned each page, searching for the illustrations, that Jillian decided it wouldn't hurt to begin reading a few of them at bedtime now. If she needed additional books later, she would write her mother and ask her to send more of the collection she had left behind.

When most of the things she needed to unpack had been put in their proper places, Jillian reached into the bottom of the trunk and pulled out a bundle of cloth. She untied the string from it, smiling to herself as Lisa watched her with burning curiosity. She hoped her treasures had not been broken during her trip.

When at last the final layer was unwound, she laid the cloth on the floor to examine its contents. Everything seemed to have survived the long journey intact. Lisa's eyes got big as Jillian picked up a large seashell and held it to her ear. She closed her eyes to listen to the familiar and soothing sounds captured within. As she opened her eyes again, she laughed at the puzzled look on Lisa face.

"Here," she said and held the shell up to Lisa's ear. Lisa looked confused. "It's a seashell," she explained. "If you listen carefully, you can hear the sound of the ocean." Lisa obeyed and Jillian could tell she was concentrating when finally a small smile graced her face.

The next treasure Jillian picked up was a starfish. This she handed to the child and watched as Lisa felt the bumpy surface and turned it over to examine the small suction cups on the underneath.

"That is a starfish." She could see in Lisa's face that she made the connection between its shape and its name. She continued, "They live in the ocean and occasionally wash up on the shore." Jillian turned to the last item in her bundle, a piece of sea glass. It was cobalt blue and had been smoothed to perfection from tumbling in the waves. She took the starfish from Lisa and placed the piece of glass in her hand. Lisa turned it over and over again, feeling its smoothness and then lifting it up to the light. The light shining through made a small reflection of blue light on the wall. Lisa's eyes got huge as she smiled.

"That's a reflection," Jillian explained as she anticipated Lisa's barrage of questions.

When they were finished examining the items, Jillian got up and placed her treasures carefully on her dresser. Then she walked over and closed the trunk.

"Well, I suppose we ought to go check on Brenn. Jenny should be home pretty soon too." She took Lisa's hand and headed for the door. "Let's go see if we have time to bake some cookies before Jenny gets home. Do you think she would like that?"

Lisa nodded her head and grinned from ear to ear. "I think me and Brenn would like it too."

Eight

Dalton wiped the sweat from his brow with the sleeve of his shirt. He had been working nonstop all morning, trying to dispel the thoughts of that woman from his mind.

For the first time in fifteen months, his waking thought hadn't been of Laurellyn and the deep pain of her loss. He had even forgotten to put her cameo in his pants pocket. Jillian had only been here three weeks now, and she was already invading the spaces in his mind where Laurellyn resided.

In frustration, Dalton stripped off his shirt and stuffed it partly in his back pocket. He leaned up against the fence post and ran his fingers through his hair. She was getting to him, threatening his sense of control. He never thought he would have these kinds of feelings for another woman again. Could Laurellyn have been right? Was he able to love again? He thought back to the second part of the promise he had made her.

"Dalton, listen." Laurellyn's breath was labored and her body weak. He felt her hand trembling as she placed it on his arm. He had turned from her when she had made the request. Turning back around, he knelt beside the bed and took her hand in both of his. He never could refuse her anything, especially not now. His heart wrenched; he couldn't imagine a life with anyone but her. "Please, Dalton," she pleaded. "I know you'll always love me, but you'll need someone when I am gone."

She took a second to catch her breath. "You have so much love left to give, so much time. You'll find another woman to make you happy." Her words brought a fresh round of tears to Dalton's eyes. He couldn't hide them—he wouldn't—they belonged to her.

"I don't want anyone but you, Laurellyn. I never have and you know that. We're forever, remember?"

Laurellyn reached her hand up and wiped a tear from his cheek. "Dalton, listen to me." She attempted a weak smile. "Now's not the time to be stubborn." His heart ached as he looked at her. Her skin was taut and pale, and the light was leaving her eyes. Life had slowly been drained from her in order to bring a new life into the world.

Laurellyn had labored for thirty-six hours before Brennan Michael McCullough was finally born. He had been two weeks overdue and Laurellyn was very small, which had made the birthing more difficult. She was weakened from the labor after which Aunt Betty couldn't stop the bleeding. Aunt Betty had helped to bring many babies into the world, and she was skilled at it, but when God chose to call one of his children home, try as she might, there was nothing she could do—not even to save the niece she cherished as a daughter. She had left the two of them alone when she felt the end was near.

Dalton did not want to accept that the love of his life was leaving him. He couldn't. The world would not be the same without the melody of her voice, her loving touch, the very fragrance of her. It would be silent and empty for him.

"Dalton." Laurellyn's voice was so weak, it was barely a whisper. "Promise me, Dalton. The children—they need a mother." Her breathing was no longer labored, and he could hardly see her chest rise at all with each breath. "Dalton, find her . . . find her for them." Her voice was so pleading. "Find her for you . . . promise me."

"I will, Laurellyn. Only for you, I will." He could not deny her the promise, even though he doubted he could ever keep it. "I love you."

With the last of her strength, and though her lips barely moved, he heard the words he would never hear again on the earth. "I'll love you forever, Dalton McCullough."

Then she was gone and he felt his heart being torn from his chest.

"Forever," he had repeated as he held her in his arms for the last time.

"Forever," the word fell from his lips now. He would love her for-ever.

Suddenly, an image of Jillian's face flashed before his eyes. Had he found her? A woman who could cause his heart to open again—a woman other than Laurellyn that could find residence there?

He ran his fingers through his hair again. He'd stated plainly to Jil-lian in his letters that he was not looking for love. He chose to advertise for a wife in the first place because he wasn't interested in an emotional or physical relationship. That's why, he presumed, she had chosen him also. He pondered on that for a moment.

Why this woman had chosen this path for herself was still a mys-tery to him. Jillian had never been married. What terrible tragedy had she endured that had made her give up on finding love so young? He knew she was a woman with a great capacity to love. She had taken to his children as if they were her own, almost like she had been waiting for them and finally had them at last. Lisa called her "Ma" right off, and he could see the smile in Jillian's eyes every time she heard it. Brenn didn't say much yet, but he had accepted her immediately and always wanted to be in her arms. Jenny stayed out of the way—either in her room, or out visiting her mother's grave. He could tell when she'd been there by little evidences such as a small bunch of flowers or some little treasure she would find on her way there. Sometimes it was something as simple as an unusually colored stone or a feather she might have found tangled in a bush.

Dalton sighed deeply. Jenny was still hardly speaking to either Jil-lian or him. Sometimes she would communicate her needs or wants through Lisa. She avoided looking into his eyes at all costs. When, by chance, he was able to catch a glance, his heart always sank at her solemn and lost look.

Jillian always included Jenny and treated her with the same love and kindness as she did the younger children, even though Jenny made it a point to let her know she was still not welcome. In this past week, though, he thought he'd seen her soften somewhat, and it gave him hope.

This slight change started around the time Jillian began working in Laurellyn's flower garden. He was actually quite surprised that Jillian's actions were having such a positive effect. Dalton had assumed Jenny would see it as an intrusion and use it to fuel her resentment. Instead,

Jenny found a hidden place to sit and watch her new mother as she worked.

Jillian was diligent, and it wasn't long before the garden began to resemble what it had once been at the hands of Laurellyn. Watching its transformation had actually been a shock to him, however, and it had caused him to remember the day he had presented the garden as his wedding gift to Laurellyn.

❧

"Okay now," Dalton whispered in his new wife's ear as he led her from the wagon with his hands over her eyes. "Don't open them until I say." It was hard to walk and cover her eyes at the same time, but he insisted. He was excited. He knew his gift would be perfect. He led her to the front of the house and then turned her away from it, so she was facing him, not the house. "Now, keep your eyes shut for a minute while I take my hands away."

"But Dalton," Laurellyn protested, but she wore a smile on her face, so he knew she was having fun.

"Just a minute more, now, don't peek!" He took his hands away from her eyes and waved his right hand in front of her to see if she was cheating. Satisfied she wasn't, he walked over to the porch and retrieved a large bouquet of wildflowers he had left there in a jar earlier. He came back around and stood in front of her holding the wildflowers against his chest. With a big grin, he announced, "Okay."

Laurellyn opened her eyes and smiled up at him. "Oh, Dalton, they're beautiful. I love them!" As he handed the bouquet to her, she lifted it to her face and inhaled the blossoms' fragrance. "Let's go put these in the house. They need more water right away. I've already got a vase ready and waiting." Before she could move, Dalton grabbed her by the shoulders. "Wait!" he grinned, quite proud of himself. "That's only part of the surprise."

He turned her around to face the house. He was still standing behind her, but he heard her breath catch in her throat. Turning to him, she threw her arms around his neck.

"Dalton, it's beautiful! I've never seen anything more beautiful. It's the perfect gift." She sighed and turned back to face the house and her new flower garden. She pulled his arms around her waist and leaned her head back against his shoulder. "It will always be a beautiful reminder

of the day we began our life together."

Laurellyn was right. The garden would always remind Dalton of her. It had indeed been her great joy, and she had spent many hours working in it. Jenny too, had spent much of that time at her mother's side while Laurellyn taught her about weeding and tending the delicate flowers planted there.

Dalton let out a sigh of frustration. Now when he thought of Jenny working the garden, he pictured her with Jillian, and not Laurellyn.

Just a week ago, when Dalton came in from working the cornfields, the scent of wildflowers—as strong as he ever remembered it being—hit him as soon as he had closed the door of the house. Their soft fragrance was always in the air outside when they were in bloom, but it was muted out in the open. There hadn't been flowers inside the house since Laurellyn died. The scent today was strong, overpowering, and filled with memories. He could see a large bouquet in the center of the table and another one in the parlor.

Jillian had just finished putting biscuits in the oven for dinner. She had looked up at him and smiled when he came through the door. She looked away when she saw the troubled expression on his face, but said nothing. When he saw her distracted by her work, he took a moment to recover.

"Look, Pa," Lisa exclaimed when she caught sight of him. "Look at all the pretty flowers we picked today. Ma says I can pick some every day if I want and bring them into the house. We even put some in my room." Then she made a face. "Brenn tried eatin' 'em, but Ma told him that they looked a lot prettier than they tasted. He didn't listen, though—just kept right on tryin' to eat 'em until Ma got him a cookie." Lisa made another face. "He let Digger lick his cookie before he finished eatin' it and ate the rest anyway! Boys are so disgusting, aren't they, Pa?"

Dalton looked over at Jillian. She was listening intently to Lisa and trying to suppress a smile. When he caught her eye, she couldn't hold back her smile any longer, and he found himself smiling too. At least the awkward moment had passed.

"Well, now, Lisa." He sat in a kitchen chair and lifted his daughter onto one knee. "I do suppose we men can be a little different at times than you women folk, but we also have some very good qualities, I like to think." He looked over to Jillian and winked. "Remember, the other day when you and Brenn were playing ball with Digger and the ball rolled into that big puddle of mud?" Lisa nodded her head. "Well, remember how you didn't want to go get to it because you didn't want to get your dress and shoes all muddy?" Again Lisa nodded her head. "Well, who went running right into the puddle and got the ball for you?"

"Brenn did." Lisa smiled and looked over at her brother, who didn't have any idea what they were talking about, but smiled back and waved anyway.

"That's right, Brenn did." He looked over at Jillian. "So you see, my little angel, we boys might be a little disgusting at times, but we would do almost anything for a lady." With that, Lisa gave her dad a big hug and hopped off his lap. She hurried back over to Brenn, giving him a big kiss on his plump cheek and a hug before sitting back down to play with him. Dalton found himself wishing Jillian might do the same to him.

Recalling that thought brought Dalton quickly back from his musings, and he chastised himself. He shouldn't be thinking those kinds of things about Jillian. It wasn't fair. They had made an agreement, and she was more than fulfilling her part to his satisfaction. He needed to discipline his thoughts before they grew into anything more.

Frustrated, he put his face into his hands. How had things gotten so complicated? Why couldn't they have remained simple? He had planned it all out. But then, he hadn't been expecting this woman—this beautiful, captivating woman, so warm and loving. She made him remember that he was a man, still young and virile.

"Blasted woman," he cursed to himself. "She's too bewitching for her own good." What he really needed to do was just kiss her and get it out of his system.

Dalton pulled his shirt from his back pocket and slipped his arms back in the sleeves, but neglected to button it back up. Then, instead of going back to work, he got up and walked determinedly toward the house.

Nine

Jillian was startled when the door to the house flew open. The children were spending the day at Auntie Betty's, and Jillian was taking advantage of the time to get ahead on her cooking for the Independence Day picnic on Saturday. Dalton had left early that morning to work in the fields, and she hadn't seen him yet today. Now, he stood in the doorway.

"Dalton, you scared me! I didn't expect you until later this afternoon."

Her eyes fell to his shirt. It hung open, and she could see the well-formed muscles of his chest and abdomen. The sight caused her heart rate to increase dramatically. She had never seen a man's bare chest before, and she was surprised at her reaction. He didn't make a move to enter the house. Instead, he just stood there in the open doorway, watching her.

"Are you hungry?" Jillian asked nervously. "I can get you something to eat if you'd like, or—" Jillian stopped talking as he took a step forward and then paused. She quickly wiped her hands on her apron and covered the piecrust she was working on with a cloth.

As Dalton began walking toward her again, the look in his eyes caused her heart to beat even faster. He tossed his hat on the table as he walked by it and came to stop directly before her. Jillian couldn't think. Had she done something wrong? He didn't appear to be angry. The look he wore was more one of resolve.

Slowly, he lifted his hand to her face and with his thumb, began to trace the outline of her lips. By now her heart was racing, and she didn't dare speak. She held her breath as he slowly slid his hand to the back of her neck and pulled her forward gently, as his head descended toward hers. He paused just before their lips met, to look at her. Unconsciously, her mouth began to water. Their lips were just inches apart and instinctively she closed her eyes. It was then she felt his lips, soft and gentle, caressing hers.

Slowly their kiss increased in intensity. It was almost as if he were searching for something, an answer to an unspoken question. Finally, she felt his hands come around to her back. Jillian's whole body began to tingle violently as he pulled her firmly to him. Her senses seemed to come alive, and she felt herself responding to his kiss, returning it with fervor. As her body took even more control, she laid her hands flat against his bare chest, and then slid them up and around his neck, entwining her fingers in the softness of his hair.

This only seemed to fuel the intensity of his kiss, and she felt herself being drawn even closer to him. Never had she imagined she could ever feel this way. Never had a man had so much power over her emotions. Then, abruptly, he broke the seal of their lips and leaned his head against the side of her face. At first his breathing was hard and fast, and she could feel his chest rise and fall, but slowly as his heart rate decreased, his breath against her skin became warm and hushed, almost like a whisper.

Dalton leaned back and looked into her eyes again, searchingly. She did not look away. Neither of them said anything as he continued to look at her. She felt her eyes being drawn to his mouth and impulsively, she licked her lips.

To Jillian's delight, in the next moment, he pulled her even closer than he had before, crushing her to him once again, his lips finding hers with a passion they had not held before. She thought the kiss would never end, but feared it would at the same time. Then, with as much urgency as this last kiss had begun, it ended. Dalton released her, walked to the table, grabbed his hat, and went out the door, shutting it firmly behind him.

Jillian struggled to catch her breath. *What just happened?* Her thoughts spun around in her head, and she questioned whether that kiss had been real. But as she closed her eyes, she could still feel the tingle of his lips upon her own. She felt the tender skin around her mouth where

his stubble had chaffed her face, and she still had goose pimples on her flesh where his arms had been around her. She didn't know what to think. She knew her feelings for Dalton had been steadily growing. She'd tried to fight them, but the way he was with his children was so endearing to her, and the immense love they had for him spoke to her heart as well.

Slowly, with each passing day, her former wounds were beginning to heal, and her heart was both softening and turning toward the man she married. Was it possible that she could be falling in love? It wasn't long ago that she swore she would never open her heart to a man again and leave it vulnerable to the pain it had endured once before.

Jillian turned back to her work and began rolling the piecrust again. What possessed Dalton to storm in and kiss her the way he had? He had been kind and courteous since her arrival, but she also suspected he spent a fair amount of time away from the house avoiding her. Dalton was still sorely mourning his first wife. He tried to hide it, but she noticed his sorrow more often than she would have liked. She remembered the other night when Dalton had come in from working in the cornfields.

Jillian was putting the finishing touches on supper when she thought she heard Dalton humming a little tune as he walked through the door. Turning to smile at him, expecting him to be in a good mood, she was taken aback by his expression. He just stood there, unmoving, with a look of shock and pain on his face. She turned away quickly, realizing that something reminded him of Laurellyn, presumably something she'd done. It pained her to see him still suffering so much, and she felt guilty when she was the instigator of his pain. Then, like a breath from heaven, little Lisa came to the rescue with her whimsical ways and changed his mood back around.

As Jillian tried to recall one of Aunt Betty's recipes for pie filling, her thoughts turned to Jenny, who was slowly coming to accept her, or at the very least she was coming to accept the idea that Jillian wasn't going away. It would still take time, but at least now there was a hope lingering in Jillian's heart that Jenny would one day come to love her as much as she loved the child. There were still battles, but in their wake, she noticed small victories. Even between Dalton and Jenny there were some ups and downs, but all in all, the overall feeling in the home was one of love and acceptance. Despite the little upsets, a comfortable peace had begun to settle.

Jillian was startled when she heard a wagon coming up to the house. Apparently she'd been lost in her thoughts for quite a while. The children must be home already.

"Ma!" Lisa hollered, as the wagon came to a stop. "Ma, we're home." Uncle Ned had to hurry and hop down to grab her before she attempted to jump out of the wagon herself. Immediately when he set her down, she ran up to Jillian and hugged her. "We had so much fun!" Lisa exclaimed. "Auntie Bet's cat Sable had her litter of kittens two days ago. They're so soft, but really tiny. Uncle Ned says we can't hold 'em yet, only pet 'em nicely on their backs. Their eyes are still closed, but Uncle Ned says they'll open in a few days. I counted five kittens, all by myself. Brenn kept trying to get 'em, but he can't hold 'em until they're lots bigger. He might squeeze 'em and hurt 'em 'cause he don't know no better. Uncle Ned says Jenny and me—"

"Jenny and I," Jillian corrected with a smile.

"He says Jenny and I can hold them in about a week as long as we're real careful. Oh, Ma, they are so sweet. You need to come next time so you can see 'em," Lisa rushed on.

"You're right, I must. It's about time I paid your Auntie Bet another visit anyway." By now Uncle Ned had taken Brenn from Jenny and put him down so he could toddle over to Jillian. She bent down and scooped him up. He put his chubby little arms around her neck and laid his head down on her shoulder. "You must have had a big day too," Jillian cooed at him and then smiled up at Jenny. "It's good to see you home, Jenny. I need to put some finishing touches on some of the pies I've made for Saturday and was hoping you could help." Jillian thought she saw a spark light up in the girl's eyes, but Jenny quickly hid it and mumbled that she needed to get her chores done. She wandered off to water the chickens. Jillian looked over at Ned. Despite Jenny's reaction, his smile was encouraging.

"She'll come around, darlin'. She's just stubborn," he said as they both watched her walk away. "Has Dalton come in from the fields yet? I need to run somethin' by him." Jillian felt a blush start to rise, but quickly tried to hide it by looking Brenn over and pretending to brush

some imaginary dirt off him.

"He came in about an hour or so ago, then left again. Didn't say where he was off to." She chanced a look at Uncle Ned, and it appeared as though he was trying to suppress a grin.

"Well then, maybe he's out in the barn. I'll go have a look-see." He turned to go.

"Make sure to thank Aunt Betty for me for watching the children today. I was able to get more done than I had planned." She paused then added, "Before you go, I'd like to send a pie home for you to sample. I'll bring it out to the wagon while you go look for Dalton." Before he walked too far away, she called after him, "If you see him, tell him supper is about ready." He didn't turn again, just lifted his hand and gave it a wave.

Jillian thought she'd heard him chuckling to himself. Shaking her head, she wondered what he found so humorous, and then turned and headed back into the house.

Uncle Ned couldn't suppress the grin any longer, and a small laugh even escaped his lips. Oh, he'd be sure to tell the missus alright, tell her that their plan had worked. They had figured if they'd give those two young'uns some time alone to themselves—well, nature would take its course.

When he saw the blush come to her cheeks at the mention of Dalton's name, he knew somethin' more than just cookin' and farmin' had gone on here today. Betty would be pleased. It was about time those two started acting more like married folk. Dalton was as stubborn as a mule and as blind as a bat if he couldn't see and take the prize he'd been given. Pausing for a moment outside the barn, he quickly wiped the grin off his face, just in case the boy was in the barn after all. He pushed opened the door.

Dalton looked up when he heard the barn door open. He'd been sitting there for quite a while. He couldn't get the thought of Jillian out of his head. The way she had felt in his arms, the softness of her skin, and the scent of her hair. But most of all, the way her lips had been eager to return his kiss. He hadn't expected that or the effect it had on him.

When he had first headed in from the fields, he'd convinced himself that if he just kissed her once, it might help to clear his head. Maybe then things would go back to normal. He told himself that when he did kiss her, it would be different—it would feel different than the kisses he had shared with Laurellyn.

He had been right—it was different—but not different like he'd imagined it would be. Instead of clearing his head, when his lips met hers and he felt her lips soften beneath his as she returned the kiss, a fire ignited within him. A passion far greater than he had ever felt before began to consume him. It had caused him to tear his lips away from her, but he couldn't release her entirely. Instead, he laid the side of his head to hers and waited until he could rein in his emotions. When at last he felt his control returning, he leaned back to look into her eyes. What was she thinking? Did she feel a similar pull toward him? Was she also trying to resist it? Then she moistened her lips, and at once his sense of control was lost as he pulled her body flush with his and his lips found her in a driven kiss that threatened to challenge his restraint. She was, after all, his legal and lawful wife. Instantly, guilt washed over him at the thought, and he released her.

"Dalton, boy, are you in here?" Dalton heard Uncle Ned's voice breaking into his thoughts. He must have brought the children home. Dalton stood up and headed toward the barn door.

"I'm here, Uncle Ned," Dalton replied as he stepped into the light cast from the open door.

"What are ya doin' out here, sittin' all alone in the dark, boy?" Uncle Ned asked.

"Just doin' a bit of thinking, I reckon the barn's as good a place as any, wouldn't you agree?"

Uncle Ned was always teasing him about what a catch Jillian was and that Dalton was a lucky man if ever he knew one. Once he mentioned that Old Man Evanston on the other side of Willow Springs had ordered himself a mail-order bride last fall, and he wasn't nearly as lucky.

"Well, I suppose every man needs to be doin' a little thinkin' now and then," Uncle Ned replied, but he hadn't missed the look of embarrassment that had crossed the man's face. To tease him a little, he added, "Anything I can help you out with? You know, I'm pretty good with advice about all sorts of things like farmin', horses . . . women."

"No." Dalton gave his uncle an exasperated look. "I'm fine, but thank you just the same." He headed out of the barn with Uncle Ned on his heels. "Can I do something for you today, Uncle Ned?" he called over his shoulder. He wasn't going to give Uncle Ned the satisfaction of seeing him squirm.

"Well, I was bringin' your young'uns back home and thought I'd check on how your crop was comin' along."

"Can't complain, I guess. It looks like it's going to be a good crop this year." He turned to look at Uncle Ned, now that the focus of conversation had changed. "Good thing too. I can use the extra money it will bring. I'm going to need a few things come next planting season, including a new horse. Old Decker just doesn't have much in him anymore, and Riley can't do the work alone." Looking up at the hot and low afternoon sun, he added, "Wish we'd get a little more rain, though. If it stays dry like this too much longer, I might be in a bit of trouble. How's everything with your crop?"

"Oh, it's about the same, I suppose. You're right about needin' rain, though." He added, "But not too much at one time or we might have other problems we don't want." Dalton nodded his head in agreement. "Well, I best be headin' on home, I suppose. I'm sure my Betty is pretty anxious for me to get back." He climbed up into his wagon and smiled to himself. *She'll be wantin' a report if anything positive has happened over here.* "Oh, by the way, your little darlin' in there asked me to tell you that your supper is about ready. She's as sweet as honey, that one. I wouldn't be hidin' out in no barn iffin' I had that pretty little thing in my house." He gave Dalton a knowing wink and started the wagon out.

"I told you, Uncle Ned, I was thinking, not hiding out." Dalton hollered after him.

Uncle Ned just laughed and kept on going. Dalton shook his head and headed up to the house.

The next evening, Dalton sat contemplating his family. Jillian read from the book of fairy tales she brought with her, something about a girl and a glass slipper. Jenny pretended not to listen as Jillian animatedly told the story, but Dalton suspected she was hanging on every word. Brenn fell asleep on her shoulder, and before long, Lisa did the same, but Jillian kept reading out loud, for Jenny's sake, Dalton was certain.

When the story was finished, Jillian laid the book out on her lap and closed her eyes to rest them, no doubt worn out from her day of hard work. Her breathing soon became soft and rhythmic and he knew that she had fallen asleep as well. Jenny quietly slipped out and went to bed. Dalton just sat watching, thinking, mesmerized by the scene before him, not wanting to disturb the serenity of it.

He often wondered what kind of life she'd led before coming here. From bits and pieces of stories he's overheard her telling the children and Aunt Betty about her life back East, it sounded as though she definitely wasn't used to the kind hard labor required of her here. Most likely, her days were spent in leisurely visits with friends and her evenings spent entertaining or attending socials and parties. By the look and softness of her hands when she had arrived, he was sure she had been raised with servants and attendants. He had watched sympathetically as she struggled to keep her hands from chafing. She had brought a jar of some kind of cream, which she kept in the kitchen window and used religiously after doing dishes or washing clothes. He tried to help make her burdens lighter by helping out where he could. He again wondered what caused her to give up a life of luxury and come here to a strange home, taking on all the responsibilities of a mother.

She was so beautiful sitting there, but it wasn't just her face or her wisps of strawberry curls escaping their pins once again, nor was it the creamy porcelain look to her skin. It was the beauty that radiated out from within her. It had been right for her to come here. He couldn't think it often enough. Dalton was elated that she loved his children so dearly. Jillian's love for them was evident in everything she did. An outsider watching would never guess that she hadn't borne these children herself.

Dalton sat quietly for a few minutes longer and then stood up. Jillian would sleep better in her own bed, and she needed the rest. Reluctantly, he walked over and lifted Lisa gently off her lap. Jillian woke from the movement and smiled up at him sleepily.

"I'm sorry, I must have dozed off," she said in a whisper. She gathered the closed book, set it on the table next to her, and stood up to follow him, carrying Brenn. They walked to the children's room and put them in their beds. Dalton watched from the doorway as Jillian softly placed a kiss on each of their foreheads as she tucked their blankets up around them. "Good night, my little angels, sweet dreams," she said in a whisper and walked past him and out of the room.

Jillian waited in the hallway as Dalton shut the door. For a moment they stood looking at each other. Try as she might, she could not keep her eyes from momentarily glancing to his lips and the memory she found there. She'd been trying since yesterday to convince herself that she had just been daydreaming, but she knew she could never have imagined such a kiss.

Dalton took a step forward, and for a moment, Jillian thought he might take her into his arms again. Instead, he abruptly turned and headed back down the hallway. When he reached the end, he stopped, paused, and then turned around to look at her. She was embarrassed that she had been caught still watching him.

"I need to bank the fire in the parlor," he said simply. "You've worked hard today and I expect you're pretty worn out, so I'll see you in the morning." Then, almost as an after thought, he said, "Good night." Without waiting for a reply, he turned and headed toward the parlor.

Jillian quickly went into her room, shutting the door behind her and leaning up against it. She took a few deep breaths and tried to calm her racing heart. She wanted him to kiss her again, wanted to feel his arms around her. What was she thinking? She was through with men, wasn't she? Things were working out wonderfully the way they were. She would not allow her heart to be trampled on again.

Forcing herself to recall Nathan Shaw and how he had deceived her, she walked over to her vanity and sat down. Methodically, she began removing the pins from her hair. Picking up her brush, she slowly began working her way through her mass of curls, as images of Nathan began to fill her mind. She felt icy fingers start to wrap around her heart again, as the images became more vivid. How could she have been so blind? Of course, Nathan had been an expert at hiding his true character. She remembered the night her whirlwind romance began.

It was the night of the Spring Ball Extravaganza. Jillian was sixteen and a half, and it was her first opportunity to attend the ball.

She wore the new emerald green dress Father had brought back from his trip to Paris. The color was perfect for her and made the green of her eyes come alive. She'd always considered herself mostly plain, but she did like her eyes and the long lashes that framed them. Tonight, as she gazed into the mirror, she thought herself almost attractive. Her strawberry curls were meticulously piled atop her head with just the right amount draping down the back of her neck. The cut of the dress was daringly lower than most of the dresses she owned, but not so low as to compromise her modesty. It did, however, compliment her recently filled out figure, and she felt excited for the evening ahead. There was a knock at her bedroom door.

"Come in," she called and smiled in the mirror as Marcus entered her room. He let out a long, low whistle.

"I'll be beating them off of you tonight, Little Sis. You're sure you want to be wearing that dress?" He looked her up and down. "I'll have my work cut out for me, protecting the honor of the most beautiful girl at the ball." He feigned pulling a sword from his waistcoat and stood in front of her with his other arm out to protect her. Playfully she swatted him on the shoulder and stood on her tiptoes to kiss him on the cheek.

"Oh, Marcus, you're the sweetest brother I have."

"I'm the only brother you have," Marcus said grinning.

"Well, if I did have another, you would definitely be the sweetest."

"If you did have another, I might not have to work so hard tonight defending your honor. I would have a comrade in arms." He gave his imaginary sword one last swipe and then gave her his most handsome smile. "Sweet as I may be, dear sister, I have come to collect you. Our carriage is ready and we will be late if we do not leave this very moment."

Jillian took one last look in the mirror, twisted a curl back into place, and then linked her arm through Marcus's.

"Well, lead the way, my dear champion. You do know how I hate to be late."

"That I know, dear sister, that I know." And with that, they were on their way, arriving at the ball with a couple minutes to spare.

Already the great hall was bustling with all sorts of different dignitaries and members of the elite class. Providence was known for its Spring Ball Extravaganza. The city overflowed with visitors this time of year, mostly nieces and nephews of wealthy businessmen and landowners. The *Providence Gazette*, a weekly paper that featured the high society "goings on" in the city, always published an article on the event the following day. It covered, in particular, the current most attractive debutantes and most eligible bachelors. It was considered most advantageous to get oneself mentioned. Some of the more outlandish youths even planned bizarre pranks to catch the attention of the reporters.

Marcus escorted Jillian into the ballroom after collecting her dance card. Immediately, she spotted Bethany Johansen and tugged on Marcus's arm to lead her in that direction. Bethany was a true beauty if ever there was one. She had curled her dark ebony hair tonight and pinned it up in an attractive style, with just enough of the rich darks curls hanging down around her neck, in a soft and enticing manner.

Bethany and Jillian had been best friends since, well, forever, it seemed. Jillian was only four when Bethany moved into the house across the street. They became instant friends, spending countless hours having tea parties with their dolls. Their other favorite activities had been exploring and pretending they were in danger of being captured by pirates.

As they grew older, they spent their days sharing secrets and talking about boys and men. They enjoyed practicing their ladylike poses and phrases for the express purpose of catching the attention of some unsuspecting member of the opposite sex.

Bethany was the only one that knew about Jillian's secret attraction to the dashing Mr. Nathan Shaw. In turn, Jillian was the only one that knew about Bethany's infatuation with her brother, Marcus. Jillian could see the blush rise to Bethany's cheeks as they neared her. She couldn't blame her friend. Marcus was both extremely handsome and endearingly charismatic. He had thick blond hair with only the slightest hint of curl, so instead of being unruly, like hers, it lay in perfect waves. He also had the same green eyes and thick lashes as she did. Marcus took pride in his physique, working hard to keep his body in perfect shape. No, she couldn't blame Bethany Johansen for falling in love with her brother. Marcus was a good catch. Both girls squealed in delight as they clasped hands when Jillian finally reached her.

"Oh, Jillian, you look absolutely divine. Not a man here will be able to resist you tonight, nor does any other girl stand a chance." Bethany pretended to pout for a moment, but her face quickly turned to a smile again.

"Don't be silly, Bethany. You know you will be the one getting all the attention. That color of blue is spectacular on you." Jillian stood back a step to get a better look.

"Well, maybe I'll get some attention from the ones you reject."

They both burst into giggles and hugged one another. Marcus spoke up then.

"I think you're both getting attention right now from the entire assembly, going on like you are." Both girls quickly straightened themselves and attempted to look proper. Bethany shyly looked up at Marcus.

"Hello, Marcus. Thank you for bringing Jillian here so promptly. You saved me from looking awfully pitiful, just standing here all by myself."

Marcus took a low bow and swept Bethany's hand up into his own, placing a very proper, albeit lingering, kiss there. Bethany blushed beautifully.

"The pleasure is all mine, my lady. I do adore rescuing beautiful, stranded females like yourself." He didn't release her hand right away. "Besides, you know our Jillian absolutely abhors being the slightest bit tardy to anything."

Jillian's smile widened as Bethany's blush deepened, this time creeping up her neck and face before settling onto her cheeks. Marcus was teasing her mercilessly. Jillian gave him a hard nudge in his ribs and he finally let go of her hand. Bethany was still speechless, so Jillian nudged her with her other elbow, but to her amusement, her friend still stood dumfounded.

"Why, Bethany Johansen," Marcus began, "the rose of your blush flatters me." He was in trouble now. Jillian dug the heel of her shoe into his foot. She saw him grimace slightly, but she could tell that it wasn't going to stop him. If he continued, he'd have Bethany so flustered it would ruin their entire evening. She had to interrupt before he said anything else.

"Marcus, be a dear boy and fetch Bethany and me something to drink, won't you? It is getting quite warm in here already, and I'm sure Bethany is as parched as I am." She gave him a look that said, "You'd better not cross me, big brother."

Marcus bowed again, low and graceful. "Ah, but your wish is my command." And with a wink, which only served to turn Bethany's face an even darker shade of pink, he turned and headed toward the refreshment tables. When Marcus left, Jillian heard Bethany let out the breath she had been holding. Jillian laughed and put her arm through her friend's, giving it a little squeeze.

"You know, Beth, you've practically grown up in the same household as Marcus. Why are you still so tongue-tied around him?" she asked.

Bethany sighed. "I don't know, Jillian. He just does something to me when he's around, and I can't think or move or do anything but stare at him. All that practicing we did when we were younger obviously hasn't paid off for me." Bethany rolled her eyes in exasperation, causing Jillian to laugh heartily again.

"Well, you do manage to change colors pretty easily," she pointed out between giggles. She tried to stop and appear more dignified. "Seriously, Beth, you're never going to get anywhere if you can't say two words to him."

"I know, I know," Bethany sighed.

Just then, Jillian caught sight of Nathan Shaw. He'd entered the room, immediately spotted Marcus over at the refreshment table, and gone to join him. Oh, how fine he was to look at. His hair was light brown with a touch of gold streaked through it, and his eyes were the color of brown sugar. Now, it was Jillian's turn to get nervous.

Usually, Jillian was actually quite comfortable around Nathan, not getting all jittery and befuddled as did quite a few of the other girls who tried to get his attention. Marcus and Nathan had been good friends since she was about ten, and he spent a lot of his time at their house. Not only had he seen her through her awkward years, they had, since they'd first met, playfully teased each other back and forth. By now, they had a fairly comfortable and open relationship with each other, except for the fact that she was secretly enamored with him, and he only thought of her as his best friend's little sister.

Jillian saw her brother nod his head in her direction and say something to Nathan. Nathan turned in her direction and caught her eye. Jillian quickly looked away, embarrassed to be caught staring. When she looked back at him, he was still looking at her, seemingly admiring her. She watched as he said something to Marcus and headed in her direction. Jillian began to fidget and Bethany, whom she forgot was standing next to her, gave her a little nudge. It was her turn to be teased. Jillian turned to give Bethany a sour, but playful look. When she turned back, Nathan was standing directly in front of her. He took her hand and demurely gave it a kiss.

"Good evening, Miss Jillian Grey." He was being ever so polite. "Might I be the first to tell you that you are ravishing this evening?" He stood back, still holding her hand, and looked her over from head to toe. "All grown up and blossomed right before my very eyes."

"Why, it is kind of you to notice, Mr. Nathan Shaw." Jillian pulled her hand back out of his and began fiddling with her dance card.

"Notice?" he said surprised. "Well, I'm afraid no man within miles of you could help but notice the great beauty you've become." She was flustered, but thankfully, she managed to keep her wits about her.

"Why, Nathan Shaw, don't you waste your practiced charms on me. I've known you too long to be taken in by your fickle and flirtatious ways. You might be able to fool some of the other women here tonight, but you can bet I won't be one of them." Unconsciously, she had stomped one of her feet to make her point. It was a habit she needed to break. When she realized what she had done, she was grateful he hadn't noticed.

"Waste?" he asked as he leaned in a little closer. "Nothing, my dear Miss Jillian, would ever be a waste on you." As he leaned back, he snatched her dance card from her hand and proceeded to write his name on every line. Shocked, Jillian snatched it back from him and looked at it.

"Why, Nathan Shaw! Now I won't get to dance with anyone but you the entire night!" She pretended to be angry, but secretly she was overjoyed.

Nathan just gave her his wide, handsome grin and turned to walk away, calling over his shoulder, "I'll see you when the music begins."

They danced the whole night, and Jillian found herself literally swept off her feet. The next morning, it was evident that the *Providence Gazette* had taken notice of her whirlwind evening. A week later, Nathan asked Jillian's father for permission to court her. Her parents were thrilled and so was Marcus. Thus began their romance.

Jillian had known Nathan for so long that after the initial shock of finding out that he had feelings for her as well, they fell into a comfortable courtship. Bethany was thrilled for her, and the two girls spent many happy hours discussing in length what it would be like to be the wife of Mr. Nathan Shaw. Jillian loved children so much, she was certain they would marry and begin a family right away. Nathan, however, thought it better that they have a long courtship. He respected her and never took liberties with her, so she was comfortable waiting for a while. She felt somewhat frustrated though that he would never do more than

give her a quick peck on the cheek when he said good night. She wished he would at least once sweep her into his arms and kiss her on the lips, but if he wanted to wait, she would respect his wishes. After they were married, they would have plenty of time for romantic kisses.

The thought of kissing Nathan made Jillian shudder and broke her from her thoughts. She was ever so glad that his lips had never touched hers.

An image of Dalton came into her mind. What a contrast! She felt her body simultaneously warm and shiver slightly with delight as she thought of the kiss they had shared the day before. Never had she imagined a kiss could be like that. Her heart sped up again just thinking about it. He didn't even have to be near her to make her feel this way.

Jillian laid the brush down, changed quickly into her nightclothes, and slipped into bed. She would allow herself to dream of Dalton tonight. Surely it couldn't hurt to just dream of him. Tomorrow she would try harder to control her feelings and be more firm in her commitment to keep romance out of their relationship.

Dalton poked fervently at the log on the hearth. He was finding it difficult to stick to his new resolve. When he had kissed Jillian yesterday, it had taken all his strength to break away and leave. He'd spent the rest of the day chastising himself for giving in to his desire and telling himself that it hadn't been fair to her. He was fully aware that she had agreed to the loveless marriage he'd offered; it wasn't right for him to suddenly expect more. But still, when she stood in the hallway just then, looking at him, the desire to kiss her, to take her into his arms and hold her, had returned with fervor.

Finished with the fire, he stood up and headed back toward his room. He stopped briefly and looked at the door across the hall where she slept. Torturing himself, he recalled their kiss one last time. Then, shaking his head to dispel the image, he opened the door to his own room and went inside.

Ten

It was a perfect day for a picnic. Lisa was so excited that she had been bouncing around all morning. Brenn was delightedly following her and hungrily examining the pies and goodies Jillian had made to take with them. Even Jenny seemed to be in high spirits. By ten o'clock, the wagon was packed, and they were ready to go.

The picnic was held at the lake a few miles away from Willow Springs. Jillian was excited to see water again. She always loved her family's trips to the ocean, and since she knew she might never see it again, she was determined to love the lake just as well.

Jillian was a bit anxious and was trying to concentrate on the children to help quell her nerves. Other than seeing some of the townsfolk at church the last few Sundays, she hadn't done any real socializing. She had met one young woman that she liked, Olivia Jenkins, the pastor's daughter. She and her father had come calling the Sunday after Jillian had arrived, and Olivia and Jillian had talked quite a bit. She was grateful that Aunt Betty had promised to stay close today and give her fair warning if anyone headed her way that she should avoid. She'd heard there were those in town not happy that Dalton was no longer an eligible bachelor.

Earlier that morning, she'd a difficult time deciding what to wear. Other than her party gowns, she'd only packed her more practical dresses. Since a picnic was no place to wear a party dress, she had finally decided on a peach colored dress she hadn't worn yet. It was just a little fancier than the other dresses she had brought. Lisa had been beside herself when Jillian had come out of the house wearing it. Jillian was pleased and looked forward to having the extra time this winter to make the girls a few new dresses of their own.

Dalton's gaze swept over her appraisingly, and she felt her pulse quicken. She pretended not to notice him looking at her. She did, however, sneak a few appraising looks of her own. He looked so handsome in his newer looking pair of denim jeans and clean white shirt, which was rolled up at the sleeves, accentuating his sun bronzed skin.

After a short wagon ride, they were unloading their things. Dalton quickly grabbed their bundles and ushered the children toward Uncle Ned, who was lying down on a blanket in the soft grass close to the lake. Aunt Betty came hurrying over.

Giving Jillian a hug, she exclaimed, "My, you look lovely today, dear. May I help you carry some of your things?"

"Oh yes, please," Jillian gratefully answered as she looked over at the tables that were bustling with women. She would be glad for the company, if not for the help.

"These pies look wonderful, Jillian!" Aunt Betty said with genuine enthusiasm. "That peach raspberry you sent over the other night was heavenly. I may have indeed met my match—in the kitchen anyway," she teased.

"You're too kind to me, Aunt Betty," Jillian replied, "It's taken me a little time to get used to baking in an unfamiliar oven, but I think I've finally mastered it."

"Well, no one can argue that by the looks of these." She gave Jillian an encouraging smile. "Are you ready to enter the hen house over there?" She nodded toward the crowd of women.

"I suppose I might as well get it over with," Jillian replied. They made their way over to the tables with their hands full. Before they reached the group, however, Aunt Betty leaned over to Jillian.

"Watch out," she whispered. "Here comes Mavis Bingham. She's a nosy gossip. You have to watch what you say around her." She quickly stopped her explanation as Mavis stopped in front of them.

"Well, hello, Betty. It's so good to see you! I missed you and Ned at church last Sunday.

"Yes, well, Ned was worried he had a cold comin' on and we thought it best to stay home. It didn't turn out to be much to worry over, thank goodness." Betty took a step to the side to go around her to the tables, but

Mavis ever so slightly maneuvered her body to block her way, compelling Betty to pause again. Mavis then turned her attention to Jillian.

"And who might this be, Betty? Could this be Dalton's new wife, come all the way over from Massachusetts?" She conducted a thorough examination of Jillian, with a slightly pinched look on her face. "She is a pretty little thing, I suppose." Jillian couldn't believe the woman was talking about her as if she wasn't standing right in front of her. "You know, my Sarah cried for two weeks when she found out Dalton up and got married. Had her heart set on being his new bride herself." She finally turned from Jillian back to Aunt Betty. "Well, to each his own, I must say." Jillian risked a quick look at Aunt Betty, who looked as if she was about to explode. Jillian was also trying very hard to bite her tongue as Mavis went on.

"Was kind of a funny thing though, him pining for his dead wife one day and then showin' up with a new one the next." Jillian was worried about Aunt Betty now. She had turned a new shade of red, but all of a sudden, she seemed to gain total control over her emotions. By the time she answered Mavis, Jillian would have thought they were having an everyday friendly conversation.

"Well, Mavis, you know Dalton, always wantin' the best of everything. Suppose that's why he chose my Laurellyn in the first place, and I suppose that's why he's chosen Jillian here now. You just can't blame a man if his search had to reach all the way to the East Coast to find him the best this time." She then turned to Jillian with a triumphant smile on her face. "Come on, Jillian, we'd best be gettin' these pies you made to the table before the judgin' begins. One of these scrumptious things is sure take the blue ribbon this year!"

They both walked around a dumbfounded Mavis Bingham to the tables and set the pies down. Aunt Betty took Jillian's arm in hers and said, "We best hurry back to the wagon to get the others things you brought." She nodded quickly toward Mrs. Bingham. "She won't bother us again today." She smiled mischievously. "Mavis has won the first prize for the past four years with her apple-cinnamon pie, but I've given her a bit to chew on." They both laughed together, and Jillian said another prayer of thanks for Aunt Betty.

By the time everyone arrived and it was time to eat lunch, the tables groaned with the weight of all the delicious food. Everyone filled their plates and sat on blankets down by the water's edge to eat.

Later, full from their ample meal, folks visited and relaxed while the children played in the water. Dalton had taken off his boots, rolled up his pant legs, and was playing with Jenny and Lisa. Brenn lay napping on the blanket next to Jillian. Aunt Betty and Uncle Ned were resting beside her as well.

The lake was beautiful with the sun reflecting off of it. There was a small island out in the middle. All afternoon, Jillian watched as boatloads of adults and children rowed back and forth from one shore to the other. The island must be a lovely place.

"Jillian." Aunt Betty broke through her revelry. "Why don't you take a walk around and enjoy the lake? It is a beautiful sight this time of year. I'll keep an eye on Brenn." Jillian didn't notice her turn and wink at Uncle Ned.

"That would be wonderful. Thank you, Aunt Betty. I won't be gone long." She stood up, brushed the grass from her dress, and started off.

"Take your time, dear," Aunt Betty called after her. "Uncle Ned and I will enjoy having the children to ourselves for a while." Jillian smiled to herself. She did love them—they were such good people. As she walked off, she turned to wave good-bye.

Dalton noticed when Jillian stood up and walked away. He'd managed to keep a safe distance away from her all day. He had dreamed of her last night.

In his dream, Jillian was running in a meadow with her hair down in all its glory, and she was calling out to him to follow her. He couldn't decide what to do and had reached into his pocket to grasp Laurellyn's cameo, but it wasn't there. He desperately felt around for it, only to realize there was a gaping a hole in the bottom of his pocket. Quickly, he looked about him on the ground to see if he could find it, but it was nowhere in sight. As he turned to head back to continue looking, he heard Jillian call his name again. When he looked over to see where she was, Jenny, Lisa, and Brenn were running with her.

"Come on, Pa," Jenny called, "come with us." Frantically, he tried to decide what to do.

"Wait for me, I'll be back in a minute," he called out to them. "I've lost something and I need to find it." Just then he heard Lisa call out to him.

"No, Pa, you'll miss it. Come see." He looked around behind him once again, but when he turned back to his family, they were gone. He woke up with a start, and his heart was beating furiously.

He'd glanced over at the table where Laurellyn's cameo lay undisturbed, just where he had left it the night before. Tears had begun to spill down his cheek as he got out of bed and knelt down to pray, the cameo in his hand. He was suddenly frightened he would lose his family if he couldn't find a way to release his hold on the past. He needed to make some decisions, and there was only one power he knew of that wouldn't lead him astray.

After praying awhile, he'd gotten up, walked to his bureau, and removed a small box. Lifting the lid, he'd placed the cameo inside. He brushed his fingers across it one last time before replacing the lid. Reverently, he put the box back in his drawer and pushed it closed. He would save it for Jenny and give it to her one day when she was older. He had received his answer.

Now, as he saw Jillian walking away along the lakeshore, he felt momentarily panicked as he remembered the dream. He was still confused about how exactly he was to go about remedying their situation. There were so many things to consider. The only thing he knew for certain was that he wanted to be a part of his children's future, and he wanted that future to include Jillian . . . completely.

After awhile, he saw Aunt Betty wave him over. While keeping a watchful eye on Jenny and Lisa, he walked the few yards over to the blanket. Aunt Betty smiled up at him endearingly.

Eleven

Jillian climbed up on a rock perched at the edge of the lake and sat down. She supposed she was on the opposite side of the lake from where the picnic was going on, but gratefully, the island in the center blocked her view. She didn't want to see anyone, or have anyone see her.

The tears burned hot and new as Jillian thought again of how humiliated she had felt. She could never understand how one person could be so cruel to another. That was something she could never tolerate, even in her elevated station back home. She prided herself on always treating others kindly and with compassion.

She had removed her shoes and stockings earlier, so she let her feet dip down into the cool, refreshing water. Strands of her disobedient hair had come loose when she had taken off in a run as soon as she was past the view of anyone at the picnic. She reached up and pulled the rest of the pins out, letting her unruly hair fall, unhindered, and tucked the hairpins into her dress pocket. Her anger made her feel rebellious, and letting her hair hang freely about her felt like an act of rebellion. She ran her fingers through to free it of some of the tangles, and then stopped to wipe the hot tears away from her face once again.

Jillian chastised herself for caring what anyone else thought of her. Only the opinions of those she loved and those who loved her should really matter. Who did that Sarah Bingham think she was, anyway? What she said was surely out of jealousy and spite, but still, it hurt her pride to hear them laugh at her the way they had.

Jillian had just waved good-bye to Aunt Betty and Uncle Ned and was walking away, close to the shoreline, when she saw a group of young women about her age sitting by a tree next to the water's edge. She recognized Sarah Bingham because she had seen her sitting with her mother and father after lunch. Olivia Jenkins was sitting with them also. Jillian was sure that Sarah had seen her approaching, but she quickly turned back to her friends and then heard her address them in a voice a little louder than would be normal, sitting in such a group.

"My mother told me that she answered his ad for a mail-order bride. Can you imagine being so desperate for a man that you'd have to answer the ad of someone you'd never met? That must mean no one she knew would have her!" Jillian froze when everyone in the group, except Olivia, burst out laughing. "Well, if you ask me," she continued, "Dalton could have done a lot better for himself. He should have asked her to send a picture before he agreed to the marriage." She then looked over at Jillian, feigning shock that she might have overhead their conversation. "Why, Mrs. McCullough," Jillian's only satisfaction was that it seemed painful for the spiteful woman to address her as such. "I didn't see you standing there. Oh, I'm so sorry if I said anything . . . Oh, dear, but I had no idea . . . . Were you standing there this whole time?" Jillian took a deep breath, ignored their stares, and hurried past them. The last thing she heard was the group of girls burst out laughing again.

Jillian's feet were getting cold, so she took them out of the water. Realizing she ought to compose herself and get back to the picnic before anyone worried about her, she stood and took a step off the rock when her foot slipped, and she suddenly lost her balance. Before she could let out a scream, she heard a splash and felt herself caught by someone's powerful arms. She looked up into Dalton's handsome face. After the worried look left him, the corners of his mouth turned up into a grin.

"Now, don't you dare laugh at me, Dalton McCullough," she scolded, causing a deep hearty laugh to erupt from him. She tried to wiggle free of his arms.

"Now, hold on there, missy! You'll make us both fall in the lake if you keep squirming around like that." Easily lifting Jillian, he stepped out of the water and onto the shoreline.

"Thank you. Now, put me down . . . please," she insisted.

"We'd better get you a little farther from the water first, just so you're safe." He laughed again and walked to a nearby tree. "There now," he said as he lowered her legs, placing her bare feet on the soft grass. As he stood next to her, he asked, "Are you all right?" He still hadn't removed his arm from around her. As she looked up into his face, he brushed the remains of a tear from her face with his free hand.

"What brings you out this far anyway? Aunt Betty and Uncle Ned sent me out to find you. Just in time too." He laughed lightly. "You might have had to return to the picnic looking like a drowned rat instead of an angel."

Jillian smiled. "Well, Aunt Betty suggested I take a walk and look around a bit. I guess I lost track of how far I'd gone." She was trying really hard to slow her heartbeat and will away the goose bumps on her skin where he was holding her.

"She told you to go for a walk, huh?" Looking as though he'd just figured something out, he leaned one hand against the tree above her head. "I think we have a couple of meddling old matchmakers watching our children back at the picnic."

"Matchmakers? What do you . . . ?" Suddenly, she understood too. "Why, those two . . . Would they really try and . . . Oh, I'm so sorry, Dalton."

Without warning, he leaned in close and brushed his lips next to her ear. "Are you really?" he whispered. Jillian's ear began to tingle, and she felt her heart take flight. He had such an effect on her! She didn't know how to answer him.

"I . . . I . . . um," was all she could get out. Dalton's lips had moved to her neck, and the heat of his breath on her skin caused her to shiver. In a moment, his lips were at her ear again, and she felt excess moisture flood her mouth.

"Well, we ought not disappoint them," he whispered. Jillian's body trembled with anticipation. His lips then found hers, and their warm caress was heaven. She felt her body melt into him, and in an instant his arms were around her. At first his kiss was soft, but slowly the passion began to increase. She was still leaning back against the tree, and as their kiss intensified, she was crushed even closer to him. She was having trouble catching her breath, but she was too overjoyed to be in his arms once again to care. She was his, her mind said over and over. She belonged to him. Her heart leapt at the thought. Finally, unable to breathe, she was compelled to put her hands on his shoulders and gently push him away. Immediately, he broke their kiss, and she took deep gulps of air back into her lungs.

"We should probably be getting back," she said softly, not looking into his eyes. "They're probably getting worried about us." He released her, and, as she stepped away, he reached down, plucked a long blade of grass, leaned up against the tree, and began chewing the end of it.

Jillian walked over to the bush where she had left her stockings and shoes. Embarrassed by her audience, since he hadn't yet taken his eyes off her, she quickly put her stockings back on. She then found a rock to sit on while replacing her shoes. When she was finished, she retrieved the pins from her pocket and began to redo her hair.

"You can leave it down if you'd like. I don't mind." Jillian looked up and saw Dalton grinning at her while still chewing on the blade of grass.

"And what would people say, Dalton McCullough, if I came walking back with you, with my hair all undone?" She gave him a stern look.

"Probably what they're already saying . . . that I'm the luckiest man in all of the state of Wisconsin." That caused her to blush, but then she remembered Sarah Bingham, and her mood once again became solemn.

"No, I don't think that's what they're saying at all." She couldn't keep the hurt look from returning to her face. He looked confused at her meaning. She ignored him, finished her hair, and stood, ready to go. He took her arm and they both started walking back together.

Neither one said anything to each other as they walked, both lost in their own thoughts. As they turned the last bend in the shoreline, they began to hear the sounds of the picnic again. Dalton felt Jillian stiffen. He wondered again what had happened that had caused the evidence of tears he'd seen earlier. He looked up at that moment and caught sight of Miss Sarah Bingham. She was staring at them and looking none too pleased. She had made more than one play for Dalton in the last year, each of which he had emphatically turned down. It wouldn't surprise him to find out that she had done or said something that had been the cause of Jillian's tears.

Dalton took his arm out of Jillian's and put it around her waist, pulling her in close as they walked past. He leaned in intimately and whispered something into her ear. She laughed and he laughed with her. Abruptly, he stopped and turned her towards him. With a twinkle in his eye, he kissed her squarely on the lips, in front of everyone, ignoring the shocked look on her face. He smiled broadly, looked up, and waved at Miss Bingham like he had just noticed her standing there. Dalton put his arm around Jillian once again, and they headed back towards Uncle Ned, Aunt Betty, and the waiting children. When they got to their blanket, Aunt Betty was grinning from ear to ear.

"Now, don't you go looking so pleased with yourself, dear Auntie. We know what you've been up to today. You haven't pulled anything over on us," proclaimed Dalton. But she didn't stop smiling. He knew she had seen the kiss he had just given Jillian.

Jillian looked around. "Where did Uncle Ned go?"

Aunt Betty's smile faded. "Well, when Jenny saw Dalton kiss you, she ran off. Uncle Ned went after her."

Jillian's heart sank. What damage had been done this time? She felt like she was finally just getting through to Jenny. She felt they were so close to finding a peaceful middle ground. Now all of that would be undone. Jillian was stirring things up instead of making them better. She couldn't bear to see the young girl's heart broken any more. There was only one way to get things back on track. She would have to avoid Dalton and squelch her growing feelings for him, for Jenny's sake. She looked up at him desperately. Would that be possible? She could tell from the look on his face that he understood their dilemma as well as she did, without putting words to it.

"It's getting late. Maybe we should head home," Jillian solemnly suggested. Lisa and Brenn looked tuckered out, and Jillian had surely had an emotional day herself.

"But they haven't announced the winner of the cooking contests yet." Aunt Betty frowned. A sudden thought brightened her face once again. "I can't wait to get a look at old Mavis Bingham's face when they announce your peach raspberry pie as the first place winner. Somebody's been needin' to knock her off her pedestal for a long time." She looked like a child waiting for a present. "Besides, Uncle Ned and I thought maybe we could take the children home with us tonight and you two youngsters could stay for the dance."

"NO!" Both Dalton and Jillian protested at the same time. Aunt Betty was taken aback, but noticed the determined look in their eyes. Something had changed and not for the better.

"I mean, Jillian's right, Aunt Betty," Dalton began quickly. "The children are tired, and they would be better off sleeping in their own beds." He looked over at Jillian for support.

"Yes, I'm feeling a bit tired as well." Jillian feigned a yawn. "If you wouldn't mind bringing my dishes home with you when you leave, I'd be grateful." She looked over at Dalton and spoke. "Maybe you should see if you can find Jenny and Uncle Ned. I'll get the other children over to the wagon and wait for you."

"But—" was all Aunt Betty could get out. Sometimes even the best-laid plans got foiled.

✦

They rode in silence back to the house. Both Brenn and Lisa were sleeping and Jenny was brooding. Jillian looked back at her. When would all ever be right with the world for her?

Jillian pondered on Dalton and his strange reaction on their walk back to the picnic. They had been casually strolling arm in arm when she had spotted Miss Sarah Bingham eyeing her—the woman was fairly glaring at them. Then all of a sudden Dalton had let go of her and put his arm around her waist, pulling her intimately close. The next thing she knew, he leaned in and whispered in her ear, "Don't ask any questions, but I want you to laugh out loud like you just heard something very funny." Too amused at his odd behavior, she complied with his request and randomly laughed out loud, which he followed up with a laugh of his own. Without warning, he turned her to face him, his eyes twinkling, and kissed her soundly on the lips, in front of everyone. She knew she must have looked shocked, but he just put his arm back around her waist like it was the most normal thing in the world, and they had continued on to join their family.

She still didn't know what he'd been up to exactly, though she suspected it had something to do with Sarah Bingham by the way he waved enthusiastically over at her immediately after they'd kissed. She had intended on questioning him about it until they'd found out about Jenny running off, and then it just slipped her mind. Now, it seemed too awkward to talk about.

The wagon turned past the gate and into the yard. Jillian was glad to be home. *Home,* she thought. Despite everything that happened, or perhaps in spite of some of it, this still truly felt like home.

Twelve

Jillian looked out at the storm clouds mounting and sighed. She wouldn't be able to work in the garden today. By the time all the chores were done, it would surely be raining. The rain would be good though. The crops had become drier by the day from the lack of rain. She could see that Dalton was worried. The corn wouldn't make it if they didn't get some moisture soon. Well, their prayers were about to be answered.

It had been a week and a half since the picnic. She and Dalton had hardly spoken to each other, and he seemed to be particularly bent on avoiding her. A few nights after the picnic, after Jillian had put Lisa and Brenn to bed, she had gone to Jenny's room and knocked on the door. There was no answer, so Jillian opened the door a crack.

"Jenny." She paused and waited for her to reply. "Jenny, can I come in and talk to you?" There was still no answer, so Jillian opened the door and slipped inside, leaving the door open a crack. Jenny was lying on her bed, just staring at the ceiling. Jillian sat beside her on the bed, and Jenny turned away from her and faced the wall.

"Jenny, I know this has been hard on you, and I understand why you're upset with me." Jillian tentatively reached out, placing her hand gently on Jenny's back. She hadn't touched the child in the five weeks she'd been here, and her arms ached to hold and comfort her. "You know, I just wish we could at least be friends." If only she knew what Jenny was thinking. What ideas and thoughts were milling around in that young head of hers? Maybe she was just as confused as Jillian and didn't know what everyone expected from her. Maybe she really didn't mind having a new ma, but just had forgotten how to act with one. Could Jillian help her remember? Suddenly, she had a strong impression to try something different.

Jillian lay down on the bed next to Jenny and put her arm around her. She felt Jenny stiffen slightly, but she ignored it. Jillian started to hum softly. It was a lullaby she had heard somewhere. She couldn't quite remember the words, only the melody that was playing in her mind and in her heart. Maybe it was a song her mother had sung to her when she was a child. She stopped trying to analyze it. It didn't matter where the song had come from, only that it felt right. She just kept humming and caressing Jenny's head and hair with her hand. All of a sudden, the words came to her and she began singing them softly over and over again. Before long, Jillian could tell by Jenny's slowed breathing that the young girl had fallen asleep. Jillian did not get up immediately, but stayed there thinking, and it wasn't long before she had dozed off herself.

When Jillian woke, she was sure it was past midnight. Jenny still lay sleeping soundly. She gently rose from the bed, tucked Jenny's blanket around her, and for the first time kissed her forehead softly, whispering "I love you, Jenny." She crossed the room and closed the door quietly.

Jillian paused outside of Dalton's room. She assumed he was inside, even if she hadn't heard him come in. She hoped he was sleeping as soundly as Jenny. He worked too hard not to get a good night's sleep. She quietly opened the door to her own room, went in, and silently closed it behind her. Quickly she undressed, climbed into bed, and fell immediately asleep.

Things were better with Jenny after that night. Jenny even silently helped a little around the house and with the cooking. A few days later, when Jillian was weeding in the flower garden, Jenny came up, knelt down in the dirt, and started working right beside her. She didn't say anything, just worked. She seemed to know what she was doing too. Then, just as quietly as she had come, she got up and left. Jillian said a special prayer of thanks that day.

The more progress she made with Jenny, however, the more distant she and Dalton seemed to become. She had barely seen him in almost two weeks, and the children were missing him terribly.

Jillian saw a flash of lightning, just over the north fields, and it jolted her back from her thoughts. A few moments later, she heard the clap of thunder that followed. The storm was moving faster than she thought it would. She would need to hurry to get her chores done.

About fifteen minutes later, Jenny came stumbling into the house out of breath. School must have let out early because of the impending rain.

"Ma, come quick!" Jillian was startled. Jenny had just called her "Ma" for the first time. She would have liked to ponder on that and what it meant for their relationship, but the next words out of Jenny's mouth caused an immediate fear to well up inside, stifling any good thoughts.

"Ma, the fields are on fire!" Jenny cried desperately.

Jillian ran to the door to look out. She could see a billow of black smoke rising up in the distance behind the barn, but her view of the north fields was blocked. Immediately, a vision of Dalton possibly caught in the flames crossed her mind.

"Jenny," she said, reaching for the coat that hung by the door and putting it on. "Watch your sister and brother for me. I've got to go help your father."

Jenny ran into her arms and began to cry. Jillian wished she could stay and enjoy holding her, but instead she broke the embrace, knelt down, put her hands on Jenny's shoulders, and looked into her eyes. "Jenny, everything is going to be okay, but listen carefully to me. You are in charge. You need to stay in the house. The fire is not close. You, Lisa, and Brenn will be safe. I will come back and check on you or send someone as soon as I can."

Jenny nodded her understanding. Jillian stood and walked over to where Lisa and Brenn had been playing minutes before. They now sat watching intently what was going on between her and Jenny. They didn't quite understand it, but they could tell something unusual was happening. Jillian quickly hugged them both and said, "Lisa, I want you to mind your sister and help her watch Brenn, okay?" Lisa nodded and put her arm around Brenn protectively, sensing her great responsibility. Jillian stood and hurried out the door.

As she headed across the yard, Uncle Ned and Aunt Betty came barreling up the road in the buckboard. They jumped down and quickly retrieved a number of different sized buckets that had been haphazardly thrown into the back.

"Quick, Jillian," Aunt Betty hollered. "Find any containers that will hold water, as many as you can carry. We can't take the wagon any closer because fire will spook the horses." Jillian immediately obeyed her, grabbing anything she could find.

As she hurried out to the fields, Jillian saw two other wagons drive up carrying their neighbors—the Collins, the Flannigans, and some others she didn't know. Quickly, she said a prayer of thanks for the additional help and asked for the rain to begin. So far, not a drop had fallen.

Jillian's breath caught in her throat when they reached the blazing fields. It appeared that close to half the crop was already burning. Her heart ached, and she searched anxiously until she finally caught sight of Dalton working feverishly, beating at the flames with a wool blanket.

Almost immediately, those present formed a line from the well to the fire, and everyone began working, bringing water to the flames to help put out the fire. Jillian kept looking up at the sky, praying that the rain would begin, even as the sky darkened and the winds picked up. Nobody spoke a word to anyone else. They just continued to work and to pray.

Jillian looked over at Dalton. He hadn't taken his eyes off the fire, but she could see the pained look, even in the profile of his face. Her heart ached for the loss of all his hard work. It was a blessing when the skies finally opened up and poured their mercies out onto the fields, dousing the flames.

Finally, when only small tendrils of smoke billowed up here and there, each neighbor came forward, one by one, and offered their sympathies to Dalton and then to Jillian, before slowly heading back to their own homes. Uncle Ned and Aunt Betty were the last to leave. Aunt Betty stepped in front of Dalton and gave him a heartfelt hug. He just stood, despondent, with his arms hanging at his side. She then walked over to Jillian and gathered her tenderly into her arms.

"I'll stop in at the house and check on the children before we head back home. Is there anything else we can do for you?" Jillian just shook her head. She didn't trust herself to speak—her emotions were too raw. Uncle Ned gave her a tight hug next.

"Everything will be all right," he said. "We farmers are strong. When life knocks us down, we just pick ourselves up and get goin' again. You both will get through this, and we'll be here to help." He grabbed her hand and squeezed it, and he and Aunt Betty headed back to the house.

Jillian turned back to look at Dalton. His back was to her, and he stood motionless as the rain mercilessly poured down on them. She wiped the rain from her eyes that was now mixed with the salt of her tears. She walked up behind Dalton and placed her hand on his shoulder.

It was as if she had just disturbed a castle made of cards. His knees buckled beneath him, and he sank to the ground. Jillian knelt down beside him and put her arms around his shoulders. Immediately, his arms came around her and he laid his head against her chest. She felt his body shudder as if the last remnants of the imaginary castle suddenly fell. She could feel his defeat in the way his body lay drained against her own. Her tears fell freely, lost in the rain that continued to fall as she tried to comfort him.

Jillian didn't know how long they sat that way. The rain had let up to a hard drizzle. Eventually, Dalton sat back up and they both stared at the blackness in front of them. Jillian had been struggling to control her body and keep it from shivering, but finally she couldn't hold it back any longer and her body began to shake violently. Dalton stood up then, lifting her up with him, and looked into her eyes.

"Thank you," he said. "Thank you for staying out here with me for a while." Jillian said nothing. She reached up and brushed away a wet strand of hair that had fallen into his face, until her hand began shaking again. He cradled it in his own and tried to give it some warmth. "We need to get you back to the house." Without letting go of her hand, he turned and started walking. "Besides, the children are probably worried."

"Yes, I told Jenny I'd try to hurry. I hope we haven't frightened her." The thought made her walk a little faster. She remembered the miracle that had happened. Jenny had not only called her "Ma," but had hugged her as well! In spite of all this devastation, Jillian found something to be happy about. She recalled Uncle Ned's words. *We farmers are strong. When life knocks us down, we just pick ourselves back up and get going.* Was he right? Would Dalton be able to pick himself back up and get them through this? They would need to be strong—she needed to be strong, both for Dalton and for the children.

Jillian suddenly remembered the money her mother had given her before she left. It was tucked safely away in her trunk. Her mother had said it would come in handy in good times and troubled ones. The fire would definitely bring troubled times, but would the money be enough to help her family through them? Yes, she knew it would. Everything was going to be all right. "Thank you, Mother," Jillian whispered to herself as she and Dalton returned to the house and the waiting children.

❧

It was Saturday—just a few days after the fire—and Dalton came home for lunch at the house for the first time in two weeks. He sat watching as Jillian patiently showed Jenny just how to knead bread dough. Jenny laughed out loud as a cloud of flour burst from the table and into her face as she plopped the dough back down.

Jenny, laughing? he thought. That was a sound he hadn't heard in over a year. Something wonderful had happened, and he sensed which night it had begun.

Dalton came in one evening after making sure the chicken coop was secured. Some critter had been getting at the chickens. It hadn't taken one yet, but already two had broken their necks scurrying around in the dark, trying to get away from whatever was after them. He didn't know what it was, and he would be on edge until he eliminated the threat. The idea of some unknown animal running around attacking things didn't sit too well with him, especially knowing his children often played in the area.

When he came back inside, the house was quiet. It appeared that everyone had gone to bed, even Jillian. He had been avoiding her lately. He didn't know what else to do. After Jenny had gotten so upset at the picnic, he was afraid his actions would ruin any progress Jillian had made with her. In order to avoid any awkwardness, he spent most of his time in the fields, repairing fences, or working out in the barn. He'd leave early in the morning, taking his lunch with him, and return home late at night, eating what Jillian had set aside for him.

It had been a difficult time for him. He missed playing with the children at night and spending time with them in the mornings. He had hardly seen them at all the last two weeks. He checked in on them every night before he went to bed, but that didn't fill the void.

He finished his supper and headed to his room. He wasn't getting enough sleep by rising earlier and getting to bed later than everyone

else. As he walked up the hall, he heard a soft melody drifting from Jenny's room. He recognized the tune immediately—it was the one Laurellyn sang to Jenny and Lisa as she rocked them to sleep when they were small babies. The door was open a crack, so he peeked inside. Jillian lay on the bed next to Jenny, caressing her hair as she sang the melody. He stood mesmerized, watching the scene before him as he listened to the familiar tune.

> Gracefully the dove spreads her wings
> And upon the wind she glides.
> Sweetly the meadowlark starts to sing
> Her beauty she cannot hide.
> Butterflies go dancing by
> And bring color to the skies.
> Wildflowers, a bloom in the meadows,
> Are rainbows to our eyes.
> And you, my child are the greatest of all,
> For you live within my heart
> And where'er we be, either near or far,
> We will never be apart.

Dalton couldn't bring himself to walk away but instead leaned against the wall outside the room and continued to listen as she sang the words over and over. Was it a coincidence that Jillian would know the same tender lullaby that Laurellyn used to sing?

Eventually, Jillian stopped singing. Dalton slipped off to his own room. As he lay down in his bed, he felt a peace settle over him. With the lullaby still playing in his head, he fell into a deep, untroubled sleep.

Jenny laughed again, and Dalton was startled from his memories. Lisa and Brenn had wandered over to where Jillian and Jenny were working, and Jillian gave each of the younger children a small piece of the dough. Lisa rolled hers around on the table, and Brenn shoved his piece into his mouth. Jenny laughed because more of it was sticking to his face than he was getting in his mouth. Dalton leaned back in his chair, sighing quietly, and contentedly watching his family for a while longer.

Things had worked as he'd hoped. By keeping his distance from Jillian and thereby not causing Jenny any more upsets, his family was healing. He watched Jillian for a moment. He couldn't help but feel he'd made the right decision because of the change in Jenny. The laughter and happiness that filled the house was a blessing that helped temper the tragedy they had experienced.

They had lost over half of the crop to the fire. It was too late in the season to replant, so he busied himself tending the surviving corn, cleaning up the debris, and getting the fields ready for planting next year. He looked over at Jillian as she smiled down at Jenny. He recalled the surprise she had given him the morning after the fire.

Jillian sat down next to Dalton after breakfast, and, after taking his hand, she placed a large sum of money into it.

"Take this," she said. "It will get us by until you bring in a crop next season, with money to spare." At that moment, he looked at the money she had given him. His eyes got wide, so she continued quickly. "My mother gave it to me before I left. It is of no consequence to me in any other way than to help our family in this time of trouble." He didn't want to take it, but he knew she was right. He had to think of the children. So he asked her to put it away, but when the time came and they had need of it, they would discuss it further. Dalton hoped that if he could possibly cut back on some other things, they wouldn't need but a small portion of Jillian's money to tide them over.

"Ma . . . Ma . . . up!"

Dalton saw Jillian beam with pleasure as Brenn spoke the words for the first time. She went to his outstretched arms at once and lifted him from the chair. Dalton had to suppress his laughter at the expression on her face when his sticky fingers found their way into her hair. Not missing the slight chuckle that escaped him, Jillian looked over at Dalton and feigned an angry glare, but he wasn't fooled. As he watched the mirth dancing in her eyes, he couldn't help but wonder how, with so much tragedy, his family seemed so happy. His heart then whispered to him that it was the woman standing before him that made it so, and he had to agree. If only things were different.

Thirteen

Jillian was hanging laundry to dry on the clothesline when Uncle Ned and Aunt Betty rode up in the wagon with the children. They had gone into Willow Springs to get supplies and had taken the children, who were overjoyed to go with them. She quickly wiped the tears away from her eyes. She had hoped that she and Dalton could talk while they were gone, but before she could think of an excuse to detain him, he had left as soon as he could after breakfast, as if he couldn't get away from her fast enough. She was finding it more difficult with each passing day to hide her feelings of hurt at his avoidance. She knew that somehow they had both come to the same conclusion—if they stayed away from each other, Jenny would not have another setback. But Jillian felt that Jenny had finally accepted her and didn't think that Jenny would react to their relationship the way she had before.

Jenny hopped down from the wagon and ran over to Jillian, smiling. What a change had overcome her, indeed!

"Ma, we stopped at the post office, and two letters were waiting for you!" Jenny held out the letters as if they were prizes for Jillian to see.

Jillian hung up the last article of clothing and dried her hands on her apron. She had been hoping a letter would come soon. She corresponded with her mother on a regular basis and had even received a few letters from Bethany, who was busy in school trying to get her teaching degree. She had also written to Marcus several times, but he hadn't written back. Her mother had said he was extremely busy with work, having recently achieved a promotion, but Jillian feared the rift between her and Marcus would never be repaired—a rift that was just one more thing the abominable Nathan Shaw had done to destroy happiness in her life. She prayed that one of those letters would be from her brother.

Jillian smiled back at Jenny as she took the letters. The first was from her mother, and to her great relief, the other was from Marcus! There was simply no mistaking his familiar handwriting. She was eager to read them, but she did not want to be rude. Uncle Ned and Aunt Betty had been watching the children all day. She needed to invite them in for some refreshments. She slipped the letters into her apron pocket to enjoy later.

"Come on in the house," she told them. "I have a loaf of sweet bread hot out of the oven, the milk is chilled, and I think a snack will do us all good. You can all tell me what's happening in town." Jillian was still uncomfortable going to town herself for fear she might run into Sarah Bingham or one of her cronies. When Aunt Betty offered to fetch some needed supplies and to take the children with her, Jillian had jumped to accept.

Everyone filed into the kitchen and sat down at the table. Jillian sent the children off to wash their hands, giving them strict instructions to clean them well. Jenny took Brenn with her to clean him up. Meanwhile, Jillian poured the milk and sliced the bread for everyone. Then she sat down and joined them.

Aunt Betty watched Jillian closely. The girl still had a troubled look on her face at times, even when she was with the children, which was normally when she was the happiest. Betty knew things had changed for the worse between Dalton and Jillian since the picnic, but she couldn't figure out how to help them. She was determined to speak to Dalton and find out what was going on in that stubborn mule head of his.

Jenny, on the other hand, had done a total turnabout. Betty was so pleased to see her smiling, playing, and enjoying life again. Jillian didn't tell her what exactly had happened to bring about Jenny's change of heart—she just hinted that it had been inspired. Betty's heart told her that somehow, Laurellyn must have had something to do with it. She often felt that Laurellyn was watching over her small family. And if the number of prayers Betty sent up on their behalf counted, she was sure

God was well aware of their needs.

"Did you enjoy having some time to yourself?" Betty finally asked Jillian.

"Yes, thank you." The young woman smiled, but her thoughts seemed to be elsewhere.

"You'll be glad to know you avoided a run-in with Mavis Bingham and that awful daughter of hers. She asked about you, ya know." This seemed to get Jillian's full attention, and she waited for Betty to continue. "Miss Sarah wanted to know how you'd been doin' since the picnic, said somethin' about how she didn't know you were standin' there. I just told her that I hadn't a clue what she was talkin' about. I told her that you and Dalton were as happy as two lovebirds could be. I went on and on sayin' somethin' about how could you not be the luckiest woman in the world with him bein' so attentive and all. Then I told her that if I had to witness you two smoochin' one more time, that I was going to threaten to go home and not come back for six months." She smiled boldly at Jillian's surprised face. "Well, I may have embellished things a little, but as soon as was possible, I asked the Lord for forgiveness." She put on her most innocent face. "I was hopin' that would be the end of it, but then she had the audacity to ask me to convey to you an invitation to her house for tea the next time you were in town." Aunt Betty shook her head in disgust. "Never did care for that girl. She was always pawin' after Dalton before he was married to my Laurellyn, even though Dalton always made it plain as day that he wasn't interested in anyone else but my girl. Then when Laurellyn passed on, rest her soul, that terrible girl started right up after Dalton again." She thought it best to give Jillian a warning then. "I wouldn't trust her if I were you, Jillian. She's always playin' at somethin'. She only ever has her own welfare in mind. You won't be acceptin' any invitations to tea from her, if you know what's best for you. Goin' to town would be a lot more pleasant if I could guarantee that she and that awful mother of hers were out of it!"

Jillian let out a small laugh. The girl had the most beautiful sounding laugh. All too soon, the troubled look came back into her eyes. Betty frowned and thought again of Dalton. *I need to have a talk with that nephew of mine*, she decided, *and the sooner the better. Somebody needs to talk some sense into that boy before it's too late.* Betty understood their hesitation as it regarded Jenny, but the little girl was finally doing great! She couldn't comprehend what the problem was now. She nudged Uncle Ned with her elbow. He'd been blissfully enjoying his snack and entertaining the children.

"We best be gettin' back—we still got afternoon chores to do." She looked at Jillian. "Now you tell Dalton I said not to work too hard. The children were telling me they've hardly seen hide nor hair of their pa in the last couple weeks. A man's got nothin' if he hasn't got his family."

She grabbed Ned's arm, pulling him out the door, and they headed for home, waving from the wagon as they rode away.

It was bedtime before Jillian got the chance to read her letters.

She opened the one from her mother first. Her mother always had a way of soothing Jillian's soul and helping her find a personal reservoir of strength to draw from. Not knowing what Marcus had to say, she felt it wise to read her mother's letter first.

> My Dearest Jillian,
>
> I hope this letter finds you and yours in good health. I so enjoyed your last letter. Lisa sounds like such a delightful child, so animated and vivacious, much how I remember you at that age.
>
> As for little Brenn, who, I might add, sounds simply adorable, fear not, my dear. I can tell you from motherly experience that their taste for eating crawling creatures does forsake them at some point. Your brother tried to convince you to eat a worm when you were about Brenn's age. You adored him as much then as you do now, and I fear you would have done it, just to please him. A pang of conscience, however, seized hold of him just in time, and you did not have to endure the vulgarity of that wiggly thing sliding down your throat.
>
> It warms my heart to hear that you seem to be making some progress with Jenny. Just be patient, my love. The loss of a parent creates a deep wound that is not easily healed. It is better that she was not at a much older age when her mother passed, or I fear turning her heart to you would prove to be much more difficult. I'm confident it won't be long before she's following you around, adoring and treasuring you as do the other two children.
>
> Now, my love, I wish to address you about another more intimate matter that has concerned me for some time now. You write mostly of the children but very seldom, if at all, mention their father.

You hinted to me in our last talk before you departed that the two of you had entered into to some sort of accordance as to the intimacy of your relationship after you married. You know my heart has grieved deeply at the pain you suffered at the hand of Mr. Nathan Shaw. I was not blind to the fact that he had been in your high esteem for quite some time. His lack of propriety, as well as the absence of his moral character, came as quite a shock to all of us having been familiar with him these many years. I know he hurt you, my love, most deeply and irreparably.

Your new husband has suffered great pains as well. Losing one's spouse is an agony that cannot be compared to any other. When a man and woman share certain intimacies, their lives are bound in a way beyond just friendship. They no longer think of themselves as one individual, but they two are entwined, and their souls share an equal space.

Living with this man, raising his children at his side, and not sharing any of those intimacies set forth by God to renew and give strength in his sacred union of marriage, I fear you will never come to fully enjoy the blessing and joy that is meant to be, and your family will suffer for it.

What will he be to you when the children are raised and gone? What will you be to each other? Open your heart, Jillian. Listen to the whisperings of your soul. You will both heal sooner if you will let love happen. I love you, my daughter. My heart yearns for you to find true happiness in this life. I miss you so, every day. May God be with you and may you continue in good health and safety. Father sends his love and wishes me to tell you that he misses you terribly.

Ever,

Your Loving Mother

With tears in her eyes, Jillian folded the letter and put it back in the envelope. She pondered on the wisdom in her mother's words. She did want to open her heart again to love and knew Dalton had already found a place there, but her fear and the commitment she had made to him before they married held her back. She wished her mother was here. She recalled how her mother smelled of rose water, and how safe Jillian always felt as she had laid her head on her mother's chest. Her mother had been and always would be such a comfort to her. She took a moment to savor her memories before opening the letter from Marcus. She would need to write her mother a letter again soon and let her know that her prediction about Jenny had come true.

With cautious excitement, she opened her brother's letter.

Dear Jillian,

It is with great vigor that I chastise myself for not having sent correspondence sooner.

I fear it has taken much time to resign myself to the immense guilt and self-loathing I feel for being, at least in part, responsible for the incalculable pain and humiliation you have suffered at the hand of that fiend and coward, Nathan Shaw. With marked soberness, I regret the time forfeited and wasted in friendship with a man of such low moral standing. If I had had any idea of his poor character, indeed, I would not have recommended him to you.

I've also suffered much guilt over your decision to throw your life away, abandoning your dreams and consigning yourself to a loveless marriage due to your loss of trust and assurance in the credence of my gender. I worry about what your life has now become, burdened with caring for another man's children and his household. I also fear other things I dare not think about.

I must say, though I am a most undeserving brother, that I miss you intensely, Little Sis. It is most unbearable to wake up each day, knowing that you will not be waiting at the breakfast table ready to receive my daily dose of teasing. I also find myself lacking anyone to be in my confidence. Who am I to gossip with about the empty-headed upper-class puppets and their constant need to boast of their frivolities?

I did, however, chance to run into Miss Bethany the other day at the university. I had forgotten quite entirely how much I enjoy teasing her, as well as that adorable blush of hers. She has not been to the house but once since you left, and that was immediately after she had returned home from her holiday in Newport. We have been in contact a few times since our meeting, which brings me to a very important question I need to put forward to you, dear sister.

Miss Bethany has asked—nay, I must say pleaded—that I request an opportunity to visit you at your home in Wisconsin. She misses you most ardently and is also quite concerned as to the state of your happiness. She has requested that I accompany her on such a trip during a break in her studies and I have agreed wholeheartedly. If you must know, Little Sis, I have spent many days worrying over your situation. I am most interested in making an acquaintance with Mr. Dalton McCullough and inquiring as to his treatment of my dear sister. Mr. Griffin, my superior at the bank, has indicated numerous times over these last months that I may take some time off, if needed. I have discreetly informed him of my concerns for you. I think he has grown quite fond of me and has granted my request for time away. We hope to leave within a fortnight, which unfortunately would not allow time for a return post from you. Will you grant us a visit, dear sister? You may send a telegram to the bank, and I will retrieve it there.

I am most anxious to see you again, dearest Jillian, and I must admit, I am looking forward to having the beautiful Miss Bethany Johansen all to myself on the long train ride there. I anxiously await your reply!

With loving fondness,

Yours always,

Marcus.

P.S. I promise not to go and break anyone's nose or blacken anyone's eye that is undeserving. We both know that Nathan was most deserving!

Jillian closed the letter and laid it with her mother's on the night-stand.

They were coming to see her—her two most treasured friends! Unable to contain her joy, she stood up and took a dance about the room.

Sitting back down on the bed, she contemplated the reality of her dream come true. Would Dalton be all right with the visit? She was sure he would be. Jenny could move into Lisa's bed for a few days so Bethany would have a place to sleep, and Marcus could possibly stay in the spare room over at Uncle Ned and Aunt Betty's. She would ride over and ask first thing in the morning. She would also need to get a ride into town tomorrow to send the telegram.

Jillian lay down on her bed, putting her hands behind her head. She hadn't seen Bethany since she'd visited her in Newport, and the pain over Nathan had still been so raw then. She thought of her mother's letter again. Could she ever rid herself of the fear and trepidation of giving her heart freely to another man? Her thoughts wandered to Nathan and the night he had plunged her heart into its present perilous state.

✤

Marcus suddenly burst through the parlor door.

"Tell me again how I'm the sweetest brother you have." He sauntered over and plopped himself onto the sofa.

Jillian wasn't in the mood to play games with Marcus just then. She was too busy pouting and missing Nathan. He had gone to Boston on business. He and his father were in the shipping business, so they traveled quite frequently, but this time he had gone alone. When a shipment would arrive, one or both of them would travel to Boston to oversee the distribution of goods and to see to the next ship's cargo. Nathan had been gone almost a fortnight, with over a week to go.

Jillian feared how his frequent trips would affect their relationship after they were married. She supposed that until the children came, she would accompany him on his trips. She was truly looking forward to the month-long honeymoon they would be spending in Cape Cod, so she could have him all to herself.

She looked over at Marcus. He sat there gloating, like he knew something that she would die to know. It was probably just some new bit of gossip, but her interest was somewhat piqued.

"Okay, dear brother, what have you done to deserve my praise yet again?" She would play his game for a while.

"Well," he said wittily, "it was all very coincidental actually." He paused in an effort to build her suspense.

"Marcus, you have already captured my interest. You've no need to toy with me," she protested.

"If you insist, dear sister," he said triumphantly. "Well, I was at the bank today." He paused. "You know, I go there quite frequently. One might think I actually worked there." He laughed at himself. "Well, actually I do, don't I?"

"Marcus, please!" He was really in a mood today.

"Well, since, you said 'please,' my pet, I will try and 'please' you." Once again he laughed at his joke. "As I said, I was at the bank this morning, when I noticed that Mr. Griffin, the bank manager, was in a very foul mood. So, being the concerned employee that I am, I approached him and said, 'Why hello, Mr. Griffin. What a wonderful day we are having today, are we not?' Now, we all knew he was most certainly not having a good day. He had been short and cross with everyone, including the patrons who happened onto

him. He turned and gave me a glare."

Marcus, ever the actor, changed his facial expression to act the part of Mr. Griffin. Jillian couldn't help but laugh.

"Honestly, Marcus, sometimes I'd swear you are still a boy. I would think that you would not want to irritate your employer, especially if he was in a foul mood."

"Now, Sis, don't go getting your feathers ruffled. I knew what I was doing. Would you like me to continue?" he said in a teasing manner.

"Yes, please do, dear brother of mine."

"Well, see, now that's better." Marcus returned to his imitation of Mr. Griffin once again. " 'And what, may I ask, is so wonderful about today?' Mr. Griffin replied to me—very tersely, I might add. So I pulled a chair up next to him, sat down and asked, 'Why don't you tell me about your day? I've heard it said that if you get it off your chest, it makes you feel better.'

"He looked at me very doubtfully and I expected him to send me away. Instead, he nodded his head and said, 'All right, young Mr. Grey, I'll give it a try. You see, I have been working on this account for months now, and some very vital and confidential paperwork was set to leave by courier this afternoon to Boston. However, the courier company sent me a message a little over an hour ago stating that two of their most trusted couriers had taken ill, and they would not be able to transport my package until the day after next.'

" 'I can see why you're so upset,' I replied, 'and I forgive you for losing your temper with me but a little while ago.' "

Jillian gasped. "Marcus, you didn't!"

Marcus chuckled. "No, I didn't. I just wanted to make sure you were still listening. Now, now, I am trying to tell a story here," he said as Jillian reached over and swatted him on the shoulder. " 'Marcus,' he told me, 'I have a half mind to send you to deliver my package.'

" 'Well, Mr. Griffin,' I told him, 'that isn't half a bad idea at all . . . if it will get me out of a couple of days of work. He reached out, shook my hand, and said, 'It's a deal, my dear boy. You can use the bank's carriage and the bank will pay your hotel for the night. Go home and ready your things. I'll send Williams over to pick you up in an hour.'

"So, by my calculations, Williams will be here in about twenty minutes." Marcus looked down at his pocket watch. Jillian rushed over to him and grabbed his hands.

"You will take me with you, won't you, Marcus? Then I can see Nathan! I know what hotel he's staying at." She looked up at him hopefully.

"Well, now that all depends, Little Sis."

"On what?" Jillian cried.

"On whether you can be ready in twenty minutes." He grinned teasingly.

"You know I can!" With that, Jillian kissed her brother on the cheek and dashed upstairs to pack.

Jillian couldn't stop smiling. She couldn't complain about the distance to Boston. Marcus was good company, and he had kept her in stitches most of the way, telling her stories and little tidbits of the latest gossip. They had arrived in town a little after sundown, and Marcus had delivered his package straight away.

"Marcus, I'm starving," Jillian said when her brother climbed back into the carriage. "Let's go to Nathan's hotel and get registered. Then we can find his room and invite to him go to dinner with us." Truthfully, Jillian was a little nervous about surprising Nathan, but she was his betrothed. There could be no harm in it.

"Anything your heart desires, dearest sister." He gave the driver the address of the hotel.

Butterflies had taken over her stomach by the time they arrived at the hotel. Marcus helped her out of the carriage, and Jillian grabbed his hand and walked anxiously to the registration desk.

"How may I help you?" the hotel clerk offered.

"We are in need of a room for the night," Marcus replied. The clerk looked Jillian over appraisingly and winked at Marcus.

"I believe I have the perfect room for you." Marcus, quickly catching the misunderstanding, corrected the clerk's misguided thoughts.

"We would like two separate rooms, adjoining please; my sister here snores and will keep me up half the night if I am not at least twenty feet away from her." Jillian jabbed him in the ribs. He was forever embarrassing her in front of people.

"Yes, sir," the clerk said. He tried to hide his embarrassment by looking closely in his registry book. "I have two rooms joined by a parlor. Will that be sufficient?"

"Yes, indeed." Marcus signed the book and took the key.

Jillian took the opportunity to address the clerk. "I was wondering if you would ring Mr. Nathan Shaw's room for me. I am Miss Jillian Grey, his fiancée." The clerk looked startled for a moment but recovered quickly.

"I'm sorry, Miss Grey, but Mr. Shaw is already out for the evening," he informed her. Jillian's face fell.

"Out, did you say? Do you know where he might have gone? Maybe we could join him." The clerk looked nervous, and Jillian was confused. Where would Nathan be spending his evenings out in a bustling town like this? Surely business hours were over by this time of night.

"I'm sorry, miss, but he did not disclose that information to me."

Jillian felt that the man was being less than honest but quickly brushed it aside. What reason would the clerk possibly have to lie to her? She would just have to wait for Nathan to return and explain. She and Marcus would have dinner in the hotel restaurant and wait for him in their rooms.

"Thank you, sir." She started to leave, but as an afterthought, she scribbled a note on a piece of paper that she took from the counter and handed it to the clerk. "Would you please give this to Mr. Shaw when he returns, and could you tell me what room he is staying in?"

"Yes, miss." The clerk flipped though the registry book and wrote the room number on a piece of paper.

"Thank you." Jillian forced a smile and put the piece of paper with Nathan's room number in her handbag. Meanwhile, she watched the clerk take the message she handed him and put it in the box with Nathan's room key.

Two hours later, Jillian paced the floor in the parlor that joined her room with Marcus's. She could hardly recall what she'd eaten for dinner. When she discovered that Nathan wasn't in, she'd lost most of her appetite and consequently had not paid much attention to the food that had been placed before her. *Where could Nathan be?* she wondered. *What does one do in a town like this to entertain oneself?* Nathan wasn't a drinker or a gambler, so thankfully the drinking houses and taverns were out. Marcus wasn't being much help. He told her he was sure Nathan had a perfectly good reason for being out and that she needn't worry. He had purchased a copy of the *Bostonian* and was currently entertaining himself by reading the society page in the winged chair by the fire. Every so often, he interrupted her thoughts to share some tale, or she would hear him laughing lightheartedly.

"Oh, I'm going to bed," Jillian finally said. She was exasperated with both Nathan's absence and Marcus's lack of concern about it. "If you hear from Nathan, please wake me, Marcus." She bent and kissed her brother on the cheek. "I don't know why I even bother. What is it with you men? You don't seem the slightest bit concerned, yet I'm sure I won't sleep a wink!" She stomped her foot and marched off to her room.

"Temper, temper, Little Sis! Stomping your foot never did get you anywhere." Jillian slammed her door and heard him laugh heartily after her.

Jillian threw herself on the bed. All of her anticipation for the evening she'd built on the long journey had been deflated. Too frustrated to cry, she got up and dressed for bed, looking about the room as she did. It was a an extremely nice room, although much too expensive, she was sure. Of course, the bank was paying the bill. Not that she couldn't afford such a room herself, it was quite the contrary, actually—her parents were very well off—Jillian just had an aversion to squandering money frivolously. Marcus, on the other hand, enjoyed the niceties and privileges of the wealthy, despite all his making fun of them. He was never wasteful or prideful though, which added to his good character. That was also another reason he worked at the bank. He was allotted a monthly allowance from their parents, like most of the other wealthy and spoiled socialites, so he didn't need to work. But Marcus wasn't spoiled, nor did he feel comfortable taking an allowance from his parents to spend on idle pleasantries. Impressively, if he wanted something expensive, he would pay it from his own salary.

Jillian finished dressing, slipped under the silky blankets, and closed her eyes, but, as she expected, sleep would not come. Her mind kept wondering where Nathan could be. Why didn't he tell anyone where he was going? What if someone had come to call? But, that was silly. He certainly wouldn't have been expecting her to show up in Boston. Marcus was probably right. He would have a good explanation as to where he was. It was not his fault she had shown up unannounced. She would stop worrying and get some rest. If not, she would surely look a fright in the morning.

Determined to cease her worrying, Jillian forced herself to relax and finally fell into a fitful sleep, but it did not last long. It was just after eleven o'clock when she woke again. Soft moonlight streamed through the fine lace curtains. The fire had gone out in her room, and she was uncomfortably chilly. It was only March, and the nights still got cold. She looked over at the hearth and saw that the wood box was empty. She had intended to have Marcus bring some wood in from the parlor, but that was before she'd stormed off. She'd been so irritated at her situation, and Marcus hadn't given her an ounce of sympathy. Jillian threw her blankets back and put on her robe. She would just have to get some herself.

As soon as Jillian opened the door to the parlor, a rush of warm air immediately brushed past her, causing her to shiver involuntarily from the change in temperature. Marcus must have stayed up quite a while after she had retired and kept the fire going. As she started to make her way over to get some wood, she heard a woman giggle obnoxiously, followed by a man's voice, deep and caressing, in the hall outside their room. Jillian shivered again, not from the cold, but because there was something vaguely familiar about the man's voice.

Something—maybe curiosity, maybe the churning feeling that had begun in her stomach—drew her to the door. Very quietly, she opened it just a crack and peered down the hall. In the dim light, she saw an attractive woman with her back against the door to a room up the hallway. She toyed with the lace on her bodice as a man leaned in closely to her. The man wore a hat, preventing Jillian from seeing but a small portion of the side of his face. The man leaned in closer, whispered something, and then brushed his lips against her ear. The woman laughed again and reached up, taking his hat from his head, but Jillian still couldn't see his face clearly.

Mesmerized by the scene before her, Jillian knew she had no right to intrude on the private interlude between these two lovers, but she couldn't tear her eyes away. She and Nathan had never shared intimate moments such as this. The man leaned in again, and the woman seductively caught his lower lip with her mouth.

Jillian almost wished that she had courage enough to entice Nathan with an intimate move like that. The gesture having done its job, the man then took the woman instantly into his arms, crushing her body to his, and kissed her with a heated passion that caused Jillian to gasp silently and a blush to rise to her cheeks, merely being a witness to it.

Jillian stepped back from the door momentarily. *I shouldn't be watching this!* Jillian thought. She had been raised to respect a person's privacy, but witnessing the woman's forwardness with this man piqued her curiosity, and she was drawn back to the door. She would only watch a moment more.

The man breathed heavily as he ended his impassioned kiss. He paused, looking deeply into the woman's eyes. He leaned forward again, and Jillian saw the woman quiver in anticipation of his kiss. When their lips met, he began fumbling with the key in the lock of his door. Jillian again felt a blush rush to her face. He broke the kiss and began lightly caressing her neck with his lips as he finally managed to unlock the door.

"Let's go inside, Lorelei," he coaxed while trying to maneuver her into the room. "Just for a little while." The woman was still trembling from his kiss, but Jillian saw her body stiffen. She straightened herself as if preparing to hold her ground.

"Now, you know very well that I'm not that kind of girl," the woman answered firmly.

"Oh, come now, Lorelei, I just want to kiss your delicious lips a little more in private. I wouldn't try anything improper, even though we are engaged now." *So they're going to being married*, Jillian thought. With his arms around the woman's waist, the man tried to coax the woman into the room again. This time, she pulled away from him with determination, which seemed to make the man angry, but he quickly recovered himself.

"You won't have to wait too much longer," the woman said. "I absolutely detest long engagements." She reached behind her and took his hands from her waist. She held them out in front of her and stepped back out of the doorway and into the hall while giving him a teasing smile. "You just need to learn a little more patience." The man mumbled something Jillian could not quite hear.

The young woman leaned in for one last lingering kiss and turned to walk down the hall, away from Jillian. As she did, she turned her head back momentarily, smiled a satisfied smile, and called over her shoulder, "I'll share your bed as soon as you marry me, Nathan Shaw, and not a moment before."

Jillian shut the door quickly and leaned her back against it. Her heart raced, and she couldn't catch her breath. Had she heard the woman right? She shook her head, as if trying to rid it of the sound of her betrothed's name coming from the lips of another woman.

It couldn't be Nathan. Not *her* Nathan! Could there be another Nathan Shaw staying at this hotel? No . . . what would be the chance of that? Her thoughts whirled back to the man's voice. It had sounded vaguely familiar, but she had never heard Nathan speak in such soft, seductive tones as this man had.

Just then, she remembered the paper with Nathan's room number on it. She had tossed it into her handbag without looking at it as soon as the clerk had handed it to her, thinking that when they returned from dinner, she would go to his room and see if he was there.

Jillian bolted to her room, lit the lamp, and searched around. Where had she laid her handbag when she had come in from dinner? Looking about the room, she saw it sitting on the night table. Quickly, she tore it open to retrieve the paper. Unfolding it, she saw a 38. She felt a jolt within her. Hers and Marcus's room numbers were 34 and 35.

Jillian left her room and walked to the door that led into the hallway again. She paused with her hand on the door handle. With great trepidation, she once again opened the door and peered down the hall. It seemed to be empty—not a soul in sight—so she quickly stepped outside, leaving the door open behind her. Jillian took a deep breath and started inching slowly down the hall, keeping close to the wall, reading silently to herself the numbers on the doors as she passed them . . . 36 . . . 37 . . . she knew before she even looked at the door that her worst fears had been confirmed. She didn't want to believe it. Through the tears that were streaming down her face, Jillian looked up at the number 38 on the door the man had disappeared through moments before.

Though her heart felt as if it had been crushed, a feeling of anger overtook her. She suddenly wanted to pound on the door and see his face, but as she raised her hand to do so, she heard him humming a tune on the other side of the door. Instead of knocking, she covered her face with her hands and crumbled to the floor. Unashamed, she let her tears flow freely. Her body was wracked with uncontrollable but quiet sobbing.

How could he do such a thing? She loved him! She had trusted him! How could he betray her like this? How had she not seen what kind of man he truly was? He had not only fooled her, but had misled her entire family. Her anger finally returned, and she harshly brushed the tears from her face. Jillian would never think of Nathan Shaw again with anything but contempt and loathing. Standing back up, she quickly escaped back to the parlor and secured the door firmly. She shivered. The parlor was cold now; all its warmth having escaped into the hall when she'd left the door open. Jillian walked hastily to her room, locked it, and leaned against the door for support. She had been awakened this night to the world and all the ugliness that could exist in it. Her dreams and hopes for the future had been stripped from her. There, sitting in the cold, having lost faith and hope in love, she gave in to the despair. Her body no longer fought the chill but embraced it, and she felt the icy fingers of hate and mistrust grab hold of and slowly lay claim to her heart.

In the early hours of the morning, exhausted from her spent tears and her weakened soul, sleep finally came. Jillian dreamt of Nathan in the arms of his lover. In the dream, they both turned and saw her watching them and began to laugh. Jillian just kept saying over and over, "I trusted you . . . Why did you do this? . . . I trusted you!"

Jillian woke with a start. The sun filtered through the lace curtains and made beautiful patterns on the wall across from her bed. Any other day, she would have stayed in bed a moment and pondered the wonder and beauty of it, but not today. She immediately climbed from her bed, washed and dressed herself, and began quickly packing her things. She took them into the parlor and set them by the door. She and Marcus had originally planned on spending most of the morning in town and heading back home to Providence in the afternoon. But now that there was no longer any need to stay, Jillian felt the need to leave forthwith.

She crossed the parlor, knocked on the door to Marcus's room, and entered. Grabbing his bag, she began tossing his belongings inside, calling him awake as she did.

"Marcus! Marcus, wake up!" He was not easily awakened, so she went to the bed and shook him. "Marcus, you need to get up. We need to leave this minute."

"Jillian? What's this all about?" he said groggily. "We have a whole day to get back home. You go meet Nathan alone. I'll take breakfast in my room."

At the mention of Nathan's name, a sob escaped Jillian's throat, and

Marcus was instantly awake. He took in her countenance, untangled himself from his bed, and walked over to her, deeply concerned.

"Jillian, what happened? Is it Nathan? Has he been hurt?" He was holding her shoulders, looking into her face. She saw the worry and concern in his face, but he would have to wait for an explanation.

"Marcus, I cannot speak about it right now. Just trust me. We must leave. We'll talk on the way home," she said quietly as she continued working.

"But, Jillian," he pleaded, "please tell me what happened. Are *you* hurt?" Jillian shook her head and fought to hold back the torrent of tears that threatened to break free.

"Please, Marcus. Not now . . . not here. I've almost got your things packed. Get dressed so that we can go. I'll be waiting." She turned and walked out into the parlor. Marcus did not argue this time; he just let her go and dressed hurriedly.

As they checked out of the hotel, Marcus kept giving his sister worried glances. Jillian was grateful that he had stopped asking questions. She knew that if he found out what happened before they left town, he would search out Nathan, who would suffer greatly for having done her harm. But she wasn't concerned for Nathan's safety. No longer would she care for anything having the least bit to do with him. In fact, he would surely deserve anything Marcus would give him. She just needed, for her own sake, to get as far away from Boston and her former fiancé as possible.

So, in less than an hour from the time she had awakened, they were headed home. She knew she would have to hold Marcus off a little while before she confessed what she had seen so that he wouldn't insist on turning around. Jillian sat glumly back in her seat, watching the scenery out the window while listening to the tapping sound Marcus was making with his fingers as he waited, not so patiently, across from her.

She had been right about him. When she finally confided the whole sordid story to him, Marcus had been so angry that he'd insisted they turn the carriage around and go back at once. It was only her pleading, bordering on hysteria, that finally convinced him that she needed to get home first and foremost. She could not endure being anywhere near Nathan ever again. For the rest of the trip home she had watched as angry flashes, along with the worried looks he intermittently directed at her, crossed his face.

When they arrived home, Marcus, uncharacteristically silent, helped her down from the carriage. He then immediately went to retrieve his horse from the stables. Before she was even inside the house, he had ridden past her at a gallop, back up the road in the direction they had come.

&

When Jillian remembered Marcus heading back to Boston so earnestly, the note scribbled at the end of his letter finally made sense. He had obviously found Nathan, but he had never confided in her what had transpired between them when he had gone back.

Jillian wondered for a moment what Nathan had done after Marcus confronted him about what she had seen. Did he marry the woman he had been kissing that night more than four months ago? She disregarded the thought instantly. She didn't care what had become of Nathan Shaw. She never wished to see nor hear of him again. Instead, she turned her thoughts to Marcus and Bethany and their impending visit. Thoughts of seeing her brother and friend again soon caused her to drift off into a contented and pleasant slumber.

Fourteen

Nathan Shaw sat in the tavern, waiting for the card game to begin. He'd already had more to drink than he should have and would have a difficult time keeping his head in the game. He had lost too much money this month already, and soon his father would notice if he kept dipping into the business funds. *Oh, what do I care. It'll all be mine someday anyway,* he thought. Besides, he'd been angry with his father ever since Nathan's reputation had been tarnished and his father refused to let him work. He said it would be bad for business because people didn't like what they were hearing about Nathan. Not only had he lost his standing with the upper echelon because of his actions toward Miss Grey and her family, someone was spreading rumors all around town about him that attacked his moral character even more.

From the far side of the saloon, he heard a woman laugh. The laugh reminded him of Jillian and sounded out of place for the dive he was sitting in. He had to look, even though he knew it wouldn't be her. The woman turned and flashed him a more-than-friendly grin. Self-consciously, his hand went to his nose, and he felt the crooked ridgeline there. He would forever hate Marcus Grey for breaking his nose and blackening his eyes. The bruising had healed long ago, but his nose would never be the same, forever marring his good looks. Bitterly, Nathan thought back on that disastrous business trip to Boston.

Everything had been going fine until the night Jillian came to see him. Nathan had been in Boston for two weeks and in between his duties with his father's business, he found himself spending time with Miss Lorelei Davis. She was an attractive little thing, and that woman did things to him. She acted the "good girl" part well, but secretly he suspected she was not as virtuous as she pretended to be. He had heard rumors. Rumors that led him to believe that she was precisely the kind of girl he was looking for.

They spent the evening together, and Nathan finally talked Lorelei into coming back to his hotel room to bid him good-night. He hoped it would finally be the night she gave in to his desires. He even played his final hand and asked her to marry him. He had made pretense of courting her for months, and lately he finally felt her defenses slipping away.

His plan didn't work out quite the way he wanted. When they arrived at his hotel, Nathan tried to seduce her with his kisses, but when he tried to coax her into his room, she stood her ground. Well, he was through with her. He never had any intention of marrying her. She had a shady reputation, at best, and she was penniless to boot. It had all been a waste of his time and money. As much as he enjoyed the little game of cat-and-mouse, he should have just found himself a nice, sassy tavern maid instead.

After Lorelei left, Nathan let his mind wander to Jillian Grey. She was the real beauty. He had always known she would grow into one. He had watched her transform from a silly, awkward girl, always following him around, into a woman any man would dream of owning. He also knew she was sweet on him and had been for a few years. He had pretended not to notice, but when the timing was right, he turned on just the right amount of charm and stepped in by her side. They were going to be married in a few months. She was just what he imagined he deserved in a wife.

Nathan hadn't allowed himself to take any liberties with her, even though they were engaged. Restraining himself had been particularly difficult, especially when he could tell she wanted so ardently for him to kiss her fully. He would make her wait in an effort to increase her desire. Deep down, Nathan feared her affection was only an infatuation—that she didn't truly love him. He feared if he kissed her now, she would realize her mistake and break off the engagement, and she was too good a catch to let go.

Besides her looks, Jillian stood to inherit a great sum one day. Her fortune was a benefit almost equal to the rest of her, especially with some of the habits he had grown so fond of. So he could wait for her affections. Besides, he had plenty of women with whom to fill his time whenever he was in Boston on business, a habit he wasn't sure he would be giving up, even after he and Jillian were married. He hummed as he thought of it.

He rose early the next morning, despite his late night. The clerk took his time retrieving his messages, irritating Nathan. He liked the evening clerk a lot better, but in his haste the night before to get Lorelei up to his room, he hadn't picked up his messages, just his key. He usually had at least a few cards or messages having to do with his business, but he knew they could wait. That morning there were three messages. One was from the manager of their warehouse, which probably meant more work for Nathan. The next message had been from Lorelei, which he ignored. He waited to read the final message until he left the hotel lobby. The doorman had greeted him as he held the door open.

"Good morning, Mr. Shaw." Nathan was not in the mood for pleasantries, so he only gave a slight nod in return. "Looks like it's going to be another beautiful day," the doorman continued, but Nathan still did not respond.

When he raised his head, he saw the backside of a nicely shaped woman climbing into an expensive carriage. Something in the way she moved and held her head struck him as familiar. He disregarded the thought and turned his attention back to his third message.

It was puzzling to him. It simply read, "Come to room 35 as soon as you get in. I have a surprise for you." Just then, a breeze ruffled the paper and he smelled a light, familiar scent. He held the paper closer to his nose to smell it again. "Jillian?" he said out loud. The paper smelled exactly of her. *That's nonsense*, he thought. *What would Jillian be doing in Boston?* The message probably wasn't even for him. That simpleton clerk probably gave it to him by mistake. He would have to talk to the hotel manager about that one. Instead of throwing the message away, however, Nathan tucked it into his waistcoat pocket. The strange message gave him an odd, unsettled feeling. "Ridiculous," he muttered. Miss Jillian Grey was waiting—probably even pining—for him back in Providence.

"My dear little Jillian, not so little anymore," he said as he thought of her, picturing her shapely figure wrapped in his arms. She would be all his, soon enough. He continued walking up the boardwalk, humming the wedding march like he had done in his hotel room the night before as he'd thought of her.

It wasn't until later that evening that he had found out that Jillian had indeed come to see him and had actually been staying in the hotel room just a few doors up from his. She had heard Miss Davis and him when they were out in the hall and witnessed the whole interlude. Of course, he hadn't known any of this until Marcus had burst through the door of the tavern and proceeded to break his nose with one solid punch. Yes, he hated Marcus Grey.

It was no matter though. He would find out where Jillian had gone. She would yet be his. He had waited too long to have her. She couldn't just walk away from him. It was of no consequence to him if she was already another man's wife. He would find her sooner or later and take back what rightfully belonged to him, in spite of her brother. He took another drink of his whiskey and tried to focus on the poker game.

Miss Lorelei Davis was angry. Her thoughts wandered once again to Mr. Nathan Shaw as she waited tables at her new job in a tavern near downtown Providence. She had spent months working him and making him want her, and finally he had proposed. She'd known the first time she'd seen him come into the tavern in Boston that he was the man she'd been waiting for. She was tired of working the tables and having all those drunken men's hands on her all the time. She hated the smell of whisky. He was her ticket out of this life, and she was catching the ride.

Deep down, Lorelei knew she deserved it too. She'd always known she was meant for finer things. Her mama had always told her, "Lorelei, you're too beautiful to be wastin' yer life in a tavern like your old ma. You need to find yourself a rich man so he can treat you like you deserve to be treated." After she met Nathan Shaw, she surely wasn't going to miss her chance to do just that.

When Nathan walked into the tavern that day, Lorelei was taking

her break in the back room. She'd watched him play cards for a while, more than a little interested in the load of money he had laid on the table.

Lorelei knew she couldn't let him see her working there if she was going get his attention, so she pretended to become suddenly ill. Frank, the bartender, was upset with her, but she promised she would work longer the next day and hurriedly slipped out the back. She waited in the dark alley until Nathan finally left the tavern hours later, a little too drunk, and watched as he stumbled back to his hotel.

The next day, dressed like a proper lady, she went into the hotel where he was staying. She had to wait almost two hours before he finally left his room and came down the lobby, where she easily caught his attention. After that, she played all the games, letting him kiss her enough to ignite his passion but never giving into his desires. He'd been wantin' her real bad. She'd had him right where she wanted him, all right.

Lorelei almost ruined everything the night Nathan finally proposed. She was in a good mood when she left him wanting more at his hotel room door. She could almost smell the expensive perfume and feel the satin gowns draped around her body. His wealth would all be hers shortly. But something went wrong that night.

Lorelei dropped by the hotel early the next day, hoping they could talk about their wedding plans, but he hadn't come down yet. She decided to wait around for him, but after a long while, she left a message at the front desk and went outside for some fresh air. A few moments later, Nathan came through the door. She stepped up behind him and got ready to surprise him when he brought a slip of paper up to his nose and inhaled deeply. Then he said a name, and the name was not hers. He tucked the message in his pocket and threw the others, including the one from Lorelei, away. She watched as he smiled a very satisfied looking smile and heard him say, "My dear little Jillian, not so little anymore."

Who was Jillian? Was Nathan stepping out on her? She wanted to race across the few feet between them, yank that handsome hair from his head, and slap that smug smile from his face. "Whoever this Jillian is, he better get her out of his mind," Lorelei thought. She had worked too hard for Nathan, and she was not about to be put off now. She would be Mrs. Nathan Shaw, no matter what!

Just then, Nathan stepped into the street and crossed the road to the tavern. Lorelei knew then that she needed to get him married to her before he left town again. Her eyes narrowed slightly. She thought her plan had worked.

Lorelei simply waited patiently—for hours—before Nathan came out of the tavern. When she approached him, she knew he was well intoxicated, in spite of the early hour.

"Nathan, darling," she began and slipped her arms around his waist, right in the middle of the street. "I've been looking for you all morning. Didn't you get my message?"

"Message?" She cringed at the smell of alcohol on his breath, "I didn't have any messages today." He lied so easily. "Must have been that morning clerk. He can never get anything right."

"Well, no matter." She leaned in closely and pressed her body to him. "You're here now, and that's all that counts really. But we do have so much to talk about. We are gettin' married, you know. We need to start makin' plans right away."

"Well, it's not a good time right now, Lorelei—I've got work to do. But if you want to come by my room tonight, I might be able to find the time to discuss it." He pulled her in close and kissed her lips. She had to hold her breath.

"I was thinking maybe we could talk over a late breakfast. You haven't eaten yet, have you?" She was hungry, and she wanted him to buy her breakfast.

"Yes, actually, I ate a bit earlier than usual." She knew he was lying again, and it made her angry.

"Well, maybe we can get together for a late lunch then?" she asked hopefully.

"To be honest, Lorelei, I think the soonest I'll be free is late this evening. We could have some dinner brought up to my room." He tried to kiss her again, but she held him off. So he was going to play it that way, was he? She was better at this game than he knew. She leaned in closer to whisper in his ear. He got an evil grin on his face.

"Why don't we make a quick visit to the justice of the peace? After all, I told you I don't like long engagements." She pressed her body even closer to him this time, saying slowly and seductively, "And when you

come home tonight, I'll be waiting in your room." She smiled when she heard him groan.

"Well, you do make it hard for a man to wait." Her heart jumped with delight. "I'll tell you what. I have some appointments right now that will take me most of the afternoon." He reached into his pocket, took out a large bill, and handed it to her. "Why don't you get yourself something nice and spend the day getting all dolled up. After all, it is your wedding day. When I get finished, I'll get cleaned up myself and meet you at the courthouse at about four o'clock." Lorelei squealed in delight and kissed him hard before heading for her favorite boutique with the money clutched tightly in her hand.

Lorelei felt anger boil in her veins at the memory. She had spent the rest of the day getting ready and telling everyone she happened across that she was getting married to Mr. Nathan Shaw that afternoon. She had even arrived at the courthouse early, so she didn't make him wait. She had waited over two hours for him to arrive, until she had finally given up and left, humiliated. Even now, she still couldn't believe that he hadn't shown up. She'd wondered if he was sick or hurt or just detained, so she had gone directly to the hotel—only to find that he had checked out earlier that day.

The next day, she had boarded a train headed for Providence. Nathan Shaw wouldn't get away with doing this. He would regret the day he had ever tried to make a fool of Miss Lorelei Davis.

He may be regretting it already.

Fifteen

Jillian was so excited that even if the wagon hadn't already been bouncing her around, she wouldn't have been able to sit still. She and Dalton had dropped off the children at Aunt Betty's and were on their way to the train station in Darlington to pick up Marcus and Bethany. She thought back with fondness on how pleasant things around the house had been. Everyone had caught on to her good mood. Even Dalton, who was spending more time at home, seemed to enjoy helping get things ready for her guests. Jillian suspected she should thank Aunt Betty for that.

The morning after Jillian had received Marcus's letter, Jillian discussed their upcoming visit with Dalton. He had told her that he thought it was a good idea and was glad that she would be able to see someone from her family. They had driven with the children over to Aunt Betty's later that day to discuss plans concerning her brother staying in their home. Dalton had offered to drive Jillian into town to send a telegram back to Marcus, but when they had arrived at Uncle Ned and Aunt Betty's house, Aunt Betty proposed that Uncle Ned drive Jillian into town instead, suggesting that Uncle Ned needed to get her a few things. She saw Dalton roll his eyes at his aunt, but he obediently stayed behind. Jillian suspected that Betty wanted some time to speak to Dalton alone. Whatever had been said that day seemed to make all the difference in Dalton's behavior the last few days, and for that, Jillian was grateful.

Jillian stole a glance at Dalton. It never failed to surprise her the way her heart began to race every time she looked at him. Her mouth watered every time she thought of his kisses. He must have sensed her staring at him, because he briefly turned his head her way and smiled. She realized she was being rude. She had been lost in her thoughts for a while.

"Dalton." He looked at her and smiled again. Her heart fluttered and she almost forgot what she had been about to say. "I wanted to thank you for allowing Marcus and Bethany to come for a visit with us. It really does mean a lot to me."

"I hope you know your family and friends are always welcome in our home," Dalton replied sincerely.

Jillian felt a stirring within her when he said "our home." It really did feel like she belonged, especially now that she and Jenny had forged a bond. She still worried, however, that he regretted his decision to marry her, especially during those few weeks he had stayed away so much. Forcing the thought from her mind, she tentatively reached over and squeezed Dalton's arm briefly.

"Well, thank you again. You've made me really happy."

Then, slightly embarrassed, Jillian hurriedly moved her hand and turned back to stare in front of her and watch the wildflowers along the sides of the road as the wagon went by. She wasn't going to start digging up her many reasons to doubt herself now. She did not want anything ruining this day. They didn't speak more than a few words more to each other the rest of the trip, but the atmosphere between them felt warm and comfortable.

At last, they arrived at the station. Jillian could hardly wait for Dalton to come around and help her down. She thought of little Lisa and the many times she had laughed at the girl for almost tumbling out of the wagon because she couldn't wait for someone to help her out. She smiled at Dalton as he helped her down and tingled at the touch of his hand.

Dalton offered his arm, and she took it gladly. Jillian glanced around the train platform and felt the flood of memories rush back, but she threw up a wall in her mind quickly. She was making better memories here today. She concentrated on the imminent arrival of the train.

Dalton offered Jillian his arm when he noticed that she looked a little unsure of herself. He realized she must be thinking of her last visit to the Darlington train station. She eagerly accepted his arm before stepping through the doors.

For a moment, he saw an anguished look overpower her features, but she replaced it quickly. He was pleased she was having visitors. He often worried about how hard it was for her to make such a break from her family, coming out here, so far away from them, to marry him. He witnessed how happy knowing they were coming made her, and he felt guilty. This past week it seemed as if a light had come into her eyes that he hadn't seen there before.

Not that Dalton thought she was necessarily unhappy living with them. The children seemed to bring her joy at least. Still, he knew that he was likely partially responsible for any sadness she might be feeling. He had broken their agreement—he'd kissed her twice—three times actually, if you counted the one for Sarah Bingham's sake. Even though he felt ashamed, the only way he had kept from kissing her again was by avoiding her. That was except for this last week, of course. She had come to life, and the sight of her dancing around the house and the sound of her laughter filling his home had made it almost unbearable, but he'd stayed close. He was finding it increasingly difficult to rein in his feelings, but he felt he must, at least for now, although there was always the potential for change.

When Uncle Ned had taken Jillian to town to send a telegram to her brother the previous week, Aunt Betty had sent the children out to play and set him down for a talk. She had strong words for him that day, and he knew she was right.

"Dalton, my boy, you know I never cared for puttin' my nose where it don't belong, but I'm needin' to speak my piece to you." She reached across the table and grabbed his hand in both of hers. "I know you been hurtin' . . . have been for a long time. I miss her too." She took her hand from his and quickly brushed a tear away. Grasping Dalton's hand again, she continued. "You have made some progress towards healin' these last weeks. I've watched you closely and it has done my heart good to see it." She looked at him sympathetically. "But boy, I know you have feelings for our Jillian and you're fightin' those feelings with all you got. Whether it's out of guilt, thinking you'll betray Laurellyn's memory, or because of some foolish—and I mean *foolish*—commitment you made to her that you would be married in name only. Boy, you've got to stop this foolishness. You're hurtin' that girl, deep down. I can see it every time I look into those beautiful green eyes of hers. She has feelings for you too, deep ones." Dalton widened his eyes and arched his eyebrow as he looked at her. "Oh, don't look at me all surprised. You know I'm right. Only a blind man wouldn't notice the way she looks at you." She shook her head. "I'm shocked by the way you been treatin' her—hidin' out all day either in the fields or the barn, while you leave her to tendin' your children all alone. And your poor children, missin' you so much." Aunt Betty shook her head at him again. "You know better than that. You're a good and sensitive man, Dalton McCullough. You got a lot to offer that woman. She and your children need you!" Dalton looked doubtful, but she patted his hand and said sternly, "You got to quit being so self-centered and start thinkin' of the ones around you."

Aunt Betty stood up and walked over to the window to check on the children. Dalton finally stood and walked up beside her, draping his arm around her shoulder. The children were sitting just outside the barn door, and all three had a kitten in their laps. Lisa was hovering over Brenn, watching him closely to make sure he didn't hurt the one he was playing with. Without saying anything, Dalton hugged Aunt Betty and walked out the door. He had a lot of thinking to do.

Ten minutes later, he found himself standing at the foot of Laurellyn's grave. It had been over a month since he'd been there. He laid the flowers he had gathered on the way at her headstone. "Laurellyn Elizabeth McCullough, Cherished Daughter, Loving Wife and Mother," the tombstone read. At the bottom was the word "Forever." Dalton looked at the words he had carved there so long ago. He knelt down and traced the letters with his finger.

"Laurellyn," he spoke softly. "I've missed you." A tear trailed down his face. "I've kept my promise. The children have a new mother, and I have a new wife." He sat back on his heels. "You would like her. She's different from you in many ways and a lot like you in others, but she loves the children like they were her own. Even Jenny, as stubborn as she is, has finally seen her goodness and has accepted her." Dalton brushed another tear away.

"Laurellyn," his voice broke with emotion. "I don't know what to do. I want to keep my second promise to you, but I don't want to betray your memory. I'm afraid I'm falling in love with her, but can I love you both? I don't know if my heart has room for both of you."

Softly, a breeze whispered past him, bringing the sweet scent of lavender and roses. Dalton breathed in deeply and closed his eyes, relishing the aroma and the multitude of memories it brought with it. Laurellyn felt so near, and yet the pain was no longer tugging at him. He felt in his heart that she was assuring him that he was free to love again. A peace and acceptance settled within him. He would always have Laurellyn in his heart, he knew that. But maybe, just maybe, his heart had grown to make room for Jillian as well.

But did she want that? Jillian had been hurt deeply somehow, and he didn't know how to help her heal enough to make a place for him. Yet, remembering their shared kisses, hope began to grow. He would be patient.

Aunt Betty was right about the way he had been treating her and the children. He had only been thinking of himself lately. He resolved to be more mindful of the ones he loved. As he prepared to leave, he kissed the tips of his fingers and pressed them against the hard stone.

"Thank you, Laurellyn, for loving us, for listening . . . and inspiring," he whispered. Then he stood and headed back toward the house to his children.

Dalton looked down at Jillian now as he held her arm, waiting for the train to arrive. Her eyes were once again alight with excitement. He noticed how quickly she was past her bad memories of the place. She was a strong woman and beautiful beyond description.

"Would you like to find a place to sit down and wait?" Dalton asked politely. "The train won't be in for another twenty minutes."

"Oh, Dalton, I don't know if I could sit still that long." He grinned. She was fidgeting around so much just standing there! Her excitement was obvious. "I suppose we should probably find a seat," she finally said. They found a bench nearby and sat next to each other. The same bench, as it happened, where she had lain not so long ago. Jillian smiled. "This seems a little familiar," she joked. Dalton smiled at her again and they settled in to wait for the coming train.

Marcus was getting a little nervous as the train neared their destination. The trip had been a good one for him. He'd always enjoyed Bethany's company, especially since she was so easy to tease. They had discussed all sorts of topics on their trip, and he was surprised to find they had so much in common. She was usually so quiet around him. He hadn't even known that she played the pianoforte. He looked forward to having her play for him sometime. Music was a great love of his.

Bethany had dozed off from time to time, and during those moments Marcus had allowed his mind to wander to Jillian. He worried about her living out in the rough frontier. He also worried about the character of the man she had married. Marcus feared that this Dalton McCullough couldn't be much of a man, ordering a wife the way he had. His mother had assured him, though, that whenever Jillian spoke of him, it was always with the highest regard. That had eased his worries, if only a little. He had gathered little from her few letters to him.

He glanced over at Bethany a moment while she slept in the seat across from him. Her face was so peaceful and relaxed—so different from the way Jillian's face had been in the carriage on the way home from Boston those many months ago. He felt a pain as he remembered the tortured and helpless expression she had worn then. Her tender heart had been shattered. When she had told him what she had witnessed, he'd been furious at Nathan and his debauchery. At first he'd insisted that they go back immediately. He could think of nothing but making Nathan pay for his betrayal. But Jillian had begged him to take her home first, and when her protests began to turn panicked, he feared for her state. She was right. She needed to get away from Nathan and what had happened. He'd decided he would make his return as soon as he saw her home safely, and he had.

A sound of disgust slipped from his lips when he remembered finally discovering Nathan in the tavern across from his hotel, drinking whiskey and playing cards. Without even giving him time to stand up, Marcus had thrown the table out of the way, causing cards and drinks to fly everywhere. Nathan just sat there, looking up at him with a stunned expression on his face. With all the anger that had been building up in him, Marcus struck Nathan with a powerful blow directly to his face. The chair he was sitting in had flown partway across the floor with Nathan's hands still tightly gripping the arms of it. It finally landed on its back, with Nathan in it, and continued to slide further across the room, upsetting another table of drinkers.

Marcus rubbed his hand as he thought of the blow he had rendered the scoundrel. He had broken two of his knuckles, but it had been worth it. After he told a bleeding Nathan that his sister had seen him the night before, his final words before exiting the tavern had been, "If you ever come near my sister again, you won't live long enough to regret it."

The train slowed as it prepared to make its stop. Before he woke Bethany, Marcus said a quick prayer that he would find Jillian safe and happy, and, most important, loved.

Jillian fairly flew into Marcus's arms. He spun her around before setting her down again. She couldn't help the tears of joy that began to flow.

"What's this, Little Sis?" Marcus lifted a tear from her cheek and held it out for her to see. "Are you so sad to see me again that I make you want to cry?" Jillian smacked him on the shoulder playfully.

"You big oaf, I've missed you so much!" She hugged him again and then saw Bethany standing behind him. "Beth, I can't believe you're here too!" Her tears began to flow more freely as she gave Bethany a heartfelt embrace.

"Me too, Jilly," said Bethany, as she also started to cry.

Marcus put his hand out to the man watching them from behind Jillian. "You must be Dalton." Jillian watched as Marcus sized him up quickly. As she glanced over at Dalton, she noticed that he was doing much the same thing.

"And you must be Marcus. We've heard nothing else but talk of the both of you for the last week. I'm glad you both made it here safely. Welcome to Wisconsin."

Jillian noticed that Bethany was now looking at Dalton. When she looked back at Jillian, she purposely gave her a dreamy look. Jillian stifled a giggle.

"Well," Dalton spoke again. "I suppose we should get going. We thought that after getting a bite to eat, we probably ought to get on the road so you can get settled in before it gets too late. It's still a two hour drive home." Dalton reached over and picked up Bethany's trunk, which had just been loaded onto the platform next to her.

"I think you're right," Marcus answered him. "If we don't get these two sobbing women out of here soon, they're liable to flood the station." The men both laughed. Marcus grabbed his bag and Bethany's valise, and everyone followed Dalton to the waiting wagon.

Dalton had borrowed a two-seated wagon for the trip from the Flannigans, their neighbors to the south. Jillian was impressed by his foresight and thoughtfulness. Remembering the soreness she experienced after her first wagon ride, Jillian had gathered some extra quilts and put them in the back. If she spread a couple out on the seat underneath Bethany, maybe she could prevent some of the soreness she had experienced.

They enjoyed a light meal at the café where she and Dalton had eaten when she first arrived, and soon they were on their way home. Marcus sat up front with Dalton. They discussed a variety of topics such as farming and the Indians that still inhabited the area. Jillian sat on the back bench with Bethany, who was telling her all about her schooling. Jillian was finding it difficult to pay attention to her friend while trying to listen to Dalton and Marcus's conversation at the same time. She was grateful to Marcus for acting civilly and for not asking any threatening questions about her welfare. She was especially relieved when they drove down the lane to Uncle Ned and Aunt Betty's, signaling the near-end of their journey. Lisa came running out of the house, followed by Jenny, who walked a little slower and more timidly.

"Pa! Ma! You're home!" Lisa ran to the side of the wagon near Jillian and began hopping frantically up and down. Dalton hurried around and helped Jillian to the ground in hopes of settling Lisa down quickly. She hugged her father and rushed immediately to Jillian.

"I'm so glad you're home. I've been waitin' and waitin' 'cause Auntie Bet says I have to ask you first. She says you have to say if it's okay. Please Ma, can we? I promise to be really good all the time. I won't tease the pigs or chase the chickens, only when you tell me to, promise. I'll even eat all my veggietables when you say they're good for me. I won't even sneak Digger in my bed when everyone's sleepin' and I won't sneak him any more chicken legs to feed him."

So that's where my fried chicken has been disappearing, Jillian thought, smiling. She had assumed Dalton was given to midnight cravings of her fried chicken. Lisa went on begging. "Oh please, Ma, can we? Can we?" Jillian looked over at Aunt Betty, who had just come out of the house carrying Brenn, with a questioning look. Aunt Betty just smiled without offering an explanation. Jillian reached down, picked Lisa up, and sat her on her hip. Although she was light enough to carry easily, Lisa was really too old to be carried about, not to mention the fact that Jillian was usually carrying Brenn around instead. But today, she picked her up in order to calm her down. She was even more excitable than usual, and that was saying a lot for Lisa.

"Now, suppose you slow down, honey, and tell me what it is you're wanting so badly," Jillian encouraged. Lisa's expression changed to one that said she couldn't believe her ma didn't know what she was talking about, especially after all that begging.

"Why, to keep one of Sable's kittens, of course!"

"Oh, of course," Jillian replied. "What was I thinking? Well," she said, setting Lisa back down, "I think we'd better ask your pa first, since it will probably be living in the barn." Lisa looked over at her pa hopefully.

"Well now, I don't know." He rubbed his chin like he was thinking about it. "A kitten is a big responsibility. You sure Digger won't mind having something taking your attention away from him?"

"No, Pa, puppies love kittens. They like to chase each other." Everyone laughed at that, and Lisa seemed to suddenly remember that there were other people watching her. Marcus walked up to her, got down on one knee, lifted one of her small hands, and kissed it.

"How do you do, little lady? You must be Lisa." For the first time since Jillian had met her, Lisa was speechless. She smiled shyly and hid behind Jillian but did not take her eyes off of him.

"Lisa, this is my brother, Marcus," Jillian said proudly. Lisa still said nothing; she only stared, wide-eyed. Marcus laughed and stood back up. Meanwhile, Aunt Betty had walked up to them, and Brenn reached out for Jillian. She took him into her arms.

Dalton had helped Bethany down from the other side of the wagon, and she walked around—a little stiffly, Jillian noticed—to join them. Jillian smiled at her friend with sympathy.

"Aunt Betty, this is my brother, Marcus, and my childhood friend, Miss Bethany Johansen. Beth, Marcus, meet our wonderful Aunt Betty." True to character, Aunt Betty gave them both a welcoming hug. Jillian looked over at Jenny, who was still standing on the porch. "Jenny," she coaxed, "come over here so I can introduce you." Jenny walked slowly

over. Marcus bowed deeply, took her hand, and kissed the back of it. Jenny turned three shades of red.

"And how do you do, m'lady?" Turning his head to Jillian, he continued, "Now, Jillian, you neglected to describe in your letters what beautiful ladies there are in these parts. I am quite sure I would have come to visit you sooner if you had." Marcus had worked his magic, and poor Jenny turned an even brighter red, if that were possible. Jillian looked at her brother endearingly. She had missed him so.

After all the introductions were made, Aunt Betty steered everyone into the house for some before-dinner refreshments. Meanwhile, Uncle Ned came in from the fields and the introductions went the rounds again. It was an enjoyable evening. Marcus entertained everyone with stories about Jillian as a child, and she and Bethany told some funny ones about Marcus, leaving Nathan out, of course. Aunt Betty had cooked a wonderful meal, and even though they had eaten a late lunch at the café, everyone enjoyed it thoroughly. Marcus even succeeded in making Aunt Betty blush with his compliments on her cooking. Jillian finally noticed Bethany trying to hide a yawn, so she stood up and began cleaning things up.

"We'd better be getting the children home to bed. I'm sure it's been a long day for you too, Marcus and Bethany." She looked at Bethany and said, "Besides, we need to get you settled in."

Lisa and Brenn had fallen asleep, so while Dalton picked up Lisa, Marcus carried Brenn, and they both headed out to the wagon. Jillian hugged Aunt Betty and Uncle Ned and thanked them both. Taking Jenny's hand, Jillian and Bethany followed the men out. Dalton had put one of the quilts into the back of the wagon and laid Lisa on it. He then helped Bethany onto the back seat and Jillian up into the front before going over to untie the horses. Marcus walked over and lifted Brenn up to Jillian. She bent down and kissed Marcus on the cheek, being careful not to wake the sleeping boy in her arms.

"Thank you, Marcus, for coming."

"I've missed you," Marcus said. "Besides, I couldn't stop worrying." He glanced over at Dalton, who was busy with the horses. "I'm beginning to think it was all for nothing." Leaning in closer, he whispered, "I think I might just like this fellow of yours. Too bad, though," he teased. "I haven't given anyone a good punch in quite a few months!" With that, he winked at her and stepped back from the wagon.

"We'll see you in the morning." Jillian called and waved as they were driving away.

"I'll be there first thing," he called. "Good night, Bethany. Night, night, Little Sis," he said before walking back into the house.

Jillian sighed and kissed the top of Brenn's head contentedly. She felt so surrounded by love that her heart was bursting at its seams.

Looking up at Dalton, she could tell he was deep in thought. Jillian wondered if his thoughts were running along the same lines as hers, considering the peaceful expression he wore.

Jillian was in love with Dalton McCullough, fully and deeply, and had been for some time. She was finally willing to admit it to herself. With the realization of what true love really felt like, she knew now that she had never loved Nathan. Her feelings for Nathan had been an infatuation. He had been flirtatious and charming, and she had been young. She'd confused her feelings of flattery at his attentiveness and being enamored with his good looks with being in love. She knew now that had he ever really kissed her, she would have realized it immediately.

As Jillian looked at the handsome and kind man sitting next to her and relished the warmth of his sleeping child in her arms, she knew she truly loved him and belonged with him. The constant stirring in her bosom and the whisperings in her heart attested to the fact that they were meant to love each other. But how she could ever tell him? Just then he looked down at her, and her heart skipped a beat. She smiled warmly at him, and he returned her smile with one of his own.

Oh, Dalton, she thought. *If only we had met in another time or by any other way, maybe this wouldn't be so difficult.* Jillian somehow knew, however, that this was how it was meant to be. She thought of Lisa and Jenny, now both sleeping on the quilt in the back of the wagon and looked down again at the sleeping babe in her arms. *Yes,* she thought again, *this is meant to be.* She could only pray and hope that there was some way for her and Dalton to finally realize the greater love that lay in store for them.

Sixteen

The next day dawned bright and beautiful. Marcus, true to his word, had ridden up on one of Uncle Ned's horses right after breakfast. He was wearing a pair of jeans, a checkered shirt, and a cowboy hat. Jillian couldn't believe her eyes. They all came out onto the porch to greet him, except Dalton, who was already out working. Hopping down deftly from the horse and sauntering over, he kissed Jillian on the cheek. Afterward, he kissed Bethany's, Jenny's, and Lisa's hands, all in succession. All three blushed, and he looked proudly over to Jillian. She gave him a pitiful look, shook her head, and walked back into the house to finish cleaning up after breakfast. He was incorrigible! He talked with the others on the porch for a while, and then popped his head through the door.

"Jillian, how about a walk after lunch today—just you and me?" She nodded her head in agreement, and he smiled handsomely at her. "Wonderful. I'm going to ride out to the fields and see if I can give Dalton a hand." Jillian looked nervous. "Don't worry, little sister, I will come and tell you first if I have reason to believe your husband is in need of a good whoopin'." She smiled at him and decided he deserved a little teasing back.

"I'm not sure you got a very good look at my husband yesterday, Marcus dear. I'm not so sure you'd be the one doing the 'whoopin',' as you say!"

Marcus faked a hurt look. "Why, my dear sister, are you telling me that you doubt my ability to be your champion after all these years of being just that? Have I been replaced?" Jillian laughed and threw the dish towel at him.

"Oh, go play in the corn. I'll see you at lunchtime." He laughed heartily and ducked back outside the door. A few minutes later she heard him ride off, whistling as he went. Bethany joined Jillian in the kitchen, picked up another dish towel, and helped her dry the dishes.

"Did you see the way he looked in those new clothes?" Bethany said dreamily. "I thought I'd just died and gone to country heaven when he rode up." Jillian laughed. Bethany had always been the more dramatic of the two.

"He's my brother, Bethany. I wasn't thinking of how good he looked," Jillian giggled. "Though, I have to admit, I was shocked when he rode up. I would never have imagined . . . ." Suddenly she was overcome by another fit of giggles, and Bethany chuckled right along with her. It felt good to laugh. By the time they stopped, their sides hurt. "Oh, Bethany, it's so good to have you both here. I haven't laughed like that since . . . ." She couldn't remember how long it had been, and the thought was very sobering. Bethany gave her a hug, and then pulled her back to look into her eyes.

"Are you happy, Jilly? Please tell me you're happy. I've been so concerned." Without warning, Bethany had tears in her eyes.

"Yes, I'm happy. I love the children. They mean so much to me already," she replied honestly.

"But do you love Dalton? Does he love you?" All of a sudden, Jillian was fighting tears too. She sat down at the table, and Bethany sat next to her.

"I do love him, Beth." She swallowed hard. "But I don't know if he loves me." The tears she had pent up over the last few weeks began to flow freely down her cheeks. "Sometimes I think he's starting to love me back, but then something always happens. He loved his first wife so much. When I first came, the pain in his eyes was so intense. After a while it seemed to lessen some, and I began to hope. One day he came in from the fields and kissed me. He kissed me like I never thought a man could kiss a woman." Jillian blushed as she remembered how it had made her feel. "A couple of days later, he kissed me again, but not since then. A man couldn't kiss a woman like that if he didn't have feelings for her, could he?" She stopped when she noticed Bethany was staring oddly at her. "What? What did I say?"

"You've been married to him for months now, and he's only kissed you twice? What's going on between you two?"

Jillian was suddenly embarrassed. She had forgotten that she had never told Bethany about their prenuptial arrangement. She explained it fully right then, telling Beth how she and Dalton were doing their best to keep the arrangement but that it was much more difficult than she'd thought it would be. When she had finished her tale, Bethany's face registered disbelief.

"That's why the two of you sleep in separate rooms?" she asked. Jillian nodded. "How do you stand it? He's so handsome!" Bethany teased, trying to lighten the mood. Jillian smiled back at Bethany. How she loved her dear friend. Jillian had greatly missed having a confidante. She stood up, gave Bethany a quick hug, and changed the subject.

"It's almost lunchtime already, and I haven't gotten anything started," Jillian complained. She quickly gathered the vegetables for the soup she was planning on making. "The men will be home soon, and there will be nothing for them to eat."

"I'll help." Bethany picked up a carrot and started slicing it. "I kind of like this domestic thing. Maybe Marcus will see me cooking and get some ideas."

"Oh, I don't think you need to worry about that, Beth. I think you put plenty of ideas into his head already." Bethany blushed and Jillian laughed. She was glad for the lighthearted mood once again.

The men came riding in on their horses about an hour later, talking and laughing. It did Jillian's heart good to hear Dalton laugh. Marcus had always been able to bring out the happier side of anyone he met.

After lunch, Dalton went back to work by himself, and Bethany offered to watch the children so Jillian and Marcus could go on their walk. They set off to the south over the meadows. After walking in silence for a few minutes, Marcus cleared his throat.

"So tell me, little sister, how have you been these few months?" He looked over at her for a second and added, "I mean, how have you really been? Don't just tell me what you want me to hear."

"Well, I've been happy—most of the time. I mean—" Jillian paused to think of how to answer him better. "I like it here, Marcus. I love the children, I love where I live, and I love this land." She lifted her arms up and held them out. "Just look at how beautiful it is. Did you ever see such a variety of wildflowers?"

"You did always love flowers," Marcus chuckled. "Ever since Grandma Lizzie came to live with us. What were you, about five years old?" Jillian nodded. "I remember how you would follow her out to the garden every day. Mother used to scold you for getting dirt stains all over your pretty dresses. She never really minded you gardening with Grandma, only she wanted you to change into something more expendable first. But you were always so impulsive and impatient. As soon as Grandma would walk by with her gardening hat and tools, you would stop whatever you were doing and follow her. You even made Bethany mad at you a time or two." He looked out at the fields of flowers again. "It's no wonder you love it here. It is beautiful." He turned and looked at her seriously. "What about Dalton, Jillian? Do you love him?"

"I've already been asked that question once today by Bethany. Did the two of you put your heads together on the train and decide what the best method of interrogating me would be?" Jillian gave him her most intimidating scowl. Marcus just laughed.

"Surely you don't think me that devious, do you?" Jillian raised her eyebrows at him doubtfully. He laughed again, louder this time, before becoming serious once more. "It was a simple question. Do you love him?"

Jillian sighed. They'd always been so close, always been in each other's confidence. She couldn't shut him out now, so she told him what she had just told Beth. She loved her husband but wasn't sure if he loved her in return.

"Are you so sure, Little Sis?" Marcus asked her intently.

Jillian looked away as she contemplated her brother's question. She noticed a white picket fence just up ahead and instantly she knew where they were. For a moment she froze. Marcus stopped walking beside her and looked at her with concern.

Taking a deep breath, she began walking again and stopped at the edge of the fence. She put her hand on the gate, but made no gesture to go inside. She felt Marcus walk up and stop beside her.

"I know he loved this woman," Jillian said quietly, her tears threatening to escape. Marcus put his arm around her. They stood in silence for a little while before he said anything.

"He told me about her," Marcus said. Jillian looked up at him abruptly. "When we were working together this morning." He looked sad. It wasn't often Jillian saw her brother look this way. "You're right," he added. "He did love her." They both stood in silence another moment.

"I think I would have loved her too," Jillian whispered.

Marcus's demeanor changed then. He placed his hands on both of Jillian's shoulders and turned her to face him. "But that doesn't mean he's not in love with you now." He looked her directly in the eyes as he said it. She thought of how much he looked like their father at that moment. Marcus released her shoulders and gathered her into his arms. She felt the tears break through, and she cried. She shed tears for Laurellyn and for Dalton and all he had endured. She cried for the children, especially Jenny and the pain she had suffered, cried for herself and for what Nathan had done to her, and for the uncertainty of her relationship with her new husband. Although she had already spent countless tears, somehow this was different. It felt cleansing. It was as though she was finally being freed from all the pain and anguish these things had caused her. Her heart began to feel lighter. Marcus said nothing. He simply held her patiently until eventually her tears were gone. With a long sigh, she lifted her head to look up at him. He smiled down at her.

"I think you've sufficiently watered the flowers around us," he teased. Chuckling, she pulled away from his arms.

"I suppose we ought to head back. The children might be giving Bethany a hard time by now," she said, smiling at the thought. "Either that, or Lisa has talked her ears off." They both laughed.

"She is a little talker!" Marcus admitted. "She can hold her own even with me."

"You haven't heard the half of it, dear brother. Since you arrived, she hardly talks at all. You've cast some sort of spell over her that has stunned her into near silence." They both laughed again.

"That reminds me. I wanted to compliment you on your cooking. I hadn't realized you were so domesticated." He patted his stomach. "Lunch was delicious—especially those biscuits."

"Oh, did you think so?" Jillian smiled to herself. "I'm afraid I can't take the credit for those. Bethany made them." She watched as he looked shocked momentarily and then grinned widely.

"Hmm, I seem to learn more about Miss Bethany Johansen every moment I spend with her." He quickened his pace. "We had better hurry back, Little Sis, so I can see what else I might find out about that lovely lady." Jillian tugged on his arm to slow him down.

"I don't think you have to worry about her going anywhere." Marcus smiled and Jillian laughed heartily.

❧

As they neared the house, Jillian could hear some commotion. She tugged on Marcus's arm to hurry him along. When they turned the corner and the barnyard came into view, Jillian's hand flew to her mouth to stifle her laugh.

The chickens had escaped their pen and were running all over the yard while Bethany, Jenny, Lisa, and even little Brenn chased after them. Brenn must have finally managed to get the latch on the door open—something he'd been threatening to do since Jillian arrived. She had counted herself lucky that so far, he hadn't accomplished it.

Just then, as Bethany was inches away from catching a hen, it flew up and startled her, knocking her down on her backside and sending her dress flying up over her head. Jillian's mouth dropped open, and Marcus burst out laughing beside her. Bethany abruptly pulled her dress back down, looked over at them staring at her, and, with an indignant look, quickly righted herself.

"Don't just stand there laughing at me! Stop it this instant! Get over here, and help us." Marcus didn't stop laughing, but he did help. Jillian did too, and before long, they had all but one chicken back in the coop.

"Hello, Pa," Jenny called, and Jillian turned to see Dalton standing directly behind her. She didn't know how long he'd been standing there watching, but by the look on his face, he was quite amused. Just then Marcus hollered, still chasing the last chicken.

"Jillian, it's headed your way!" Just as she turned, the chicken took flight, heading directly toward her face. Startled, she backed up quickly, lost her balance, and fell back into Dalton, sending them both backwards into the nearby water trough.

Immediately, Marcus and Bethany both doubled over with uncontrollable laughter. Jenny and Lisa fell down in a fit of giggles. Before long little Brenn, who didn't like to be left out, started laughing as well. Only two members of the group weren't laughing, and then much to Jillian's chagrin, only one of them wasn't.

Jillian struggled and finally managed to get herself off of Dalton and out of the trough. He made no immediate move to get up. He just kept laughing right along with the rest of them. As she stood there dripping, Jillian looked over at her brother and felt her temper rising.

"Marcus Grey, you did that on purpose!" Marcus's expression instantly became one of innocence, but he wasn't fooling her.

"Come now, Little Sis, how could I have done that on purpose?" He grinned mischievously. "I don't . . . speak . . . chicken." Everyone started laughing again, which only caused her frustration and embarrassment to increase.

"Oh, you make me so angry sometimes, you scoundrel!" She stomped her foot. "Why you are still such a boy, I will never know!" She ran dripping wet into the house and to her room, where she could still hear the sounds of laughter coming from the yard below.

Marcus walked over and held his hand out to Dalton. He took it and Marcus pulled him out of the trough. Still laughing, Dalton asked, "Did I just see her stomp her foot? I seem to remember her doing that once before."

"If you haven't noticed, Dalton, our girl has a bit of a temper. She can be a real spitfire, if you really manage to get her goat," answered Marcus.

"I trust that you know what you're talking about." Dalton slapped Marcus on the back. "Well, I guess I best be getting out of these wet clothes. Do you suppose you could round up that last renegade chicken?

"I'm sure I can manage it." Marcus headed in the direction of the barn where the lone chicken was idly plucking at something on the ground.

"Thanks for completing my day with a good laugh," Dalton called over to him. "It's been much too long," he added with conviction as he walked into the house to change.

Marcus put the last hen away and looked over at Bethany. She had just finished brushing the dirt off the children and was trying to brush the dirt off the backside of her dress. He walked over to her.

"Do you need me to help you with that?" Her head snapped up and she blushed with embarrassment.

"Honestly, Marcus, Jillian's right. I think you are still just a boy sometimes!" A mischievous look crossed his face again, and Bethany, knowing what Marcus was capable of, looked suddenly worried.

"If I were still just a boy, Bethany Johansen," he growled with a smirk on his handsome face as he walked closer to her, unknowingly causing her heart to race, "I wouldn't be strong enough to do this." Swiftly, he reached down, scooped her up into his arms, walked quickly to the water trough, and dropped her in. A look of complete shock registered on her face as she was suddenly engulfed in the cold water. "There now," he said with finality, "you and my sister always did like to do everything together." With that, Marcus turned and walked toward the house, picking Brenn up on his way, and motioned to the two astonished little girls to follow him inside.

Seventeen

Jillian rolled over in bed and stretched. Mornings always came too soon on a farm. She realized she'd slept a little late, so she got up and dressed quickly.

A week had already passed, which meant she only had three more days with Marcus and Bethany. She and Bethany had given the men the silent treatment for a day after the water trough incident. Then Jillian had realized she was wasting precious time with her brother. Though he had apologized on numerous occasions, she still wasn't certain he felt remorseful enough, but she finally forgave him anyway. She had forgiven Dalton for laughing as well. Bethany followed suit and was soon back to swooning over Marcus. Jillian walked into the kitchen, which almost smelled of fried eggs. Dalton and Marcus were both dressed and talking at the table.

"Good morning," she said, smiling. She looked over at Marcus. "You're up early."

"Dalton and I are going out to do a bit of riding around this morning," Marcus explained.

"Oh?" she said with a questioning look. "Anything interesting out there I should know about?"

Marcus answered quickly. "No, I just wanted to see a bit more of the land around here."

"Well, I'll make you some breakfast so that you can be on your way." She turned and started gathering the things she needed for hotcakes.

"No need, Little Sis. Dalton here has already made me some breakfast." Jillian raised her eyebrows again and looked over at Dalton.

"What? I can cook—a little anyway." Dalton looked out the window. "I was on my own for a while."

Jillian was instantly flustered. She hadn't meant to upset him. She thought of her walk with Marcus on his second day here. She hadn't missed the rather fresh looking flowers lying at Laurellyn's headstone. They hadn't been more than a week old. She wondered how often he still went there. Dalton stood up.

"Well, Marcus, we best be on our way." He took his hat off the hook by the door and placed it on his head. Marcus stood up and did the same but then walked around the table and kissed Jillian on the cheek.

"We should be back by midday, Little Sis. Maybe you could convince Bethany to bake some more of those delicious biscuits. The more I eat, the more I think about putting a ring on that girl's finger!" Jillian beamed and playfully swatted him on the behind with her wooden spoon as he walked away.

While Marcus waited outside, Dalton saddled his horse, a chore that took longer than usual because Dalton's thoughts went to Jillian. He envied the relaxed and playful relationship she shared with her brother. He thoroughly liked Marcus and their friend Bethany. Their visit had been a welcome change, bringing fun and laughter to his home once again. He noticed how Jillian's eyes always seemed alight with joy these days. He suspected it was because she felt loved and valued by her brother and her friend.

The thought caused guilt to well up inside him. She had treated him a lot better than he had been treating her. He wasn't proud of the man he had been of late. He needed to do right by his wife. Slowly, he led his horse out of the barn toward Marcus, who had climbed up on his horse and was patiently waiting. When Marcus had asked him to go riding around to look at the available land in these parts, Dalton wondered what the man was thinking. This morning he intended to find out.

"Well, Marcus," he said, as he swung his leg over the saddle, "are you ready to see some of the most beautiful land God ever created?"

Marcus grinned. "I'm counting on it!"

Jillian sat down at her vanity that evening. She was especially tired and looked forward to getting a good night's sleep. The men had come home from their ride just before the noonday meal. After they had eaten, they headed out to the fields to work for a while. She was glad to see Dalton and Marcus getting along so well. Jillian was just taking her hair down when she heard a soft knock at her door.

"Come in!" she called. Dalton had ridden over to Uncle Ned and Aunt Betty's home after dinner. He had a matter to discuss with Uncle Ned, and he hadn't returned yet. Marcus had taken Bethany out for an evening stroll, but Jillian had heard Bethany come in a moment ago, and then she'd heard Marcus's horse ride off, so that meant it was either Bethany or one of the children at the door.

"Jillian, am I disturbing you? Can we talk?" Bethany asked softly.

"Of course, Beth, come in." Jillian finished letting her hair down and began brushing it.

Bethany floated into the room and dramatically fainted backward onto Jillian's bed, bringing her hand to her forehead. Amused, Jillian turned in her chair and gave Bethany her full attention. Bethany sat up and smiled.

"He kissed me, Jilly. We were just standing there on the porch and all of a sudden, he took me in his arms and kissed me." She lay back on the bed again, and then just as quickly sat back up. "Not just a little peck, either. I thought that I was going to faint dead away, right there."

Jillian laughed as she got up from her chair, sat down on the bed next to her closest friend, and took her hands.

"Oh, Beth, I'm so happy for you!" She released her hands and gave her a quick hug. "I knew he would eventually get up the nerve, but it certainly took him long enough." Jillian smiled genuinely at Bethany. "I have never wanted anyone but you for a sister."

"Don't be silly, Jilly. He only kissed me! He didn't ask me to marry him." Bethany stood up, walked over to Jillian's vanity, and sat down. Jillian turned to face her.

"I know my brother, Beth. He never would have kissed you in such a way if he wasn't thinking about marrying you." Bethany squealed and ran back over to the bed to hug Jillian.

"Do you really think so?" she asked excitedly.

"Yes, silly. I know so," Jillian answered. "Now you'd better go get some sleep so I can get mine. I get up a lot earlier than you, remember?" Bethany gave her friend another long hug and danced to the door. Before leaving, she turned back to Jillian.

"I love you, Jilly. Thank you for letting me come and visit you. It's been a dream!"

"I love you too, Bethy. Now get," Jillian teased.

Despite what she said about needing her sleep, Jillian lay awake for a long time. She was genuinely happy for Marcus and Bethany. They were both wonderful people and deserved all the happiness life could afford. But her thoughts kept turning back to Dalton and herself. She thought about the times he had kissed her, how he'd caused her whole body to tremble with exhilaration. It had been so long since they had had any physical contact at all. Even when he helped her into or out of the wagon, he let go of her hand as quickly as possible. She wanted to be close to him, wanted him to hold her like he had before. Sighing deeply, she rolled onto her side and held her pillow in her arms. Would they ever have their chance at happiness?

"I love you, Dalton." she whispered to no one. At last, she closed her eyes and fell asleep.

Jillian held on tightly, not wanting to let go. She had started crying the moment she woke up and realized what day it was. She could feel her brother's heart beating beneath his lapel. Marcus's checkered shirt and denims had been replaced by his usual clothing. Bethany stood off to the side. They had said their tear-filled good-byes earlier, before Marcus arrived. Now she was having a hard time letting her beloved brother go. She knew she was being selfish by wanting him to stay— Mother and Father were surely missing him too—but she didn't know when she would ever see him again. It was he who finally broke their embrace. Marcus put his hand under her chin, lifted her face up, and wiped the tears from her eyes.

"You're going to cause a flood with all those tears, and then you'll have Dalton upset with me. First a fire, then a flood!" he teased.

"Marcus, don't try to make me smile. I don't want to today. You're both leaving, and I can see no earthly reason to be happy," she complained.

"Oh, but you're wrong, dearest sister of mine. There's always a

reason to be happy, even in good-byes. If there were no good-byes, then there would be no hellos. You see?" He smiled at her. "Besides, I don't want to remember a frown on your face as I ride away. I might think you don't like me anymore." Marcus pretended to pout.

Jillian whimpered, "You know that's not true."

"Well then, give me a smile so I can remember my beautiful sister just as she ought to look," he coaxed.

"I just wish we had more time! I wish I could ride to the station with you both, but I can't leave Brenn." The poor little boy had come down with stomach pains in the night. He seemed so little and helpless that she couldn't bring herself to leave him and she didn't want to risk having Aunt Betty or Uncle Ned catching anything from him either, so Dalton was going to take them to the station alone. They also wouldn't have to borrow the Flannigans' wagon this way. She knew it would be for the best, but it was still difficult.

They all walked down the porch steps and over to the wagon. Jenny and Lisa were crying now too. Marcus opted to forgo the proper kisses reserved for ladies and gave them both hugs and kisses on the cheek instead. They were now extremely fond of Marcus and would miss him terribly. Jillian gave Bethany one last hug, and before letting her go, she whispered in her ear, "As soon as he proposes, you be sure to send me a telegram right away."

Bethany blushed deeply. Marcus gave his sister a quizzical look before stepping past her to help Bethany into the wagon. Jillian winked at him, trying to tease him a little. When Bethany was seated, Marcus walked back over to Jillian and took her into one final embrace.

"Are you telling secrets about me, Little Sis?" he whispered, just loud enough for her to hear.

"No secrets, dear brother, only predictions." This made him raise an eyebrow, and she smiled widely at him. He hopped onto the wagon seat with Bethany and Dalton.

"Now, that's the look I want to remember," he declared.

Dalton flicked the reins, clucked to the horses, slowly turned the wagon around, and headed down the road away from the house.

Jillian watched as three of the most important people in the world to her rode away. She turned quickly and dismally gathered the children back into the house.

❧

Jillian looked out the window yet again. It was late, and she was worried. Marcus and Bethany's train didn't come through until five-thirty, so she knew Dalton would get home late, but it was already after nine, and he should have been home over an hour ago.

She went to check on the children. Lisa and Brenn were sleeping soundly, but she knew Jenny would still be awake. The two of them had spent the evening completing the last of her makeup work, and then they took turns reading from the book of fairy tales. By working together each evening, Jenny had not only caught up but was excelling in her studies. Earlier that evening, Jenny had been concerned when her father failed to return, especially because Dalton had promised to read to her when he got back. Jillian knocked lightly on the door to Jenny's room and peeked inside. Jenny was sitting up in her bed with her arms wrapped tightly around her knees. Her head was down, so she guessed the girl was still worried about her father. Jillian walked over and sat next to her on the bed.

"Hello, sweetie. Are you ready to go to sleep now?" Jenny looked up, and Jillian could see the tears welling up in her eyes. Jillian gathered her in her arms. "There now, don't cry. Everything is fine. Your father has been delayed is all. He'll be home soon enough." Jillian tried to soothe Jenny's worries, even though her own were growing with every passing minute. Finally, Jenny lay down and fell asleep, and Jillian tip-toed quietly from the room.

Immediately she looked out the window again. It was almost ten o'clock. Jillian grabbed a quilt from the chair and went to the hook by the door. Reaching up, she grabbed Dalton's coat, slipping her arms into it as she opened the door and went out. She shivered briefly. The nights were getting cooler now. Jillian sat down on the porch steps, leaned against the railing post, and laid the quilt over her lap.

"Where are you, Dalton?" she whispered into the night air. She leaned forward, put her elbows on her knees, and covered her face with the sleeves of his coat to keep her nose warm. She breathed in deeply, inhaling his familiar scent.

Before long, Jillian found herself fighting sleep. She didn't want to go back inside until Dalton was safely home, so she took the quilt from her lap, tucked it under her head, and lay down on the porch steps, deciding to rest her eyes for just a minute or two.

Dalton wearily drove the wagon past the gate and made his way toward the house. Old Decker's bridle lay on the bed of the wagon along with his rifle. What had started out to be a very simple trip to the train station had turned into a long and tedious ordeal.

Dalton delivered Marcus and Bethany at the station with plenty of time to make their train. He waited there until the train was out of sight, and then wasted no time in heading back home. When he was about a third of the way there, he felt the wagon drift to the side of the road. He had been lost in his thoughts again, something that had been happening often lately, and had allowed the reins to go slack. Old Decker, who seemed to be getting lazier by the day, had decided that since he hadn't felt a tug on the reins for a long while, he would try his luck at grazing on the tall grasses along the side of the road. Dalton quickly pulled the reins tight to the left in order to center the wagon on the road again, but not before Decker's right front leg fell into a deep gopher hole. The wagon jerked to the side as the horse fell lame. Dalton heard the front wheel crack.

Dalton unhitched both horses, led Riley to the back of the wagon, and tied him up. Retrieving his rifle from under the wagon seat, he walked back around to where Old Decker lay in obvious pain.

With a heartfelt sigh of grief, he lifted his rifle to his shoulder. Killing his own horse was one of the most difficult things a man had to face. A man got quite attached to his livestock out on the frontier, and Old Decker had been a good old horse, although somewhat of a rascal at times. He was saddened to see him have to go this way. Laurellyn always had a soft spot for him, especially since he hadn't been treated well by the gambler who had sold the horse to his father. The children were sure to miss him too.

"Good-bye, old friend," Dalton murmured softly. He took careful aim, slowly pulled the trigger, and in an instant, Old Decker was gone.

After dragging his dead horse's body from the road with the aid of the surviving horse, he walked back to his wagon and assessed the damage to the wheel. The break was beyond his ability to repair. Luckily, another wagon happened by just then, heading toward Darlington, and its owner was willing to take his wheel for him and drop it off at the blacksmith's. So, after moving his wagon farther off the road, Dalton climbed atop Riley and followed the other wagon back into town.

By the time the wagon wheel was repaired and delivered back to Dalton's wagon, it was past nine. It took him the better part of another hour for him to secure the wheel to the wagon again in the dark. He knew Jillian and the children were probably worried, so he drove toward home as fast as he dared with Riley being the only horse pulling the damaged wagon.

Exhausted, Dalton pulled the wagon to a stop as quietly as he could near the barn and set the brake. He looked back at the house, noticed a light still on, and then saw a figure lying on the porch. Trusting Riley would stay put, he quickly jumped down and walked over to the house.

When he got closer, Dalton saw that it was Jillian on the steps. He looked down at her, so adorable sleeping there curled up in his old coat. She was so beautiful. The strands of moonlight that filtered through the porch roof caressed her face softly, making patterns on her cheeks. She looked so peaceful that he did not want to wake her. He knew she had been through a lot today, with her brother leaving, caring for a sick child, and then having to worry about him.

Dalton reached down and lifted her easily into his arms. She was so light, almost like a child. He felt her shiver in her sleep. Under the coat she wore only a thin nightgown, and he could feel the cold skin of her legs through the fabric. He hoped she had brought warmer clothing than this with her, because the winters here could be harsh.

Dalton carried her into the house and up to her room. Pulling the bed covers back, he laid her down carefully so as not to wake her. He gently pulled her arms out of his coat slowly, one at a time, and set it aside. Then he laid her back down and reached for the blankets to cover her. When his hand briefly brushed against hers, she unexpectedly grabbed a hold of it, rolling over on her side and pulling his arm around her. Dalton froze.

"Dalton, you're home," she whispered. He could tell she wasn't awake. She was talking in her sleep, but still, he did not pull his hand away. She gripped it firmly. He maneuvered himself fully on the bed and lay on his side next to her. *What am I doing?* he thought. He decided

to stay for a while longer, until she fell into a deeper sleep.

He watched her breathe slowly and admired the way her thick eye-lashes lay softly against her cheek. He was tempted to trace the brow above her eye with his fingers. Her hair lay in splashes on the pillow beside him and smelled of roses and wildflowers. Dalton breathed the scent of it in deeply. She burrowed more deeply into her blankets, releasing his hand, but he made no move to leave.

Dalton couldn't resist taking a strand of her hair delicately between his fingers and feeling the softness of it. Before he knew what he was doing, he lifted the hair from her neck and kissed the ivory skin that lay hidden there. He paused for a moment when he felt her body quiver. She snuggled her body in closer to him, and from her dreaming lips came the whispered words, "I love you, Dalton."

Jillian felt something soft and warm brush against her neck. Instantly, she was awake and aware that Dalton was lying beside her. She had been dreaming of him moments before, and now he was here. She felt his lips travel to her ear briefly before finding their way back down her neck and to her shoulder, lingering there. Trying to lie still, so as to not break the spell, she felt herself tremble despite her efforts. He paused. Slowly, she turned her body so that she could meet his eyes in the moonlight. She couldn't miss the passion in them, and her heart beat faster.

Dalton brought his hand to the side of her face, and he softly caressed her lower lip with his thumb. As his head descended to hers, she instinctively closed her eyes, and immediately his lips were soft and wet upon her own. Suddenly, it was as if there was a burning within him, and he could not quench his thirst. His kisses became deep and demanding. Jillian answered him with her own growing passion. They kissed with a mutual need and intensity.

All at once, he broke the seal of their lips and laid his head down on the pillow next to hers. His breathing was hard, and she could plainly see him fighting for control. Groaning audibly, he turned his back to her and sat up on the side of the bed.

Putting his face in his hands, Dalton pinched his eyes tight and tried to think. How did he end up here? Her confession of love had been his complete undoing. He wasn't a fool. He knew she was dreaming, but it had been a long time since he had heard those words from the lips of a strong, beautiful, compassionate woman. His mind tried to reason an excuse for his behavior. They were man and wife, legally and lawfully married in the eyes of God. Regardless, he felt shame course through him.

He had given his word. She came to his house without fear of being molested. He was a man of honor and they had agreed before she came as to what their relationship would—and would not—be. Dalton stood up without even turning to look at her. "I'm so sorry," he said quietly and left to tend to his tired horse.

Eighteen

Miss Lorelei Davis looked at the address scribbled on the piece of paper in her hand and then glanced again at the massive estate through the closed iron gates. If there was any doubt that she had received the correct address, it was vanquished when she saw the sign hanging above the gate. It read "Grey Manor."

Tentatively, she pushed at the gate and walked onto the exquisitely manicured grounds. She was especially nervous to be here, but she felt she had no choice. If this was indeed the family of Miss Jillian Grey, she needed to warn them. Lorelei wasn't a bad person, and she certainly didn't want to feel responsible for something evil befalling any person—except for maybe Nathan Shaw—including this unknown woman.

Lorelei approached the massive door and rang the bell. Moments later a well-dressed butler opened the door and gave her an odd look. Ever prim and proper, he asked, "May, I help you, miss?"

Lorelei shifted nervously before replying. "I'm looking for a Mr. Marcus Grey."

The butler looked her over from head to toe. "Is he expecting you?" he questioned.

"N-no, sir," Lorelei hesitantly responded, "but I have an urgent message to give him."

"I'm afraid that we don't expect Mr. Grey back until tomorrow morning, Miss . . . ?" He looked at her expectantly.

"Miss Davis," she informed the man. Lorelei started to fret. What should she do? Nathan was already on the train. He would be there the day after tomorrow.

"I can take the message for him, if you like. I will be sure that he gets it upon his arrival," the butler offered.

Lorelei felt that she didn't have much choice. "Well, I planned on giving it to him personally."

"I can fetch you a pen and paper if you wish to leave a note," the butler suggested.

Lorelei was relieved. Yes, she could write a quick note, and then she would get out of the city. She was tired of being in Providence. Besides, Nathan scared her, and she wanted to be as far away as possible when he came back.

While the butler went back inside the house, Lorelei looked around the yards. Yes, this was exactly how she wanted to live. She had made a mistake in choosing Nathan Shaw, but she wasn't washed up yet. Just then, the butler returned and set the paper and inkwell on the outside table. Lorelei took the pen from his hand, dipped it in the ink, and wrote out her warning. She blew on the ink until it dried, folded it, and handed it to the man.

"You will make sure he gets this the moment he gets back?" She looked at him sternly, hoping to covey the importance of it.

"Yes, Miss Davis," he replied firmly.

"Good! Thank you, kindly." She turned and walked down the steps and back toward the gates.

It wasn't until she went through and closed them behind her that she finally felt a weight lift from her shoulders. She had done all she could to help the poor girl. Now it was out of her hands. She recalled what had happened two nights past.

Knowing Nathan's weakness for gambling and whiskey, Lorelei found a job right away in one of the more popular taverns and started spreading rumors about him. Nothing that wasn't true, as far as she was concerned. He was a cheat and a liar, and his word could not be trusted. Those weren't good things to be said about a person in a city like this. She had also spoken of his association with women of questionable character and how he fancied sullying their reputations. She was angry with him for humiliating her and was determined to make

him pay. Quite quickly, his name was on the black list of both those in high society as well as those who were not.

Eventually word started filtering back to her that Nathan had it in for whoever was ruining his good name. Lorelei wasn't worried. She had been careful about how she'd gone about spreading tales about him.

She was working at the tavern when Nathan suddenly walked through the doors and glared at her. She wasn't worried until she saw the daggers in Nathan's eyes. She decided it would be best to be coy and feign ignorance, on the slim chance he had just happened into her tavern.

"Why, Nathan Shaw, what a surprise it is to see you here!" She walked over to him. "Can I get you something to drink?" She knew immediately that it wasn't by chance that he was here. He grabbed hold of her wrist and dragged her toward the door. "Let go of me, Nathan, you're hurting me!" she protested.

"I don't think so." He spoke to her through clenched teeth. "Not until you and I have a little talk." The tavern's other patrons thought it was only a lover's quarrel, so no one offered to help her as he led her to the door. Once outside, he dragged her into the alley on the side of the tavern and held her against the wall with one strong hand.

"What do you want, Nathan? Let me go before I scream." Nathan took his free hand, held it tightly over her mouth, and leaned into her. His body was crushing her.

"I hear you haven't been saying very nice things about me." She shook her head vehemently, but it didn't do her any good. "Oh, don't lie to me, Miss Lorelei. I know it's been you. You've already caused me enough trouble." His face was so contorted with anger that she was frightened of what he might do. "You know, if I hadn't been with you that night, she never would have known. It's partly your fault that my dear, sweet Jillian broke off our engagement." Lorelei's eyes got big. "Oh, that's right." He paused. "You thought I was going to marry you." He laughed hysterically, and the sound of it sent frightening chills throughout her body.

"You meant nothing to me! It was just a game—one I was disappointed at not winning." He leaned close like he was going to kiss her, but pulled away again. "Jillian saw us together that night, me playing my game and you playing yours." He paused dramatically as once again Lorelei looked taken aback. "Oh, did you think I believed anything you told me? I knew what you were all about the moment I saw you. But what I didn't count on was you messing things up for me."

He's insane! Lorelei thought desperately, but he kept going on.

"She must have heard you say my name. I didn't even know she was watching until the next day when her brother"—Nathan paused long enough to make a hissing sound with his throat—"the high and mighty Mr. Marcus Grey, came and broke my nose."

Someone stumbled by just then, and Lorelei tried to make a sound to get his attention. Nathan pressed his hand harder against her mouth, causing tears to come to her eyes. He just stared at her for a moment. All of a sudden, his voice turned sweet and milky.

"Come now, Lorelei. I hate to see a woman cry. Please don't cry." He took his hand off her mouth and wiped the tears from her eyes. "I've made her cry, too. That's why I'm leaving for Wisconsin tomorrow—to bring her back. She's sad, and I intend to make her happy again. She loves me, you know. She has loved me since she was a child."

Lorelei stood frozen, wide-eyed. She was no longer crying. This was worse than when he was angry. He kept rambling. "She belongs to me. I'm going to get her back, and we'll go away together. She doesn't belong to him. She could never love him." His voice was growing angry again. Lorelei looked around desperately for a way to escape. "They won't take her away from me." His lip curled. "She's mine!" he shouted and looked back down at her. Instantly, his voice was soft again and he brushed his fingers across her face, wiping away an imaginary tear. She shuddered at his touch. "I've made you cry." He brought his fingers to his lips, and then he dropped both of his hands to his sides and walked away, leaving her standing alone, stunned and shaken in the alley.

Lorelei was still trembling badly when she went back into the tavern. Without saying a word to anyone, she gathered her things immediately and went home. She planned to leave Providence first thing in the morning.

Sometime during the middle of her sleepless night, Lorelei's conscience began to bother her. Maybe she was partly responsible for sending Nathan over the edge. What if he did something crazy to that poor girl? She knew she should warn her somehow, but Nathan said she was living in Wisconsin. He did mention a brother, Marcus Grey. And she knew her first name, Jillian. She would do right by this woman.

Lorelei turned and looked back at the grand house one more time. "Good luck, Miss Jillian Grey. I pray he does not find you," she said before walking away and heading to the train station.

The sun was filtering into Jillian's room. She opened her eyes and groaned. Staying in bed longer would have been wonderful, but she knew she had more to do than she could possibly have time for. As she tried to sit up, her muscles ached in protest. Unfortunately, she had come down with the stomach sickness yesterday morning that Brenn had had the day before. She had spent the better part of the day either emptying the contents of her stomach or unmoving in bed. She hadn't even felt up to comforting the children after they learned of poor Old Decker's fate.

Her stomach growled, and with no small effort, Jillian managed to sit up on the edge of the bed, but didn't move any further. Her head pounded. If she were still living with her parents, she would have crawled back under the covers, but people were counting on her here. She was needed. As it was, Dalton had to miss an entire day of work in the fields to care for the children because Aunt Betty was unavailable. Mrs. Collins, another neighbor, had reached the end of her confinement, and Aunt Betty was helping with the birthing. She wasn't due home until later today at the earliest.

There was a knock at the door, and Lisa poked her head in for a moment, then quickly backed out, shutting the door. Jillian could hear her scurry back down the hall. She didn't know what Lisa was up to, but she did know that if the children were already up, it was later than she thought.

Jillian was just about to attempt standing when she heard another knock. She could hear the girls whispering outside the door. This time Jenny poked her head in and smiled. Jillian smiled back weakly. All at once, Jenny was gone again, but only for a second this time. Lisa pushed the door open and held it while Jenny carried a breakfast tray inside the room.

"Mornin', Ma," Jenny said shyly.

"Mornin', Ma," Lisa echoed.

"Pa said we should bring you some breakfast when you woke up, 'cause you'd be real hungry." Jenny walked over and stood in front of her with the tray.

"And you're awake now." Lisa noted and walked over to stand beside the bed.

Jillian smiled down at her. "Yes, I'm awake."

"You need to sit back so I can put the tray on your lap so you can eat your breakfast in bed." Jenny informed her.

"Oh, is that what I'm supposed to do?" Jillian quizzed her with a smile.

"Uh-huh," Lisa answered this time. "That's the way we always do it 'round here when we is sick."

"When we *are* sick," Jillian corrected.

Lisa nodded and then continued, " 'Cept Brenn. He's still too little."

Obediently, Jillian sat back in the bed, and Jenny placed the tray on her lap. She looked down at the food before her. There was a bowl of some sort of soup, a piece of bread, and a glass of milk. Off to the side, there was a small vase with a few wildflowers in it. She reached over and caressed one of the petals thoughtfully.

"I picked the flowers myself," Lisa offered. She came closer to Jillian, leaned over, and looked at the food on her tray, wrinkling her nose. "You really gonna eat that stuff?" Jillian nodded her head. "It don't look real good to me. Pa made me hotcakes. They wasn't as good as the ones you make, but I just put some extra syrup on." Lisa licked her lips. "I tried to get Pa to let me bring you hotcakes—not that stuff—but he says you can't eat hotcakes today." She wrinkled her nose again. "It has veggietables in it, you know. I saw Pa put them in. He cooked them first and mashed them up." Lisa leaned in conspiratorially. "Maybe so you wouldn't know they was in there," she whispered. She peered into the bowl of soup again. "You real sure you want to eat that?" Jillian smiled and as if in answer to her question, her stomach growled again.

"Lisa, I think you'd better leave your ma alone long enough to get something into that noisy stomach of hers." Jillian looked up, startled at the sound of Dalton's voice. She blushed as she thought again of his last visit to her room. With her sudden illness, she hadn't had the time or the strength to analyze his abrupt departure that night. Dalton stood leaning in the doorway watching them.

"But Pa," Lisa grumbled, "I want to see if she really eats it!"

"Now, Lisa, do as I say," Dalton said firmly. He looked over at Jenny. "You too, Jenny. Why don't you both go see what Brenn's up to before he tears the house apart."

"Thank you, girls!" Jillian called as both girls started toward her bedroom door.

As Lisa walked by him, still grumbling, Dalton reached down and ruffled the top of her hair. When Jenny walked past him, he put his hand on her shoulder to stop her, moved it under her chin, and turned her face up to look at him. "You were a lot of help to me, Jenny, both yesterday and today. I'm real proud of you. Now, run off to school." Jenny smiled up at him before giving him a big hug and skipping the rest of the way out of the room.

Dalton remained in the doorway, looking at Jillian for a moment. She suddenly realized how frightful she must look, and immediately her hands went to her hair.

Dalton smiled. "How are you feeling this morning?"

"Much better, thank you." Realizing how silly she must look, she dropped her hands back down in front of her. "And thank you for the food. It really does look wonderful." And as if by perfect timing, her stomach growled once more. "My stomach thinks so too," she added with an embarrassed grimace.

Dalton laughed as he walked over and sat on the edge of the bed. Without looking up, he reached over, took one of her hands in his, and began tracing the lines on her palm with his finger. It sent a familiar tingling sensation up her arm, and she felt goose bumps appear as she watched him. If he noticed, he didn't say anything. She heard him take in a deep breath and let it out again.

"Jillian." It was the first time he had called her by her given name, and her heart responded to the sound of her name from his lips. He finally looked up into her eyes. "I was thinking that maybe when you're up to it," he paused a moment before continuing, "that is, if you would like to—" He looked back down at her hand and began tracing the lines again. He took a deep breath again and looked into her eyes once more. "The thing is—I've been thinking about a lot of things. Things we've said to each other and things we haven't." He paused again, but didn't look away this time. His eyes were mesmerizing her, yet she was keenly aware that he was still playing with her hand. He had no idea of the effect it was having on her. Obnoxiously, her stomach would not be ignored any longer, and it let out an angry roar. Dalton dropped her hand and stood up.

"I'll go so that you can eat," he said quickly and started to go.

"No, wait!" This time Jillian grabbed his hand desperately and looked into his eyes, pleading. "Please Dalton, don't leave. Sit back down for a moment." Dalton obeyed and sat down again on the edge of the bed. This time she looked down before saying, "I think you're right. We do need to talk." Gathering her courage and looking back up at him she added, "Really talk." Dalton slowly let out his breath like he'd been holding it.

"Okay. Good. When you're feeling better, we'll take the children over to Aunt Betty's and then we'll take a ride, spend the day together."

Jillian wanted to shout, "I'm ready now!" but her body didn't agree, so instead she just said calmly, "That sounds perfect, Dalton."

He released her hand, stood up, and walked to the open door. Before going through, he turned and said, "You need to take the day to rest. I'll manage the children just fine. Let me know if you need anything."

"Thank you," Jillian replied gratefully. He smiled at her once more and closed the door behind him.

Nineteen

Nathan Shaw stepped off the train and looked up at the sign above the platform that read "Welcome to Darlington, Wisconsin." He grinned to himself. *It won't be long now*, he thought, *but first I need a drink.* His hand went to his face. *And perhaps a shave. I want to look my best for Jillian.*

It didn't take him long to find a saloon and quench his thirst. He would have rather stayed for a game of cards, but he needed to find the barber and ask around about Jillian. He patted his breast pocket and felt the thick billfold there. By now his father had probably discovered that he was missing a rather large sum from the safe. Maybe Nathan would have the chance to double some of his money later on tonight.

After tipping the barber handsomely, Nathan walked out onto the boardwalk. He noticed a group of woman trying to catch his eye, and he sauntered over to them, removed his hat, and gave them a graceful bow.

"Good morning! And how are you beautiful ladies doing on this fine day?" There was a round of giggles, and one of the women stepped forward slightly and offered him her hand. He took it gallantly and placed a firm kiss upon it.

❦

Sarah Bingham couldn't believe her luck. They had ridden into Darlington only a short time before to attend a concert given by a traveling opera group that would be performing later that afternoon. Already, the most handsome man in town had noticed her and had come over to speak to them.

"How do you do, sir? I do agree with you, the day is fine indeed." She gave him an inviting smile.

"And with whom, may I inquire, do I have the pleasure of becoming acquainted today?" He had not released her hand as of yet. He was flirting unabashedly with her.

"Miss Sarah Bingham. And you are . . . ."

"Mr. Nathan Shaw," he bowed again, "at your service."

Nathan saw that Miss Bingham was immediately taken with him, and he was hoping she had some information that would aid him in his quest.

"I was hoping one of you ladies might be able to help me." He paused as the group looked at him expectantly. "I am looking for a friend of mine, a Miss Jillian Grey?"

The enamored look on Miss Bingham's face immediately fell.

"Miss Grey?" she answered. "Do you perchance mean Mrs. Jillian McCullough?"

"McCullough?" Nathan felt the anger well up inside him instantly, but he forced himself to remain calm and keep up his pretenses. "Yes, I'm sorry, I did mean Mrs. McCullough." He forced himself to laugh. "We've been friends since we were children and she is so recently married, I sometimes forget to call her by her new name." His anger was causing him to tremble. He needed to end this conversation quickly. "Do any of you by chance know how I might find her place of residence?"

Miss Bingham's face had turned to stone, and Nathan knew she wouldn't help him any longer. She spoke for the group when she answered him firmly.

"I'm sorry, Mr. Shaw, but I don't think we can help you. Come, ladies. If we don't hurry, we'll be late for the performance." As they started to walk away, one of the girls in the group stopped and walked back over to him, even as Miss Bingham gave her a fierce scowl. She was a little plainer than the others, but he still gave her a winning smile, hoping to gain some information from her.

"How do you do, Mr. Shaw?' She held her hand out to him and

he politely kissed it. She smiled, and her cheeks colored. "I am Miss Olivia Jenkins. My father is the reverend over in Willow Springs, a couple hours from here. I apologize for the rudeness of my friend." She paused as she looked quickly over her shoulder to make sure she was not being overheard. "How do you know Mrs. McCullough?" she asked. He assumed she was just being cautious.

"Like I said, we're childhood friends from Providence. I was away on business when she was married and was unable to attend the wedding," he lied. "I had a break in my schedule and decided it would be a good time to visit and offer my congratulations." She seemed convinced by his feigned sincerity.

"Mr. and Mrs. McCullough live on a farm on the other side of Willow Springs. If you can find your way to town, anyone there can direct you the rest of the way."

"Thank you kindly, Miss Jenkins. I am much relieved to know I will soon be reunited with my dear friend. You have done me a great service today, my good lady." She looked embarrassed at his praise.

"I am glad I was able to help you, sir," she gushed.

"Indeed, you were," he smiled gratefully. "Indeed, you were." He bowed again, and she hurried back to her group of friends. Nathan headed toward the saloon, smiling a very satisfied smile.

Two days later, Jillian was feeling well enough to go on her planned outing with Dalton. She was worried about Dalton missing another day of work, but he assured her that since the cornfields were now half their original size, he had more free time on his hands.

Jillian put on the same peach dress that she had worn to the picnic and stood in front of her mirror. She was glad that some color had come back into her cheeks. Instead of pulling her hair up, she decided to wear it in a loose braid down her back.

The children were excited to be going to Uncle Ned and Aunt Betty's. Today was the day they were going to be able to bring their kitten home. It was finally old enough to leave its mother, and Dalton had agreed to let it live in the barn.

After they dropped the children off, Jillian and Dalton headed over to Willow Lake. Jillian wanted to go again, despite her unpleasant experience there. She was determined they would have a good time making happy memories to replace the bad ones. She had packed a picnic lunch of fried chicken, potato salad, and a peach pie for them to share for dessert. Her body was still trying to overcompensate for her food depravation while she was sick, and she was looking forward to the feast.

As Riley leisurely pulled the wagon along, Dalton was being both charming and entertaining. When they finally arrived, they walked about the lake and played in the water for a while, splashing and laughing. They both felt relaxed and comfortable in each other's company. When Dalton walked back to the wagon and came back carrying a set of fishing poles, Jillian laughed.

"I've seen those things, but I've never actually used one."

Dalton raised an eyebrow at her. "You're joking. You lived so close to the ocean and you never went fishing before?" He sounded genuinely surprised.

"Well, Marcus did try to get me to go once on one of our vacations to the beach, but—" Jillian paused.

"But what?" he encouraged.

"Well, I always thought it was sort of inhumane, putting a live creature on a hook only to be eaten by a fish that was going to be eaten by you." Dalton laughed out loud. "Well, I was a bit younger then."

"How young?" he asked when he had stopped laughing.

"About ten." Dalton chuckled again and she laughed too.

"Well, ten is a very tender age, especially for a girl." He looked her over teasingly. "I think you've grown up a bit since then. Have you changed your mind?"

"Maybe," she teased back, grabbing one of the poles and heading down toward the lake.

Jillian actually had fun learning to fish, although she made Dalton bait her hook each time. She didn't catch anything, but Dalton caught three healthy looking trout. He seemed pleased with himself.

Lunch was delicious. Afterward, they relaxed on a blanket under a large tree for a while. Dalton stretched himself out, put his hands behind his head, and closed his eyes. Jillian, leaning her back up against the tree and knowing he couldn't see her, watched him intently. Every once in a while, a muscle in his cheek would twitch, as though he was thinking of something that made him want to smile. Suddenly a swan glided down from out of nowhere, landing gracefully on the lake and catching Jillian's attention. It was beautiful here.

"Did you and Laurellyn come here often?" Jillian surprised herself by asking her question aloud. She wasn't even sure Dalton was awake to hear it.

Dalton opened his eyes, sat up, and looked at her. His gaze followed hers to the lake, and he saw the swan resting peacefully on the water. He seemed to understand the reason for her question.

"Yes, but mostly before we were married. She did love this lake, though," he answered quietly.

They both sat in silence for a while, each lost in their own thoughts.

Then the swan suddenly took flight over the island and startled Jillian.

"What's it like over there?" she asked curiously.

"On the island?"

"Yes. I saw quite a few people boating back and forth from there at the Independence Day picnic."

"Would you like to go over and see?" he asked. "There's usually a boat tied up somewhere along the shoreline."

"Yes, I would like that very much," she replied.

Dalton stood up and offered her his hand. She took it willingly, and after he helped her up, he didn't let go. Instead, he laced his fingers in hers, and they walked toward the lake's shore. They followed the shoreline for some distance before finding the small boat tied up. Dalton helped Jillian in first, untied the boat, pushed off from the shore, and deftly hopped in.

It didn't take very long for Dalton to row to the island's shore. When they reached it, he got out first, tied the boat up, and helped Jillian out. He took her hand again as they walked up the shore.

Jillian's breath caught in her throat when they reached the top of the incline and looked around. There were only a few trees here, but the whole island was a carpet of flowers. Most of them were wildflowers, like black-eyed Susans with their bright yellow blooms, and butterfly weed with its frilly orange petals. There were purple lavender and delicate white aster blooms. Every color of the rainbow was represented in its entire splendor.

"How beautiful!" she whispered reverently.

"Yes, beautiful," she heard Dalton say, but when she looked over at him, he was looking at her instead of the flowers. She felt her cheeks grow hot. Suddenly shy, she turned away and tried to concentrate on the scene before her.

Dalton let go of her hand, and they walked in the direction of a fallen tree some distance away. Every now and then, Dalton bent down and picked a flower until he had a nice bouquet in his hand.

When they reached the log, Dalton motioned for her to sit down. She did, and he sat down beside her, resting his arms on his knees and leaning forward slightly, holding the bouquet out in front of him. Jillian watched as he fingered their delicate blooms one at a time. He pulled a single stem out of the middle and brought it to his nose, inhaling its sweet fragrance. Afterward, he brought it back down in front of him, but instead of adding it back to the bunch, he held it slightly away from the others. It was a delicate white flower with a yellow center.

"You know, these were Laurellyn's favorites." He was quiet for a moment before he spoke again. "It's unique and delicate and different from the rest, with a fragrance all its own." He inhaled its scent once again before going on. "When I fell in love with her, I knew there would never be anyone else in the whole world like her." Jillian could tell he was fighting to keep his emotions under control.

"When she died, I thought my whole world had died with her. I didn't want to live in a world without her. If it hadn't been for the children, I would have holed myself up somewhere and shut everyone out." He paused briefly. "But as I held my sweet boy in my arms that night, I knew I still had a part of her with me, and I vowed I would try to live for them. It hasn't been easy, what with all the constant reminders of her around." She wasn't sure, but Jillian thought she saw a single tear escape his eye and start down his cheek.

"She made me promise before she died that I would remarry and find someone to love again, someone to love our children. She was sure there was someone out there for me." His voice broke slightly. "I didn't think I could ever love another woman, but I couldn't withhold the promise from her that last night." He paused for a moment before he began again. "As time passed, I knew I had to try to find a mother for our children. They deserved that much. That part of the promise I knew I could keep. That's why I chose to do things the way I did. That's how I found you." He looked up at her for a moment and then looked back down again.

"I thought I could live with another woman, keeping my wall of memories built safely around me and still be able to be there for my family." Dalton sat upright. He looked at her once more and after laying the single flower on the log next to him, he placed his hand gently on the side of her face. His touch took her breath away and her heart raced. He continued softly, "What I didn't count on, was you, Jillian."

Dalton took his hand away and drew another flower from the bouquet. He held it to his nose, inhaling deeply. The flower was a soft purple with long slender blooms. "Both are so different," he mused, "but each is so beautiful in its own unique way."

He continued, "I don't know what I was expecting, but it certainly wasn't you." He chuckled to himself, a little self-consciously, and then became serious again. "When I first saw you at the station, I felt myself drawn to you immediately, even before I knew it was you I was looking for. Every emotion I thought I'd experienced with Laurellyn suddenly came alive, along with some I never even knew I possessed. And I fought it. I fought it with everything I had." He set the bouquet down and with his free hand began to gently caress the lavender petals of the single delicate bloom he held.

Jillian gently placed her hand on his arm. She couldn't believe what he was saying. Could he possibly love her as much as she loved him? Her eyes became moist as the tears found their way to the surface.

"I can't fight it anymore, Jillian. When I look at you, everything you are draws me to you, no matter how hard I try to pull away." He turned toward her. "I know you had your reasons for coming here the way you did. For a long time, I wondered what terrible thing had happened to you that turned your precious heart away from love. Marcus told me what happened, and it explained everything." She was taken aback, but not angry. Dalton continued in a rush, "Don't be upset with your brother—I asked him to tell me. He would not have betrayed your confidence had he not been worried about your happiness." By now, continuous tears were falling from her eyes.

"I'm not angry," she replied quickly to relieve his worrying.

"I know it might take you more time to get over what that man did to you, but I am willing to wait." He reached up, wiping the tears from her cheeks, and then letting his thumb brush across her lips.

Jillian's heart soared as she grasped his meaning. "I don't need any more time, Dalton. I realized long ago that I never loved Nathan. I am long past any feelings for him, except contempt." She saw the look of hope that leapt into his eyes and placed her hand tenderly into his. "There is only one man I have ever truly loved."

Dalton circled his arms about her waist. Immediately, her arms were around his neck, and when their lips met, she could taste the salt from her tears. It wasn't bitter though, for they weren't tears of pain but tears of joy. When their kiss finally ended, she rested her head against his chest.

"I love you, Dalton McCullough. I think I was always meant to love you."

"I love you, too, Jillian McCullough." His arms tightened around her and she felt safe, secure, and most of all, loved.

Marcus Grey unfolded the note in his hand. He had only returned moments before from delivering Miss Bethany Johansen safely home from their holiday. He had spoken privately with her father, and he smiled to himself as he thought of the answer he had received. He leisurely made his way home, knowing his parents wouldn't be there to greet him or hear his good news. They were away on a holiday themselves.

The instant he walked in the door, Thomas, their butler, handed him a note along with a quick description of the woman who had written it. Marcus wondered who the woman had been and what business she might possibly have with him. He glanced at the signature at the bottom of the message. He was not familiar with a Miss Lorelei Davis.

The note was brief, but the meaning was clear. Marcus felt fear and anger rise within him simultaneously as he read the words hastily scrawled upon the paper.

Dear Sir,

Though you are not familiar with me, we do have a common acquaintance, one whom I fear is a great danger to your family, especially your sister, Miss Jillian Grey. I witnessed certain threats made by Mr. Nathan Shaw. I fear he is not right in his head, and I know for certain he has already left on the train to Darlington, Wisconsin. Although I may be partly responsible for his poor state of mind, I do not wish for any harm that may come to your sister to be upon my conscience. I regret that you were not home when I came to deliver this message, because of its urgent nature. I myself do not wish to

be around when Mr. Shaw returns, so I am leaving forthwith. I only pray you receive this message in time to save her from danger, as Mr. Shaw is most determined to yet make her his.

Regards,

Miss Lorelei Davis

Marcus quickly folded the message, hurried to the writing desk, and began writing a note.

"Thomas, come quickly!" When the butler arrived at his side, Marcus ordered, "Hurry to the stables and have Stephens saddle my horse immediately. I must ride into town and send this telegram at once."

In less than ten minutes, with the penned note in his pocket, Marcus mounted his horse and galloped through the gates of Grey Manor.

Twenty

Nathan found it easy enough to discover where Jillian lived. The people in the small town of Willow Springs seemed anxious to find out more about the new addition to their community, especially Mrs. Mavis Bingham, a pushy and arrogant woman who had riddled him with questions as soon as he had inquired about his long-time friend.

Nathan purposely misled the town busybody about his relationship with Mrs. McCullough. In return for her new arsenal of delicious gossip, Mrs. Bingham provided him with detailed directions to the McCullough's farm. The next morning, Nathan rode out to the farm and sat watching the house.

The man he presumed to be Dalton McCullough came out of the house and worked on getting his horse hitched up to his wagon. Nathan observed him as he worked. He couldn't quite see the man's face because he had his back turned, but he looked well built and strong. A spark of jealously ignited within Nathan. When he first heard the rumors about Jillian's marriage, he assumed the worst of a man who looked for a wife via advertisements in a newspaper. He never once thought he might have some actual competition. The man whistled while he worked. Evidently, Jillian made him happy. The thought fueled Nathan's jealousy even more.

A little girl, about four or five years old, came running out of the house a little later, carrying a pup. She set it down, and it began barking and running around, trying to get her to play with it. Nathan realized the dog might be a problem. He was thinking about how he could handle it when he saw McCullough, finished hitching the wagon, pick up the girl and head back inside the house.

Just then, Nathan thought about the man waiting for him at the saloon back in Willow Springs. He was glad that he had brought him down from Darlington with him. He'd figured he might need a little help, and he'd been right. Mr. Charles Fitzgerald, "Chuckles," as he kept insisting he be called, had lost big to him in a card game his first night in town. Nathan had been lucky that night. He liked the gambling establishments out here. He had been a little fish in a big pond back in Boston, but here the tables were turned. Chuckles had taken his bluff, bet big, and in the end, he owed Nathan more money than he had claim to. That's when Nathan had given him an alternative way to pay off his debt. Chuckles actually seemed eager to help when Nathan mentioned the names of those he was looking for. That had led to a most interesting conversation. The fat, pudgy, old thing wouldn't be much good in a fight, but Nathan could think of a few other ways he could be of some use.

The door to the house finally burst open, and two girls hopped down the porch steps and clambered into the back of the wagon: the child who had come out before and an older one. Next, McCullough came out, carrying a small boy of eighteen months. He walked over to the wagon and then looked back at the house expectantly. Nathan's gaze had gone to the door as well.

When Jillian walked through the door, Nathan's pulse quickened. He'd almost forgotten how extraordinarily beautiful she was. Her strawberry curls were pulled back into a braid, and some loose strands hung softly about her face. She carried a picnic basket in her arms. She looked at McCullough and smiled. Nathan clenched his fist as Jillian walked over to him, setting the basket down at her feet. Taking the hand he held out to her, she smiled again as he helped her up into the wagon, saying something to her as he did so. He handed the boy up to her. She laughed and cradled the wiggly boy, kissing the top of his head, while McCullough picked up the basket, untied the wagon, placed the basket next to the girls, and climbed up to sit next to Jillian. The wagon pulled out and headed away from Willow Springs.

Jillian looked happy, but Nathan knew she really couldn't be. *She's only known this man for a few months*, he reasoned. She and Nathan had grown up together. He had made her smile and laugh more times than he could count. He closed his eyes and pictured her at the Spring Ball Extravaganza—how beautiful she was, the way she had looked at him. He remembered how her body had felt in his arms as they danced. She loved him. He knew it. He had foolishly hurt her, but she would forgive him. She was just confused. When he explained that the other woman meant nothing to him, she would want him back.

Nathan thought of how she had held the baby boy in her arms and kissed the top of his head. She seemed to be taken with that man's boy and it wasn't even hers. She had always loved children; she'd even talked about them when they had been engaged. Nathan hadn't really wanted any, at least not right away, but if she wanted a child that badly, he would let her have one. He was getting anxious to talk to her. He needed to get her alone so they could make their plans.

A little while later, Nathan heard the wagon coming back up the road. They had obviously dropped the children off somewhere because they were no longer with them. Nathan crouched down lower in the brush so he wouldn't be seen. As they rode past his hiding spot, he got a better look at Jillian. She was looking at the man, and Nathan didn't like the look he saw in her eyes. His breathing became harsh as he felt his anger surge. He needed to talk to her soon, that much was certain. Jillian was his, and they belonged together. Soon they could leave here and start their life together.

McCullough didn't turn the wagon into his gate, but instead headed toward Willow Springs. They were obviously heading out somewhere together. Despite his urge to follow them, Nathan made his way back to the tree a little way off the road and retrieved the rented horse he had tied up. Looking back down the road where he last saw the wagon, Nathan made his way back to town to make his plans with Chuckles.

Later that same afternoon, Nathan stood in front of the house again, waiting. He could hear the muffled whimpers of the pup at his feet. It was tied up in the old flour sack he had found in the barn. Nathan figured Jillian would return soon, so all he had to do was stay hidden until she did. The plan was to wait until she was alone, maybe while Dalton was seeing to his evening chores, and snatch her then. Chuckles was holed up out of the way with their horses right now, but

when it got darker, he was supposed to come closer to keep watch and back Nathan up. At any sign of trouble, he was to send one gunshot into the air. Nathan reached down, picked up the noisy, squirming bundle, and headed out toward the fields behind the barn.

Jillian snuggled up and rested her head on Dalton's shoulder as they headed back home to pick up the children. At some point during the day her hair had escaped its braid and she had not bothered to redo it. Dalton seemed to like it down, and all she wanted to do was make him happy.

The day had been a dream, more than she had ever hoped for. After their confessions of love, the day seemed to fly by. She unconsciously brought her hand to her lips, remembering the kisses they'd shared.

They talked about everything: their childhoods, their education, and their families. They had laughed at each other's mishaps and adventures, and she had cried when he spoke of losing his mother and father. They had even talked of Laurellyn some. Jillian felt close to her in her own way and wanted to know more about her. Her love for Dalton and the children had somehow strengthened that connection. Finally, they had spoken of their hopes and dreams for their future and made plans together. Today was a day to celebrate.

A thought suddenly struck her, and she excitedly turned to Dalton. "Dalton!" He jumped slightly, and she figured he must have been as deep in thought as she had been moments before. "I'm sorry. Did I startle you?" she asked. She didn't give him time to answer before continuing. "Would you do something for me?" Dalton pulled back on the reins, brought the horse to a stop, and turned toward her.

"I would do anything for you," he answered with a wink. She looked up into his handsome face and smiled before speaking further. How she got so lucky, she didn't know.

"Well, I was wondering, since it's on the way, if you would drop me off at home first before going to pick up the children." She smiled at the plans she was making in her head. "That way I could get a head start on supper and maybe do something extra."

"Well, that depends, I suppose," he said teasingly.

"On what?" She raised an eyebrow up at him.

"On whether that something extra might just be something extra sweet. You are the best cook this side of the Mississippi." Jillian blushed at his compliment.

"Why, Dalton McCullough, are you trying to flatter me?" She looked up and fluttered her eyelashes at him, causing him to laugh heartily. He bent down and kissed her soundly before starting on their way once more.

"Why yes, I believe I am, Mrs. McCullough. I think I've been a little too short on compliments these last few months. You can expect to get your fair share and more for a while." Smiling, she linked her arm in his and laid her head back on his shoulder. Fifteen minutes later they turned onto the road that led to their house.

Nathan heard the wagon coming up the road. He crouched low behind the side of the barn, ready to make his escape quickly if he was caught. They were back a little earlier than he had expected. He watched as the wagon pulled up to the house, and McCullough hopped down, came around, and helped Jillian down.

McCullough didn't let go of her though, and Nathan watched as he pulled her close to him. Nathan fought the urge to fly over there and make McCullough take his filthy hands off of his woman. Who did this man think he was? Nathan braced his hands on the corner of the barn to keep himself from taking his revenge before it was wise to do so. He would wait until the time was just right to make him pay.

Jillian's hands were on Dalton's chest and she could feel his heart racing. His back was to the wagon and her body was crushed closely to him. He was kissing her ear, and it was sending shivers down her neck and spine. His hands traveled to the back of her head, and he laced his fingers in her hair. Bringing his face down before hers, he looked deeply into her eyes. She blissfully anticipated his kiss and was not disappointed. His lips were eager and held a passion more intense than she had experienced before. Never had she felt so wanted or needed.

Abruptly, the wagon jerked behind him and their kiss suddenly ended. Dalton groaned. Apparently, Riley was impatient to either be on his way or unbridled and set free for the night. Dalton released her, took her hand, and walked her reluctantly to the door.

"I suppose I ought to head over to collect the children," he said dejectedly.

"Before you leave, do you have any requests?" Immediately, Dalton grinned slyly. "About dessert, I mean," she quickly clarified. He grinned again, and she playfully smacked him on the shoulder. "Oh, you know what I mean!"

"Surprise me. I like surprises—well, good ones anyway." He bent down and gave her one last lingering kiss before walking back and climbing into the wagon. "Be back in a little while," he called as he waved goodbye.

Jillian leaned her back against the door, wrapping her arms around her middle as she watched him drive away. Once he was out of sight, she danced into the house and began taking down pots and pans and pulling out ingredients. Her face was beginning to ache from smiling so much, but she wouldn't change a single moment of this heavenly day.

Dalton took in a deep breath and exhaled it slowly, trying to calm his racing heartbeat. He maneuvered the horse back toward the center of the road and realized he needed to concentrate on driving the wagon instead of daydreaming. He seemed in the habit of having wagon troubles when distracted by thoughts of his beautiful wife, and he certainly didn't want any problems tonight that might delay his return home. He kept picturing her beautiful face before him, and his hand still tingled from the touch of her skin. Their day together had been better than he had imagined. Euphoric almost! He wished he had listened to his heart sooner.

Wondering what she had decided to make for supper, his mouth began to water. He hadn't been joking. Jillian was a wonderful cook, even better than Aunt Betty. He smiled to himself. He might be better off keeping that secret to himself though, at least from his aunt.

Dalton grinned wider as he thought of all the things they had done today. She hadn't caught a single fish, but he had enjoyed watching her as she excitedly reeled in the line whenever she felt the slightest tug. He remembered the fish in the pail in the back of his wagon. He should have left them with her to fry. At least this way he could leave one for Uncle Ned and Aunt Betty to have for their supper.

After pulling up to Uncle Ned and Aunt Betty's house and setting the wagon's brake, he hopped down with the bucket of fish. All three children were in a huddle playing with the kittens. Brenn had one by the tail, and Dalton smiled when he heard Lisa scolding him. He had almost forgotten that they would be bringing one of the little fur balls home with them, another pet to be cherished by his children. That thought made him remember something. When he had dropped Jillian off, Digger hadn't come running to greet them as usual.

"I wonder where that crazy pup has gone off to," he said quietly to himself. An uneasy feeling came over him, but he brushed it aside. He wasn't going to allow anything to ruin this day for him.

Just then, the girls noticed him and came running with a black and white striped kitten between them, the other kittens forgotten and left to the mercy of Brenn.

"Pa, look! This is our new kitten." Lisa called first.

"At first we couldn't decide which one, but Uncle Ned taught us how to flip a coin," Jenny added.

"We named her Whiskers, Pa! Isn't she sweet?" Lisa cuddled her face up to the kitten and handed Whiskers to Jenny for her turn. Dalton's heart swelled as he watched Jenny hold the soft, furry kitten up to her cheek. Jillian had done this for him—she'd brought his happy little girl back to him.

"Listen, Pa. She's purring." Jenny held the kitten out to him. Dalton reached out and stroked the kitten's fur and then leaned in close to listen to its purr. Instead of a soft, rumbling sound, he heard a kitten cry out loudly. He looked over at Brenn, who was holding an unhappy black kitten up by the tail. Dalton handed Whiskers back to Jenny, along with the pail of fish and hurried over to rescue the kitten, with Lisa close behind him.

"Kitty!" Brenn cooed as Dalton gently took the unhappy kitten from his hands and handed it to Lisa. Lisa cuddled and started checking for wounds immediately.

"Brenn, you need to be nice to the kitten," Dalton found himself saying, even though he knew Brenn probably didn't understand a word. It was mostly for Lisa's benefit.

Suddenly, a buckboard came flying up into the yard at full speed, and he heard Uncle Ned yell "whoa" as he pulled the horses to a sudden stop. Uncle Ned jumped down quickly and hurried over to the group. He hastily pulled Dalton away from the children, who were all staring at him in wonderment. They'd probably never seen him move so fast! At any another time Dalton might have found the thought funny. Uncle Ned handed Dalton a telegram marked "URGENT."

"I was just getting ready ta leave town when Mrs. Pruitt came runnin' out of the telegraph office with this note in her hand and said it was for you. Said it came this afternoon, but she couldn't find anyone to bring it out.

"I didn't read it, but I suspect she did, because she informed me I should fly like the wind ta get it to ya," Uncle Ned said, breathlessly.

Dalton felt a sense of foreboding as he opened the telegram. It was from Marcus.

Dalton—
Received word Nathan left for Darlington—
Possibly arrived yesterday—
Source says he's not in right mind—
Protect Jillian—
Prayers are with you—
Will wait for word—
Marcus.

Dalton's face went ashen.

"What is it, boy?" Uncle Ned grabbed a hold of his arm.

"It's Jillian. She's in danger." Immediately, he thought again of Digger's absence, and an icy fear gripped him. "Uncle Ned, I've got to go and make sure she's all right." He raced for the wagon.

"Don't worry about the children," Uncle Ned said. "We'll keep an eye on 'em." As an afterthought, he called after Dalton as he raced away, "Hurry, boy!"

Nobody had to tell him that. Considering the feeling that had settled in his gut, wild dogs couldn't stop him from hurrying. He stopped thinking and started praying.

Twenty-one

Jillian was measuring flour into a bowl when the door burst open.
Expecting to see Dalton, she turned with a smile. Her breath caught
in her throat, and she froze when she saw who was standing there.

"Nathan Shaw!"

He looked much the same, with the notable exception of the crook
in his nose and the frightening look in his eyes. "What are you doing
here? I mean . . . h-how did you know where to find me?"

Nathan didn't say anything. He just stood there. Jillian was getting
more nervous by the second, so she asked him again, more forcefully
this time, "Nathan, what are you doing here?"

His face softened slightly. "Jillian, my love." He smiled at her, but it
was not the smile she remembered. "I'm here because of you."

"Because of me?" She didn't understand.

"Of course, because of you." He started walking toward her. "You
ran off, and I couldn't find you for months." He stopped and began
absentmindedly running his fingers back and forth along of the edge of
the kitchen table. "Is that any way to treat your betrothed?"

Jillian felt the fear in the pit of her stomach begin to grow. "Nathan,
you must have heard by now, I'm already a married woman."

Nathan narrowed his eyes and started walking slowly toward her
again. Jillian slowly backed away from him until she could move no
farther.

"Jillian, Jillian, what will I do with you?" he said patronizingly.
"You know we were always meant to be together. You have loved me

forever. On more than one occasion I overheard you confess your love for me to your friend Bethany. Why, you've loved me from the first day that wretched brother of yours and I became friends." His hand went to his nose, and he stopped directly in front of her. "He broke my nose, you know. I have yet to repay him for that," he hissed. Jillian instantly went on the defensive, her fear forgotten when he threatened Marcus.

"As I recall, you deserved that," she said a bit too snidely. "I saw you—you and that . . . that woman—you with your hands all over her when you were going to be married to me. And you . . . you wouldn't even give me a proper kiss, even though you had been courting me for better than six months! You disgust me!" She knew she had gone too far when she saw the anger in his eyes burn brighter.

"I regret that, Jillian, I truly do. It wasn't because I didn't want you. Oh, I wanted you, all right." He picked up a strand of her hair and put it to his nose, inhaling deeply, chuckling when Jillian shuddered. "You smell just like I remember you. I wonder if you feel the same."

Jillian's skin began to crawl as he reached out towards her. "Nathan, don't you touch me!" she told him firmly. She tried again to back away, but he had her pinned against the counter with his hands on either side of her. He leaned his face in close.

"You always wanted me to kiss you. All those nights that I walked you home." He was taunting her. "I could tell that's what you wanted." Jillian struggled to get free of him, and his face contorted and turned ugly. "Why did you let him touch you? I saw his hands on you. You don't even hardly know him, and you let him kiss you like that." His breathing became harsher. "I could kill him for taking liberties with you. You belong to me, Jillian, not to him. That's why I came to take you away with me. We can still be married." His face softened slightly. "I saw you holding his baby."

Jillian's head began to spin. That was early this morning. How long had he been watching them?

"We could have our own," Nathan continued. "I know I didn't sound excited when you talked about children before, but I've been doing some thinking, and all I want is for you to be happy. You can see that, can't you?" He smiled wickedly, and she began to panic. "I'll show you I know how to make you happy, Jillian." He leaned closer, as if he were going to kiss her.

"Nathan, you're not listening to me." Jillian pushed hard against his chest to hold him off. "I'm already married. I'm not going anywhere with you!"

He wasn't listening to her. It was as if he was in his own world. "I'm ready to kiss you now. After all those months of waiting, I'm finally going to grant you your wish, sweet Jillian." He leaned in closer, almost reaching her lips. Turning her head to the side to keep from screaming, Jillian caught sight of the crockery bowl filled with the flour she'd been measuring. Reaching her arm under his, she tried to grasp hold of its side. It was just beyond her fingertips. Suddenly, she felt him kiss her neck. With all her strength, she pushed hard against his chest.

"Nathan, let me go this instant! You have no right!" she yelled, panic stricken.

"I have more right that he does," he growled.

"You're wrong, Nathan," she shouted at him. She leaned with all her might, reached out, and finally felt her fingers clasp the edge of the mixing bowl. She flung it up at him, hitting him hard in the head.

Stunned, Nathan stumbled back, momentarily giving Jillian enough time to break free and run out the open door. She stumbled on the porch steps and fell. Before she could get back up, Nathan had her by the arm again.

"Why are you making this so difficult?" he hissed at her between clenched teeth. "You know you belong to me. You need me!"

"I don't belong to anyone, least of all you, Nathan Shaw!" Jillian dug her fingernails into his hand to make him release her. "And I only need Dalton! He will be here any minute, and I suggest you get out of here before he does."

A gunshot rang out in the air, and Jillian's eyes widened as her heart froze.

"I don't think he's going to make it, my dear." Nathan laughed maniacally.

"You wouldn't dare!" she protested.

"No, but my partner might." Jillian felt dizzy. Who was he talking about?

"Oh you know him." He was playing with her. "I ran into him in a saloon in Darlington, and when I told him who I was looking for, he jumped at the chance to help me." Jillian still couldn't understand who he was talking about.

"He told quite the tale about you, actually," he continued, "how

you came running over to him in the train station, flirting with him like you were interested, then acting shocked when he took you up on the offer. Said he got his nose broken over it, wanted to get back at the man that did the breaking. I figure he has done just that." Nathan started to laugh again. "I couldn't imagine you behaving that way, but I was glad for the help!"

Jillian felt her knees weaken and saw the world around her start to blur. Nathan's laugh was the last thing she heard before passing out.

Without wasting any time, Nathan bent down, threw her over his shoulder, and ran out into the cornfields behind the barn.

Dalton's heart pounded faster as he raced the wagon toward the house. Just before he got to the house, he heard a gunshot. Panic seized him, and he feared the worst. He saw that the front door was wide open as he turned into the gate. He drove up to the house and pulled the wagon to an abrupt halt. Flinging himself down, he ran into the house. It was empty, but there was a broken bowl on the floor and flour scattered everywhere. Fear gripped his heart even tighter. He ran back out the door. They couldn't have gone too far, especially not on foot.

Dalton forced himself not to panic. He wasn't going to lose her, especially not now. He ran in the direction he thought the shot had come from. After several minutes, he heard the whinny of a horse. Crouching down low, he parted the thick brush, fearful of what he would find. To his surprise, waiting in the clearing with two horses tied to a tree was none other than Mr. Charles Richard Fitzgerald III. Dalton made a sound of disgust. The man was as low as a snake.

Quietly, Dalton snuck in closer. Chuckles had his back to him. The horses, still rustling around from gunfire, were making a lot of noise. Dalton was able to get but a few feet away from the man unnoticed. He suddenly stood up and cleared his throat loudly. Surprised, Chuckles turned quickly around.

"Let's see if this makes you laugh, Mr. Chuckles," Dalton said and slammed his fist into the man's stomach, causing him to double over. Dalton then rendered a deep uppercut to the jaw, causing Chuckles to fall flat on his back with a loud thud. Dalton reached down with both hands and, standing over him, grabbed both sides of the hideous suit and lifted the man's face within inches of his own. "I'm only going to ask you one time, and you'd better know the answer," he barked. Chuckles's eyes got big. Dalton continued, "Where is Nathan Shaw?"

"Down . . . down at the house. That's where he said he would be! At the h-house or in the fields." Chuckles began to shake as Dalton narrowed his eyes. He wasn't much help—there were fields everywhere.

"You'd better pray he hasn't harmed one hair on my wife's head. I'm not finished with you." Dropping the pitiful man back to the ground, Dalton walked over to one of the horses and took a rope that was hanging from the saddle. He quickly secured Chuckles's arms behind his back. After untying the two horses from the tree, he chased them off before sprinting back toward the house.

Dalton stood frantic in front of his own home. He looked around for any sign of a struggle, all while praying desperately for some guidance. Finally, with no definite clue where Nathan would have gone, he decided to head in the direction that he would take if he were trying to hide from view quickly—the cornfields directly behind the barn. He hadn't gone more than a few yards into the corn when he heard a whimpering sound. On the ground in front of him he saw something moving. He ran to it and found Digger tied up tightly inside a flour sack. The pup was glad to be set free and began to eagerly lick Dalton's face.

"We don't have time for that now, Digger. We got to find Jillian. Do you think you can help me?" Dalton put Digger back down on the ground and after sniffing around for a moment, the pup took off into the fields like the devil himself was on his tail. Dalton followed closely after him.

Tiring, Nathan set a limp Jillian down and leaned over with his hands on his knees to catch his breath. It was not easy running between the stalks of corn, let alone running with a bundle. Jillian stirred at his feet. In a minute, he would have to fight with the stalks and with her. How had he gotten himself to this point? If only she would come to her senses! Nathan needed to find a way back around to the horses.

He heard Jillian moan and watched as she opened her eyes. At first she looked confused, and then the look of fear returned. He knelt down beside her.

"Jillian, listen to me. I know I was a fool. I promise you, that woman didn't mean anything. None of them did." Her eyes widened with surprise. She didn't think he fully realized what he had just confessed. "I just want you back. Let's go find a place to be together. I have money." He took out his money pouch, and Jillian was sure her face registered shock. Nathan continued, "We could go anywhere, start over."

Jillian finally found her tongue. "Nathan, you need to stop this. You don't know what you're saying." She realized he still wasn't hearing her, but she tried once more. "I don't love you, Nathan." Finally, he seemed to focus on her words. "I never did. I was just young and confused," she continued. Tears were falling now, tears of fear and pity. "I'm sorry, Nathan, but I just don't love you." He reached down and wiped a tear from her face.

"Please don't cry, Jillian." He looked tenderly at her, and she felt some hope rise within her. "I don't want you to cry."

"Nathan, let's go back to the house and talk this over." She quickly prayed that the children were still safe at Aunt Betty's. "Everything's going to be fine." She thought about the large sum of money he had and could only imagine where it had come from. "Your father and your mother must be worried about you." He got a faraway look in his eyes. "I'll have Dalton drive you back to the station so you can go home." She said a prayer that Dalton was all right. Suddenly Nathan was angry again. He stood and pulled her up with him. He started down the long rows of corn, dragging her along behind him.

"We need to hurry. We don't want to waste any more of our time together," he urged.

"Nathan, please listen to me. I don't love you. I—I love Dalton. He is my husband." Nathan spun around to face her.

"You don't need to pretend anymore. I'm here now. You don't need him. You don't need anyone but me." He pulled her into his arms and tried to kiss her again.

Jillian screamed and struggled to get away. Unable to free herself, she started shouting angrily at him. "I hate you, Nathan Shaw! I will never go anywhere with you. I despise the very sight of you."

Nathan raised his hand as though to strike her. She put her arms in front of her face, shut her eyes tightly, and waited to feel the impact. Instead, a hand came out of nowhere and grabbed Nathan's arm, flinging him away from her. She distinctly heard a crack as Nathan fell hard to the ground. She dared not look.

Dalton frowned at the man sprawled up against the cornstalks. He fought to control the anger that surged through his veins. Nathan didn't seem to be moving, so he turned to Jillian. She was standing with her arms still protecting her face. He reached over and took her into his arms to still her shaking.

"Are you all right?" he asked gently. "Did he hurt you?" She clung to him tightly and sobbed his name. He kissed her hair and her tear-stained face. With his hands on her cheeks, he turned her face to look at him. "I was so frightened for you when I heard the gunshot. I thought I'd lost you." He wiped the tears from her cheeks with his thumbs and softly kissed her lips.

"Nathan told me that you had been shot." She looked at him incredulously. "He was acting out of his mind. I'd never seen him like that before. Oh, Dalton, I was so afraid!" He pulled her tighter into his arms as she began to sob again.

"Hush now. I promise, I'll never let you out of my sight again." As she lifted her head to look at him again, she noticed a movement out of the corner of her eye.

"Dalton, look out!" she shouted. Instantly, Dalton spun around.

"She's mine, McCullough," Nathan said, staggering toward them. He was breathing heavily, and one arm hung limply at his side, but still he lurched forward. Before she even saw him draw his arm back, Jillian heard Dalton's fist make contact with Nathan's face. He fell solidly to the ground, this time out cold. She sat down on the ground, relieved it was finally over.

Dalton knelt down by Jillian. Suddenly, the puppy came flying through the stalks, landed in her lap, and began licking her face.

"Oh, Digger," she murmured as she snuggled the puppy close to her. "I haven't seen you since we got back. Where have you been hiding out?" Dalton laughed, and Jillian looked up at him.

"I'll have to tell you that story later." He stood up and helped her to her feet, putting his arm around her for support. "Right now we'd better get back to the house."

As they walked past the last row of corn stalks, Uncle Ned and the sheriff came riding up. Uncle Ned quickly dismounted and hurried forward.

"Dalton, Jillian, are you all right?"

"We're fine, Uncle Ned, thank you," Dalton replied wearily.

"When I heard the gunshot, I went ta fetch the sheriff. Luckily, he was already on his way, havin' heard about the worrisome telegram from Miss Pruitt. Of course, she'll never admit ta reading it." Dalton half smiled at Uncle Ned and looked over at the sheriff, pointing to the cornfields behind him.

"There is a man out cold in the fields there with a broken arm and maybe even a broken nose. I imagine you'll want to take him in for questioning."

"Another one?" Uncle Ned said incredulously. "We already found a man wanderin' down the road with his hands tied behind his back, wearin' the most hideous lookin' suit I ever saw."

Jillian looked at Dalton and then back at the sheriff.

"Chuckles?" Jillian looked up at Dalton questioningly. He nodded.

"Who?" the sheriff asked.

Dalton shook his head and answered, "Sheriff, if it's all right with you, we'd like to wait a day or two to give you our account of what happened. I'll explain everything to you then."

The sheriff nodded. "I'm happy to keep them at the jail until you feel up to it."

Dalton turned to Uncle Ned. "Would you mind sending a telegram to Marcus, letting him know Jillian's safe?"

"Sure will, Dalton. Oh, and Hank Collins came over when he heard the gunshot too and I asked him ta see ta your horses and wagon. Why don't the both of you head back ta the house and make an early night of it? Looks to me like you both could use some rest." he winked at Dalton. "We already got the children settled down over at our place, so I'll drive 'em back sometime tomorrow mornin'."

"Thank you," Jillian said and gave him a weak smile. They started back toward to the house while the sheriff and Uncle Ned headed into the cornfield to fetch Nathan.

When they walked into the kitchen, Jillian looked around at the mess.

"I suppose I ought to clean this up." She walked over and started picking the broken pieces of the bowl off the floor.

"I'll help you," Dalton offered. In no time, they had put everything to rights. When they were finished, Dalton took her hand in his, and they walked out onto the front porch to watch the sunset.

After awhile Dalton spoke. "We need to enjoy as many of these as we can before winter sets in." He said it almost to himself, as if it were only a thought that wasn't meant to be spoken out loud. "Jillian?"

"Yes, Dalton."

"I was thinking about our wedding and how it wasn't very special for you." His handsome features looked saddened at the thought. "I'd like to say some things to you right now, if you don't mind." He brought her hands to his chest and held them there.

"I don't mind," she answered softly.

"I want to thank you for coming here, for being the wonderful woman you are. You have picked up the pieces of my broken family and put us back together. I want to thank you for the love and the laughter you have brought back to our home and for your love and concern for my . . . *our* children. I wish I could find all the words to express the way that makes me feel." He gently caressed her hands beneath his.

"I'm sorry if I ever said or did anything to hurt you in any way. I'll try to make it up to you." He released her hands, put his arms around her waist, and took a deep breath. "Jillian, I promise to love you always and be there for you when you need me. You have opened my heart and taught me how to love again. I'll be forever grateful for that." By now Jillian was weeping softly as his tender words touched her soul. "I had lost all hope of happiness, and you have given that hope back to me. I will love you always. You are my life." He gently placed both of his hands on either side of her face and kissed her lips sweetly.

"Dalton." Jillian looked deeply into his eyes for a moment before continuing. "You thank me, but it is *I* who should thank *you*. Heaven smiled on me when I found you. You are the one who wrote those tender and endearing letters to me when I was still in Providence. Your words made me fall in love with you and your children before I ever stepped foot off the train. You brought me here and gave me so many reasons to find happiness in life again. You taught me that a wounded heart is no match for a heart that gives freely. You've given me peace and content-ment and joy beyond words." She put her arms around his waist.

"Dalton, I promise to always cherish you and to be your closest friend. I will do whatever is in my power to give you as much joy and happiness as you have given me. I will care for and raise your children as my own and love them even more than if I had brought them into the

world myself. Thank you, Dalton, for the gift of love you have shared with me. I love you."

He pulled her close, and she laid her head against his chest. She listened to his heart beat and felt his chest softly rise and fall with his breathing. She let her own breathing fall in rhythm with his. Truly, they were now one, and Jillian vowed to remember this moment forever.

Twenty-two

"All aboard who's coming aboard!" Jillian heard Dalton call from outside the house. Jenny, who was holding Brenn, and Lisa, who stood at their side, hurried out the front door as Jillian dried her hands on her apron and hung it on the hook by the basin. She walked to the window and looked out. Dalton was helping the children into the wagon. It was Thanksgiving Day, and they were headed over to Uncle Ned and Aunt Betty's. Despite the setback from the fire, the harvest went well, and they got a good price for the remainder of the corn crop. Along with a small portion of the money Jillian's mother had given her, there would be plenty to get them by until the next harvest. They would celebrate together with gratitude this day.

"I have so much to be thankful for," she said softly to herself and placed her hand over the middle of her stomach. She smiled at the secret she would share with her family after their meal. She had told Dalton earlier that morning as they lay in bed. He had held her as they talked and made plans for the new baby, speculated on what it would be and what would they name it. Her parents and Marcus would be elated. She planned on posting a letter as soon as she could. She thought of the letter she had received from Marcus two days previously.

Dearest Jillian,

I pray all is well with you, Dalton, and the children. Mother and Father wish me to send their love. This will be our first Thanksgiving apart, which saddens me, but I know you are truly happy at last. That knowledge alone brings me great joy.

I have glad news to share with you that I know you will be jubilant to receive.

Jillian reflected on the telegram she had received from Bethany a week prior to receiving Marcus's letter and smiled.

I have made a proposal of marriage to one Miss Bethany Anne Johansen and to my great delight, she has accepted. We are to be married in the spring. I have other news for you as well, which I hope you will find pleasing. I have purchased a parcel of land not far from your home. Bethany and I plan to relocate there a month after the wedding. I am desirous to try my hand at cattle ranching and make a living for myself!

Father was hesitant at first, but I have been able to sway his opinion in my direction. Mother was a bit harder to convince, but since she realized you and I would be so close, she has been more agreeable. She is currently working on Father, trying to persuade him to visit in the spring after we move out west. She has her work cut out for her, since you know as well as I do how he hates to travel by train.

As for myself, I plan on trying to make a visit or two much sooner to begin work on a home for Bethany and me. Dalton has already agreed to help, Uncle Ned as well. Yes, I spoke to him about my plans when we were visiting in August, and he agreed to keep my secret. I did not want to get your hopes up unnecessarily if things did not go as planned. Please forgive me my little deception.

Finally, Little Sis, I want to tell you that I love you. You have always been more than just a sister—you're a dear and worthy friend as well. I am overjoyed to realize that we have both found companions that are both worthy and auspicious to share our lives. I look forward to raising our children side by side and the friendships I know they will enjoy.

Your Loving Brother,

Marcus

Bethany hadn't mentioned them moving here. Jillian had immediately run to find Dalton and share with him the good news.

Now, Jillian looked down at the pies she had made for Thanksgiving dinner, including the one from the recipe that had won the first prize ribbon at the Independence Day picnic. She feared she had forever made an enemy out of Mrs. Mavis Bingham, the poor woman. She almost felt sorry for her. After being the town gossip and busybody for so many years, she was now the subject on the tips of everyone's tongues. They were all wagging about her daughter and the infamous Nathan Shaw.

In a rare moment, Jillian allowed her mind to drift to thoughts of Nathan. He had spent almost two months in the Willow Springs jailhouse after the night he had tried to kidnap her. Unbeknownst to nearly everyone in town, Miss Sarah Bingham had been visiting him daily, nursing his wounds and bringing him pies and other homemade goods. She had obviously had a change of heart and decided he was worth her time after all. Jillian shook her head. She alone knew how deceptively captivating he could be.

On the day after he was released, both he and Miss Sarah disappeared. A distraught Mr. and Mrs. Bingham received a letter some three weeks later from their daughter saying she and Nathan had married and joined a wagon train heading west. Nathan wanted to try his hand in the goldfields of California.

Jillian had forgiven Nathan long ago and truly wished he would find happiness. Maybe one day they would meet again and all that happened between them would be resolved. Dalton stuck his head around the door, interrupting her thoughts.

"Hello, beautiful." He winked at her. "Are you coming?"

"Yes. We just need to get these pies out to the wagon." Jillian smiled at him, and he came fully through the doors and put his arms around her. "Maybe we should leave a pie or two at home. We surely won't eat all those today," he teased.

"Dalton, you have such a sweet tooth!" She slipped her arm though his. "Well, you can rest easy. I've already baked you your very own pie. It's on the sideboard cooling off."

"I am the luckiest man in the world, Mrs. Jillian McCullough," Dalton said as he pulled her in a little closer and leaned in for a kiss.

She was sure she should argue that it was she who was the lucky one, but just then she was content to let him kiss her.

Epilogue

Jillian drove up to Marcus and Beth's home. She was glad Dalton had taught her how to drive the team so she could ride over to visit her brother and sister-in-law occasionally without having to take Dalton away from his work. After they were married, Marcus and Bethany moved out to Wisconsin to a parcel of land about three miles south of Dalton's farm. They now had a beautiful home.

Her parents had finally ridden out on the train, much to her father's chagrin, for an extended visit. It hadn't taken him long to decide it had been worth it, though. He simply adored his grandchildren, especially little Lisa, who he was sure could talk an ear off a cornstalk. The children loved spending time with their grandparents. It had been good for Jillian to have her mother close again too. Her mother was an excellent seamstress and was finally able made good use of the fabric Jillian brought from Providence. The children had loved the new clothes she fashioned for them. Lisa was particularly darling in her blue print dress with the tiny pink roses. Her parents got along famously with Uncle Ned and Aunt Betty and promised another visit in the near future. It had also given Jillian great pleasure to have them all celebrate her birthday together.

Jillian set the brake on the wagon, climbed down, and retrieved the soup and fresh-baked bread she'd brought with her. Bethany had been feeling ill lately, and Jillian had been concerned. After enjoying their meal, Bethany told her she probably wouldn't be feeling quite herself for another seven or eight months. Jillian smiled, thinking about the good news. Marcus would be so thrilled when he found out.

Dalton didn't have much work to do in the fields that morning, so he had offered to stay home and watch the children. He was repairing the barn door when she drove up. The children were sitting together nearby, playing with Whiskers' new batch of kittens. It was her third litter, and she supposed in about four weeks they would all have to head into Willow Springs to see if they could find homes for each of the furry creatures. She wished she could find the tomcat responsible for Whiskers' frequent offspring and find it a good home, far away from their farm.

Jillian set the brake, hopped off the wagon, and ran over to Dalton. She threw her arms around his neck and kissed him. Dalton stopped what he was doing and put his arms around her, pulling her close. That is, as close as her rounded belly would allow.

"What did I do to deserve such a reception?" he teased, and she gave him another kiss.

"I have good news. Bethany is expecting. I am so excited. They've been so worried she'd not be able to have a child. I've been praying for them, and now I'm finally going to be an aunt." He grinned at her news and she added, "And you'll be an uncle!"

"When's the baby due?" Dalton asked.

"In January," she replied. "I was thinking on the way back over here, wouldn't it be something if she had twins?" She wiggled out of his arms and took a few steps forward to look at the children playing. Dalton came up behind her, putting his arms around her again and placing a hand on each side of her rounded belly. He leaned his chin on her shoulder.

"Yes, that would be something," he said, looking over at the two strawberry blond, curly headed, twelve-month-old boys nestled next to Jenny and Lisa. Just then, Caleb grabbed a kitten by the tail and suspended it in the air. Calvin quickly did the same.

"Caleb, Calvin," Lisa scolded gently, freeing the kittens' tails from their chubby little fists. "You must be nice to the kittens or you'll hurt them."

"Be nice to kitty, brothers," Brenn added firmly.

Jillian smiled and sighed deeply as her heart swelled with gratitude. Who would have thought that her life would have taken her here, to this beautiful piece of land? How could she have ever fathomed the love

she would feel in the arms of the man who held her at this moment? She had been given so much more than she could ever have dreamed of: a husband she loved and adored, as well as these beautiful children who brought such joy and happiness in their wake. She sighed again, as a now-familiar feeling of peace and contentment enveloped her. There was another person she felt grateful to as well.

Thank you, Laurellyn, she thought, *for your part in this*. Just then, a soft breeze blew past, and Jillian thought she could smell the fragrance of lavender and roses.

About the Author

Prudence Bice has loved writing her entire life. Born in Orange County, California as one of eleven children, she always felt drawn to stories that spoke to and kindled her romantic heart. Having overcome tragedy in her own life, the inspiration for her first novel was sparked by her desire to ignite true romantics everywhere with a wholesome, feel-good story about the power of love in rising above the pain and suffering from loss.

Prudence resides in St. George, Utah, with her husband, Ray, and their four daughters and one son. Her hobbies include drawing, photography, music, writing, and, of course, reading anything she can get her hands on! Currently she is majoring in English at Dixie State College and loving it. The future is bright, she says. Every day she wakes up with a prayer in her heart and a story in her head. She never thought life could be so good!